NEVER A LADY

ANNA AYSGARTH

ISBN: 978-1-955784-11-5

Published by Satin Romance
An Imprint of Melange Books, LLC
White Bear Lake, MN 55110
www.satinromance.com

Published in the United States of America.

Cover Design by Ashley Redbird Designs

To Fionn

CHAPTER 1

London, 1827

Charlie rubbed the face of the sovereign absent-mindedly, something he had done so often he had almost worn it smooth. It was not the original sovereign given to him by the Duchess of Bainbridge, Miss Helen Rockingham as she had been known then. That sovereign had been his change of fortune, but he always kept the first sovereign he made as profit as a reminder of who he was and where he had come from.

He stretched his long legs in front of him and stared into the flames, touching the sovereign once more. Looking at him now, no-one would guess his humble beginnings. He had been a street boy, an urchin, until a chance meeting with Miss Helen had led him to a job at Hatchard's, the book-sellers. Mr. Hatchard had seen his potential, and within weeks, Charlie was no longer just doing odd jobs in payment for learning to read, he was living above the shop, earning a living, and being educated. He discovered he had a talent for figures and his newly learned skill of reading led him to devour Mr. Hatchard's daily copy of *The Times* as well as anything else he could lay his hands on. The good and plentiful food served by Mrs. Hatchard saw him quickly develop from a skinny, scrawny boy into a tall, powerful, young man.

His first investments had been small and careful, bringing in small rewards, and by twenty-one he had garnered enough profit to take bigger risks. By three-and-twenty, with the help of a loan from the duchess, he had made several thousand pounds investing in canals and ship building before opening his own brokerage. Further investments in land with coal and mineral mining rights led to him adding a bank to his portfolio. Some thought he was lucky, but he knew that his luck was due to rigorous research and ensuring he was aware of technical developments so that he was always ready to invest in potential. Developments in science and technology particularly fascinated him. Consequently, by six-and-twenty he had accumulated a sizeable fortune.

Although they were usually contemptuous of self-made men, the ton accepted Charlie. What fascinated them was the fact he apparently did not care whether he was accepted or not. There was even a rumour he had turned down a title, which was true. He was not impressed by titles, especially when he saw some of the fools who owned them. Yet he also numbered among his friends the owners of some of the highest titles in the land, up to and including the prince himself. Perhaps that was what fascinated society; Charlie Hampton was an enigma to them.

"Bloody hell," he grunted as he pushed one of the logs further on to the flames with the toe of his boot, releasing a shower of sparks. He poured himself a brandy from the side table. He, who had maintained rigid control over every aspect of his life, who pragmatically made decisions based on logic rather than emotion, now found it spiralling out of his control, and what annoyed him even more was that one of the reasons, the main reason if he were honest, was entirely of his own making.

A few weeks previously, Charlie had been at White's. He had been particularly pleased, as the land he had recently bought in Yorkshire had a rich seam of coal running through it. Coal was going to be essential in the power of the future. He had seen some of the new steam engines working and was convinced they would change both the way things were produced and the potential for new transportation. So convinced was he that he had invested money with several engineers, though some associates said he was foolish to believe that people would ever trust in rocks and water when horses were much more solid and dependable.

Contracts had been signed and celebrations were in order. His closest friends, Lords Harper and Silcock, had started by the time he joined them and were already on their third bottle of claret.

"Congratulations, Hampton, I hear this latest deal will make you richer than the King himself," Harper slurred.

"Kings of England and France together," Silcock added, slopping wine into a glass and handing it to Charlie.

"Soon have more money than parliament," Harper continued. "Should we need to go to war again, you can pay."

"War is too costly," Charlie replied evenly. It had taken the lives of two of his brothers, so he was acutely aware that the cost in human life was more significant than the money to be made. He never invested in anything to do with war. He would have no blood on his hands.

"Ever the serious one," Harper grimaced. "Come now, man, have some more of this. It's time you celebrated. Silcock, pour him another."

"The trouble with you, Hampton, if I may say so, is that all you ever think about is making money. What's the point?" Silcock asked, pouring another generous measure of claret. "You need to enjoy the fruits of your labours, man. Drink more wine. Come, tonight we'll go to Madame Belle's where there will be plenty of women to offer distraction. No matter what your pleasure, Belle's girls do it all," he grinned cheekily.

Charlie's smile was thin. "I think not, gentlemen." In the early days, when he had begun to make serious money, he would have gone with them, happily taking the pleasure Belle's girls gave, but for some time now, drinking and whoring had bored him.

"Ah," said Harper, "do I detect a man who, having made his fortune…"

"And ours," Silcock put in.

"And ours," Harper agreed. "A man who has made his fortune," he repeated, "is now looking for a wife, so that he has someone to inherit after he's gone. Must have someone to inherit, otherwise, what's the point? And a bastard by some common woman just wouldn't be enough, is that it?"

Charlie looked at Harper in surprise, for a man who was frequently drunk and usually completely insensitive, he had shown an uncanny insight. It was time, he considered. He wanted a well-bred young lady who would grace his dinner table and bear and raise his children. A son who would inherit and build on his empire and a daughter, perhaps. Such a woman ought not impinge on his life. In exchange, he would provide for her comfort and luxury. He could not think of a more practical arrangement. They would both benefit and there would be none of the emotional entanglement that came with the notion of love. A noble lady would surely have no expectation of love and partnership, and he had seen love firsthand and could not conceive that the rewards were justified by the cost. His own parents had married for love and that had been a disaster. He shut down the thought and refused to return to it.

"So we must find you a suitable bride."

He jerked his head round at Harper's words, the last thing he wanted was for his friends to even know he was contemplating marriage, let alone try in their misguided and he had no doubt clumsy way, to help him. "Even if I were thinking of matrimony, which I am not, I am quite capable of finding my own wife," he replied.

"No, no, we are your friends. We want to help," Silcock put in. "A toast to your future bride," he said as he raised his glass.

Charlie raised a dark eyebrow. "I would not trust you two to choose my neckcloth, let alone my wife."

"I am hurt," Harper thumped his chest, "as one of your closest friends, I only want what is best."

"Best for whom?" came a voice followed by a man who sat with elegant ease at their table.

Sir Taylor Rufford. Charlie's eyes narrowed, since he had beaten Rufford in a deal a year ago there was little love lost between them. Rufford was an inveterate snob and had not forgotten the insult to his pride having been bested by someone of lower status. The fact that the land had since yielded a fine seam of coal had added fuel to the fire.

"Hampton here wants to find a wife," Silcock explained, grinning.

Sir Rufford's eyes glinted with malice. "I doubt that any woman of quality would want to associate herself with young Hampton," he drawled. "Better to look on the streets of Cheapside, or better still, St. Giles."

"Steady on, Rufford, Hampton has the blunt to secure a match with any woman," Harper shot back.

Rufford inclined his head. "I daresay, it is no secret he has money enough," he paused before adding, "but no breeding."

"Sod your breeding, Rufford, clearly any brains were bred out of your family generations ago. Along with the family fortune," Charlie heard himself saying, he would not usually have risen to the bait, but a bottle of claret had loosened both his control and his tongue.

"Really?" Rufford drawled. "Well then, what about a wager, if you are so confident? By the end of the season, you must have secured the hand of a woman of quality. Obviously, it will have to be some woman whose family is in need of cash, for no others would look at you, I suggest Lady Jane Whistowe, the Honorable Kathryn Hadfield, even Lady Caroline Omrod or her sister Lady Susan, or perhaps Lady Elizabeth Morgan. Their fathers are all in need of funds." There was a pause before he added, "Shall we say £1,000? Come, Hampton, I am making this easy for you. Whistowe is within a whisker of bankruptcy, Hadfield's castle is all but fallen down, Omrod has already had to provide three dowries and his lands have never been enough to support him, and Morgan as everyone knows, is mortgaged to the hilt, any of them should welcome your proposal with open arms. If you are as confident as you think you are, it will be the easiest £1,000 you have made this year."

"Very well," for the second time, Charlie heard himself speaking. "But let us make this more interesting: if I win, I'll have the money and Rufford III," he challenged, calculating even an idiot like Sir Taylor Rufford wouldn't gamble his famous racehorse, virtually the only asset he owned.

"Done," he replied, "But if the lady or her father refuses you, as well as the money, you must marry her maid, who surely would have no objection to the union."

"Capital, capital," Harper guffawed. "Bring brandy," he yelled to a passing servant. "An excellent wager, Rufford, I had no idea you could be such a joker."

"Don't be ridiculous, a lady knows what she is getting into in the marriage mart, but a maid? I refuse..." Charlie began to argue before his voice was drowned out by the men's laughter.

As far as Charlie could remember, that was what had occurred. He hoped to God as he pocketed the sovereign and poured another brandy, that Rufford had indeed been jesting.

CHAPTER 2

The searing light hit Charlie's eyeballs like a knife. "Good morning, sir," Pearson, his butler, said as he opened the final drape with a flourish. "Your coffee is by your bedside, sir, your bath is drawn and Lords Harper and Silcock have sent messages they need to meet you at White's at your earliest convenience."

"What the devil time is it, Pearson?" Charlie rasped, his head pounding as though Pearson had inserted an axe with every word he spoke. Damn the Lords Harper and Silcock. Twice in three nights they had got him foxed, to say nothing of the evening a few weeks earlier when the ridiculous wager had been made. Nothing had been said about it since, so he was hoping it was but a distant memory. Either way he now had a clear understanding of the phrase 'drunk as a lord.'

"It is your usual time of rising, sir, six of the clock," Pearson replied, sounding hurt. "You left no instruction to the contrary."

"Of course, Pearson. I apologise, I was with Harper and Silcock last night and we were…"

"Carousing, sir?" Pearson provided helpfully.

"Rather an old-fashioned word, Pearson, but as good as any." Charlie took a sip of his strong, specially imported black coffee, instantly feeling more human. "What was that about Harper and Silcock?"

"They request you join them at White's at your earliest convenience. Something to do with developments in the betting book."

That had Charlie's full attention. He had not been to White's since Rufford had thrown down the challenge. It would seem that the wager had not been forgotten, the ton were no doubt on to the wager like wasps round a honeypot. Pearson took a deep breath, "There is also a message from your grandfather's lawyers requesting an appointment."

Charlie did not break his step as he strode, naked towards his bathing room. "I have no interest in anything my grandfather or his lawyers have to say, either now or at any time in the future. Please convey that point clearly, Pearson," he finished, over his shoulder.

"As you wish, sir, as I have done so with the previous requests."

"Perhaps this time, they'll get the damned message," Charlie grunted as he slammed the door.

It would be difficult to get to White's early. He had meetings all morning with his estate agents, a meeting with other investors in the afternoon, and he had promised to attend the opera with the Duchess of Bainbridge. White's would have to wait.

The meetings, as usual, overran and he had to rush to change for the opera. He slid into the Bainbridge box as the overture started. The duchess grinned and tapped his arm with her fan "Late again Charlie, I was beginning to think you were not coming. Detained by a lady, perhaps?" she whispered.

Charlie groaned. "News travels fast. I thought you only arrived in town today."

Duchess Helen giggled. "It is the talk of the ton. Honestly, Charlie, if you looked up from your accounts from time to time, you would know the gossip. It is particularly important when one is at the centre of it."

"Is the name of the lady also public?" Charlie asked at the intermission.

The duchess shook her head. "No, James knows because he spoke with Harper. He, Harper and Silcock know each other from school days. But," she added, "according to James, the betting book is filling up fast with eligible ladies."

"Damn. I had hoped that Rufford was jesting, at least in part."

His old friend grimaced. "I do not believe Rufford knows how to jest, and he certainly never forgets a slight or a perceived one. I have no notion of what he thinks you have done to anger him, but he is out for revenge, Charlie."

"I am beginning to realise that."

"Why on earth did you take on this wager?"

"Equal parts of stupidity, arrogance, irritation, and alcohol," he replied.

"Quite apart from its utter stupidity, it reflects badly on your reputation with women, Charlie. I know there are many men who regard women as inferior creatures, and frankly treat their horses with greater consideration than they do their wives, but I thought better of you," she admonished him. "Especially this bit about marrying some unfortunate maid who is being dragged into this mess through no fault of her own."

"You are right of course," he replied, feeling relieved when the performance began again.

Unfortunately, Helen was not easily dismissed.

"What do you plan to do?" she asked, as soon as the opera was concluded.

He shook his head. "I am not sure yet, I think the first thing I must do is find out the damage at White's, if you will excuse me?" He rose and kissed Helen's hand. "I shall see you at the Sisson ball tomorrow?"

"Of course. James is looking forward to talking to you about some engineer he has found. He will be here directly, once the house has risen. He takes his duties in the Lords very seriously."

"I'm glad to hear it, James and Robert are worth more than most of the rest of them put together." He bowed and left the box.

"Oh, Charlie," Helen murmured, "what have you done?"

CHAPTER 3

Clara grimaced as she saw the broken cup and saucer in the grate. When Lady Elizabeth smashed her chocolate cup in the morning, it was generally not going to be a good day.

"There you are Blackburn, I rang for you an age ago. What took you so long?" her ladyship demanded.

Clara bobbed a curtsey. "I am sorry your ladyship, but Mr. Harmer stopped me to ask if you would be dining at home this evening."

"Harmer is merely a butler. Next time, ensure that it is Harmer who is kept waiting, not I."

"As you wish, my lady." It was most definitely not going to be one of Lady Elizabeth's better days.

Clara had thought when she left the foundling hospital where she had grown up, that her luck had changed. A position as a lady's maid was definitely a step up and she was pleased to leave the regimentation and endless rules behind. The warden at the foundling hospital had arranged the position after the last lady she'd worked for had married and received a new maid of her husband's family's approval. "Lady Elizabeth will be a demanding mistress," she had said, "but if you are obedient and quiet, you will be successful. For a girl in your place in society, it is a wonderful opportunity." Yet barely a fortnight as Lady Elizabeth's maid, Clara knew that she had jumped from the frying pan into the fire, but respectable work was not easy to come by and she had no doubt that Lady Elizabeth would have no hesitation in dismissing her without a character. So she stayed in her place, bearing the situation, until she could think of something better. But it was not pleasant, even with the wages.

Clara had known she was different from the other girls at the foundling hospital from an early age. From time to time, a package would arrive for her with new clothes, or shoes, sometimes even cakes or sweetmeats came which she was only too pleased to share with the other girls. Treats of any kind were rare and treasured. The orphans were not treated poorly, but there were many of them and treats and affection were in short supply.

One day, when she was about fourteen, after having private lessons she was not to share with the other girls, she asked the warden, "If I am truly an orphan, why do I receive these gifts? Does that mean that somewhere I have a family?" The warden considered for a moment before replying, "When you are of an age to understand the consequences, I will tell you. But for now, you must concentrate your efforts and energies on the training I have arranged for you as a lady's maid. You will be required to attend on the Baroness Eizhoven under the direction of Barrett, her maid, at seven o'clock each morning and return here at ten o'clock or when Barrett dismisses you." There was no point in persisting, the warden always did just as she said.

The day Clara finally left for permanent employment with Lady Elizabeth, the warden had summoned her. "You asked me once about family, Clara. In truth, I cannot tell you everything you want to know, not until you reach your majority at twenty-one, but I will tell you this: Your mother was a lady of quality, but she apparently fell in love with an unsuitable man and you were the result. She was sent away and you were brought here as a baby. Her parents found a man willing to marry her, but it was on the condition that there was to be no further contact."

"Then who sends the gifts?" Clara asked.

"I believe them to be from your grandparents. They insisted you be taught a skill so that you would always have the means to support yourself once you were old enough, hence your domestic training as a lady's maid."

"But if they didn't want anything to do with me, why send things over the years?" Clara wondered.

The warden looked at her steadily. "That, I cannot know. In my opinion, and it is only my opinion, it would have been kinder to cut off all contact."

"Perhaps they loved me, in spite of all," Clara ventured, voicing the hope of orphans the world over.

"Perhaps. Perhaps they felt guilty, perhaps they felt it their duty. Whatever the reason, we do not know and speculation is pointless," the warden replied crisply.

"Do you know my mother's name?" Clara looked at the warden steadily. The woman returned her gaze. "I do not, and even if I did, you know I could not tell you. Be satisfied, Clara," she added in a softer tone. "You know more about your family now than most of the girls here."

The older woman hesitated before unlocking a small drawer in her desk, removing a slim box and handing it to Clara. "This is yours, it came with you, but our instructions were only to give it to you when you were about to go out into the world."

Clara drew out the delicate silver chain from which dangled a finely crafted locket, she held her breath as she carefully opened it, but there was nothing inside.

"I do not understand." She looked at the warden questioningly.

"Return on your twenty-first birthday and all will be clear, but for now, that is all I can tell you," the warden replied.

Clara thanked the warden and picked up her small valise. "Just one more question, is my name really Clara Blackburn?"

The warden thought for a moment before replying. "Clara was the name your mother chose, Blackburn was given to you here. Do not forget to return to us on your twenty-first birthday."

Clara nodded, for there was nothing else to do.

Clara busied herself picking up the broken china, thinking about the past few years of employ with Lady Elizabeth. She was now almost twenty-one, just slightly younger than her employer.

"What are you doing, Blackburn? The housemaid can do that," Lady Elizabeth snapped, bringing Clara back to the present.

If my mother was a lady, I only hope she was better than you, Clara thought.

"Come, now, Clara! Lady Sisson's ball is tonight and I must be prepared!"

A quarter-hour later, no less than seven ball gowns lay discarded on the floor before Lady Elizabeth decided on the ice blue silk with dark blue roses embroidered into the waist and hem. She gradually grew more calm as Clara dressed her hair with pearls and feathers as Lady Elizabeth directed.

"I believe I shall be married by Christmas, Blackburn, what do you say to that?"

"That would be wonderful my lady. Who is the lucky gentleman?" Clara replied, racking her brains to think which gentlemen had come courting recently.

"No-one I should normally consider, but I have it from an impeccable source that Mr. Charles Hampton is seeking a wife."

"Mr. Hampton?" Clara tried to keep the surprise from her voice. She thought Lady Elizabeth would settle for nothing less than a lord and would rather marry a toothless duke with a paunch and an ear horn if she could be addressed as "your grace."

"I doubt you would have heard of him since he is not one I would usually associate with, not noble by any means. But he has other qualities I feel bound to consider."

"Like money, your ladyship?" The words were out before Clara could stop herself.

Lady Elizabeth picked up her hairbrush and rapped it smartly across Clara's knuckles. "Do not be impertinent, Blackburn. That should have been beaten out of you at the orphanage."

"I am sorry, my lady," Clara replied contritely, lowering her eyes so Lady Elizabeth could not see the annoyed expression on her face.

Lady Elizabeth's family possessed an ancient name and title, but their estates did not bring in enough income to maintain the lifestyle they felt they rightly deserved. Lady Elizabeth needed to make a brilliant match and at nearly four-and-twenty, time was running out, as each season, younger, fresher-faced, richer debutantes arrived. It was not that Lady Elizabeth wasn't a beauty, for she was. Her fair hair and blue eyes set in her delicately featured face had turned many men's heads. But when they got to know her better, her sour demeanor and quick temper put them off. No man wanted a shrewish wife.

Clara had learned that Lady Elizabeth had not always been like this. She'd learned when chatting with Cook that Lady Elizabeth had been a happy, laughing, witty girl and had attracted a proposal from Lord Peter Eyre. However, when he learned he would not be marrying an heiress, he had withdrawn before the engagement had been made public.

"I shall overlook your impertinence this once, Blackburn. You are far from irreplaceable."

"Thank you, my lady." Clara resumed her duties, fastening the brilliant sapphires around Lady Elizabeth's neck. They were the only jewels of note the family had been able to maintain.

"Mr. Hampton is a very wealthy man, it is true," Lady Elizabeth scrutinised her appearance in the glass. "He will provide the funds and I shall provide the breeding to raise him into society. I shall ensure he pursues a peerage. I see no reason why he should not. Once I have produced an heir and if I must, another child, we shall go our separate ways."

"But what about love?" Clara blurted out. "Surely you ought to feel affection for each other?" Having been alone all her life, she had dreamed one day of finding someone to love and to be loved in return.

Lady Elizabeth laughed. "Blackburn, surely you know by now that love matches have little place among people of quality. We marry to increase our estates, lengthen the reach of our wealth and influence. Usually, our parents decide who is to marry whom, though my own father has been somewhat remiss in that department. My own parents," she mused, "barely knew each other when they married, I believe they met only a handful of times before the wedding."

"What if you do not suit?" Clara persisted. She found the attitude of the ton completely bewildering, although she had little knowledge or experience, she knew she wanted more than the ladies of the ton seemed to be willing to settle for.

"We shall suit well enough to do our duty. The important thing is that he should offer for me, the rest will follow." She peered into the mirror, refusing to wear the spectacles that lay on the dressing table. "Now, more rouge."

When she was finally satisfied, Lady Elizabeth considered her reflection once more in the glass. "That will do, Blackburn, now run along and ready yourself. Your grey, I think, I shall need you to assist with my hair and in the retiring room."

Clara bobbed a curtsey. Having spent three hours on Lady Elizabeth's toilette, she had about ten minutes to complete her own.

"And be quick about it," Lady Elizabeth yelled after her.

Nine minutes later, Clara peered at herself in the small, cracked piece of looking glass she had salvaged from one of Lady Elizabeth's rages. She had done her best, her chestnut curls were held in a taut topknot over which she had rammed her white maid's cap, though as usual, a few tendrils had escaped.

She was not a beauty like Lady Elizabeth, but her green eyes were large, fringed with thick dark lashes, her nose was small and straight, and her mouth generous. She would do, not that anyone would be looking at her. She even doubted that were all the maids to be lined up, Lady Elizabeth would not be able to find her. She could do nothing about the grey dress, she had inherited it from a previous maid who had obviously been smaller. It stretched uncomfortably over her breasts and pinched her waist, but grey had been Lady Elizabeth's order and grey it would be.

She stuck her tongue out at her reflection and ran lightly down the steps to help Lady Elizabeth and her mother into the coach.

CHAPTER 4

*L*ady Sisson's balls were always lavish affairs and this was no exception. Thousands of candles burned in the eight huge chandeliers that dominated the ballroom, every surface seemed to have an elaborate candelabra at its centre, their flames multiplied a hundred fold in the many ornate mirrors hanging on each wall. The women looked like exotic, hothouse blooms in their rich ball gowns, jewels of every cut and hue sparkling as they whirled and spun on the arms of the more soberly dressed gentlemen.

Charlie felt all eyes on him as he strode across the ballroom to join his friends.

"Ah, here is the man of the moment." Harper grinned and handed him a glass. "It is that ghastly punch with a little extra."

"To make it remotely worth drinking," Silcock explained.

Charlie took a large swig before coughing. "That is quite a lot of added extra," he spluttered as the brandy hit the back of his throat. Sobering quickly, he added, "What possessed the pair of you to open the betting at White's?" It was the first time he had managed to catch up with them since he had left the opera, as when he'd arrived late at White's, they had already left.

"We did not start it, Charlie. Rufford opened it. We just added names," Silcock explained, looking pleased with himself. "Rufford said there should be sufficient names otherwise there would be no sport, it increases the odds you see," Harper added.

Charlie took a deep breath. "You do realise that because of this ridiculous wager, every time I dance with a woman, or even look in her direction, not only will the gossips have a field day, but the betting will go wild. How am I even expected to court any woman with half the ton cheering me on to succeed and the other half willing me to fail?"

There was a pause before Silcock put in, "You did take the wager, Charlie."

"I was foxed."

"That is how most bets come to be placed," Harper said, and turned to his friend. "Your father literally bet his boots that he had bigger feet than Lord Waverly."

Silcock laughed. "Had to walk home in his stockinged feet. And your father wagered his horse could jump a six-foot fence."

"Damn near broke his neck." Harper laughed. "The horse clearly had more sense as it took one look at the fence and dumped pater in the ditch."

"Either way, have either of you considered what this ridiculous wager could do?" Charlie asked testily. "There are any number of desperate young women who will now be emboldened and try to compromise themselves."

"I do not believe you need worry about your reputation, Charlie. Where women are concerned, they seem to rather like a chance to reform a rake."

"I am not thinking about my reputation," Charlie thundered. "I do not give a monkey's arse what people think of me, but if some foolish young woman manages to compromise herself with me and I do not make an offer, I shall end up being called out and forced into a marriage. I might as well buy a house on Hampstead Heath and be done with it."

Silcock looked at Harper. "To say nothing of how the House of Lords will be decimated. That would mean further bets, though to be honest Hampton is a better shot than most of the angry papas who will be forced to call him out, lords or not."

"Well, here is your first chance to settle the matter." Harper nodded towards the door. "Lady Elizabeth Morgan has just arrived."

Charlie turned. She was a beauty, there was no denying it, but he was beyond the age where he was excited by beauty alone. As she moved gracefully across the floor, he decided to seek an introduction, then he would ask her to dance and if she was remotely suitable, he would offer for her. She was a member of the ton so she knew how the marriage system worked. It would be a business transaction like any other, and he would win the bet, gaining an extra £1,000 and some of the best horseflesh in the country, as well as besting Taylor Rufford once more.

"Ah, Mr. Hampton, I see you have noticed the lovely Lady Elizabeth, let me introduce you." Charlie had not noticed Sir Taylor Rufford's approach. "Quite a beauty would you say?" Charlie nodded.

"Of course, she has been out for a couple of seasons and I should imagine, more than willing to accept your suit."

"You know her?"

"We are distantly related," Rufford responded.

"Then why do you not marry her?"

Rufford grimaced. "Unlike you, Mr. Hampton, I need to marry a suitable heiress."

Charlie's eyes narrowed slightly, there was much about Rufford he loathed, but why was he so intent on pushing him in Lady Elizabeth Morgan's direction? Something did not make sense and Charlie was determined to find out what.

He allowed Rufford to escort him across the room.

As they approached, Lady Elizabeth turned and flashed them a dazzling smile. "Ah, Taylor, I have not seen you in an age! How is your dear mama?"

He bent over her hand. "Mama does tolerably well, thank you. Elizabeth, may I present Mr. Charles Hampton."

Charles bowed. "A pleasure, Lady Morgan."

"Oh, please call me Lady Elizabeth," she fluttered her fan.

As the orchestra started up Charles felt obliged to ask, "Are you free for this dance, my lady?"

Elizabeth glanced at her card. "I believe I am, Mr. Hampton."

He felt himself tense as she took his arm. He would use this opportunity to find out if she and her relation had colluded against him.

CHAPTER 5

*A*s she took his arm, she felt his muscles tense beneath her touch and smiled. This would be easy enough. Later in the evening, she would ensure they were found alone together, compromised if necessary—though she had to admit, he was attractive enough that that wouldn't be a chore—he would have to propose and her life would be secured. He was a handsome devil she had to concede, having him in her bed would be no hardship at all. She would have to remember to thank Taylor for sending him in her direction. Whatever he was up to, she decided that come what may, she would marry Charles Hampton and deal with her cousin when necessary.

"I believe it is customary for a gentleman to at least look at the lady he is partnering." Elizabeth's voice held an edge.

"My apologies my lady, I confess I am not much of a one for small talk."

"Evidently," she pouted.

Charlie frowned as he searched his mind for a topic they might have in common, he mentally rifled through the names of the women he knew, hoping for inspiration.

"What book are you currently reading, Lady Elizabeth?" he asked, inspired by the Duchess of Bainbridge, confident he had hit on the winning topic. Women seemed to spend a great deal of time reading novels.

Her brow furrowed. "I am not one for reading Mr. Hampton, in fact, since leaving the schoolroom, I doubt I have read a single book. I am, however, partial to reading the fashion plates. A woman of the ton simply must keep up with the latest fashion, do you not agree?"

"But you are an accomplished young lady by all accounts?"

"I paint, I sing, I play the pianoforte, whether I am accomplished would be for others to decide."

She was not making this easy for him. "I also ride to hounds, produce a fine embroidery stitch and arrange flowers," she continued. "All the qualities I have been led to believe that would make me a perfect wife."

He could not deny it, everything she said was what was generally accepted as the necessary qualities for an accomplished young woman who would indeed make an excellent wife. There was no doubt that Lady Elizabeth Morgan had the potential to be the perfect choice for his wife. She would grace his arm at social functions and his table when he entertained, and once she had produced an heir or two, they would both be free to go their separate ways. She knew how society worked, there would be no tedious romantic attachment, so long as he provided handsomely, she would keep her end of the arrangement.

"Tell me, Mr. Hampton, is it true that you are finally considering accepting a title? The rumours are that His Royal Highness has offered everything up to an earldom," she simpered, though he knew well that the gossips knew it had been a dukedom.

Charlie's lips thinned as he recalled the meeting with the prince. The prince had wanted to push a title on him so that he could join the court as an equal. The prince had even said that he could use men like Charlie in the Lords.

Charlie had refused, knowing that he would never be seen as an equal even with a title, especially since he owned many of their mortgages. He'd considered what he could do with the power that came from being a lord, like improve the lives of the poor by fighting for decent wages and education for all children, but he had little reverence for titles. It was the lack of a title that had ruined his father's life, though he had no intention of allowing Lady Elizabeth to know anything about that.

"The title does not make the man my lady," he replied quietly.

Elizabeth's lips thinned. "I assure you, Mr. Hampton, anyone who wishes to consider himself a person of quality has a right, if not a duty, to accept a title."

"There are many men I do business with, talented men, who have become rich and powerful without titles," he countered.

"Men such as you?" she asked.

"Indeed, men such as me," he agreed.

"And are beautiful women queueing up to marry them?"

He glanced round the room, where groups of young women were watching his every move. "Oh, I think I may say they are. It would seem wealth attracts young women almost as much as a title," he said with a laugh. He despised himself for saying it but despised even more the system where desperate young women were sold off by their fathers and brothers to the highest title, regardless of the lady's happiness.

"But are the women you speak of women of quality? Or are they just fortune hunters who would marry a goat if it could shower them in diamonds?" As she spoke, Charlie noticed the coldness in her blue eyes and the natural downturn of her mouth.

"I don't know, my lady. I'm sure you would be more adept at knowing than I," he replied with a lightness of tone that disguised his sentiment which was completely lost on Lady Elizabeth.

"Most of the women here would marry you for a florin," she shot back.

"And you? What is your price? Rather more than a sovereign I imagine."

"If you are making an offer of marriage, sir, you must speak with my father."

"It is a little early in the evening to be talking of marriage, my lady, I hardly think a three-minute waltz is sufficient time for us to make such a decision," he said lightly, before escorting her back to her parents. Lady Elizabeth might have the qualities required of a ton wife, but there were other qualities he had glimpsed that ensured she would never be the wife he desired.

It took longer than he liked to cordially excuse himself from the grasping hands of ladies and their families, even needing to dance with other ladies after he'd finished his dance with Lady Elizabeth. He'd finally escaped and retreated to a quiet room he was sure Lady Elizabeth would never enter.

Charlie was glad of the respite his host's library offered him. The constant whispering behind fans and pairs of eyes that followed his every move were beginning to irritate him. He could cheerfully have bludgeoned Harper, Silcock, and Rufford for suggesting the damned wager, but he had only himself to blame. No-one had forced him to take the bet.

As he was pouring himself a generous measure of brandy, he became aware that he was not alone. Sitting in one of the winged armchairs by the marble fireplace was a young woman in a dove grey gown. One foot was tucked underneath her as she concentrated on the book she was reading. He could not help but observe her for a moment, her Titian-red hair was done up in a tight chignon from which one or two tendrils had escaped, one of which she absently twirled through her fingers as she read, completely absorbed in her book.

The light of the candelabra highlighted the gold glints in her hair. It was, he noted with fascination, not one uniform colour, but had hints of both gold and reddish hues, like autumn leaves. Her profile showed a small, slightly upturned nose and a delicate chin. He found himself wanting to see the rest of her face, especially her eyes. Green he decided, he could never resist green eyes.

Whether he made a slight movement or whether she just became aware of him, he could not tell, but she suddenly jumped up, the book flew out of her hands and she was scrabbling on the floor for her shoe. She hastily scooped up the lace cap and rammed it on her head before curtseying.

"I am sorry, my lord. I know I shouldn't be in here. I wasn't doing any harm, I promise you."

He could see by the look in her eyes she was terrified and he knew why, a servant would never be permitted to sit in this room. Frankly, they would only be permitted in to work. In some houses, he knew, servants had to get from room to room by a series of internal tunnels and corridors with secret doors. If they were ever seen, they either had to turn to the wall or, in some cases they were dismissed.

He held up a hand. "You have no need to fear, miss, I will not be telling anyone you were here."

Clara bobbed another curtsey. "Thank you, my lord," she said gratefully as she hurried towards the door.

"Wait."

She turned.

"I do not see why you should leave on my account," Charlie said easily.

"Sir, you know as well as I that I should not be here. If my mistress were to find out, she would dismiss me instantly."

"Then let us make it our secret."

CHAPTER 6

*C*lara eyed the mysterious lord who had chanced upon her infringement on the library. She considered his offer. She had just re-dressed Lady Elizabeth's hair after the dance with Mr. Hampton and would not be needed, probably until the end of the ball. She had done her work and was bored by the usual maids' gossip and, being barred from keeping herself busy in the kitchen, had already grown tired of fending off the attentions of young footmen. Why not stay where it was warm and peaceful?

"All right, for a few moments."

"Good." Charlie smiled a boyish grin that made her heart flutter in a dangerous way. "Perhaps you could take off that awful hat thing you're wearing."

Clara smiled. "Cannot do that my lord. My mistress would have apoplexy."

"Then we will not tell her." He reached out and deftly removed her cap before pocketing it. He looked at her seriously for a moment. "That's better," he said, his eyes amorous in a way that caused her to blush and look away.

"No wonder your mistress makes you wear that hideous thing," he muttered, his breath deepening in a way that frightened and excited her.

He took a sip of brandy. "Come and sit and tell me about your mistress."

Clara hesitated. If Lady Elizabeth ever found out she had left the ladies' retiring room, she would be in great trouble. If she knew Clara was sitting in the library alone, chatting with one of the ton, Clara fully expected to be on the next ship to the colonies.

"I am not sure I should, my lord, or more to the point, I am sure I should not."

"I will tell you what, I will tell you my name, you tell me your name and we will sit here like two old friends having a conversation."

Clara thought for a moment, this might be the most interesting thing that happened to her, ever. She smiled. "All right, my name is Clara."

"And mine is Charles, Charlie to my friends. Pleased to meet you, Clara." He held out his hand. When Clara went to shake his, he caught her small hand and kissed it, Clara giggled, feeling giddy at the danger of their interaction. "Likewise, Charlie. My mistress is to marry someone called Charles," Clara went on, "A Mr. Charles Hampton."

Charlie's ears pricked up. "Is she indeed?"

Clara nodded. "Apparently it is all to be settled tonight, he is going to propose at the ball."

"And has this Mr. Hampton been a regular visitor to your mistress to court her?"

Clara shook her head. "Not that I know. All I know is, he is looking for a wife and Lady Elizabeth has decided it will be her. I will never understand the way these lords and ladies arrange these things."

"Would that be Lady Elizabeth Morgan?" Charlie asked.

"Yes, Lady Elizabeth is my mistress." Clara's eyes widened as she realised her error. "Oh no, you're Charlie, Charles...Mr..."

"Charles Hampton," he provided helpfully.

Clara clapped her hand over her mouth. "I have said too much, I really must go."

As she stood they both clearly heard voices on the other side of the door. "He is definitely in there. I saw him enter about ten minutes ago," came the muffled tones of Rufford's voice.

"Then give me five minutes," Lady Elizabeth's voice declared as the door handle depressed.

Within seconds, Charlie had pulled her into the window alcove and closed the curtains so they were completely hidden from view as the door opened. Every nerve Clara possessed was jangling, partly at the thought they might be discovered at any moment, and partly at the fact that her nose was pressed up against the impeccable white shirt of Mr. Charles Hampton, soon to be the fiancé of her mistress. She was so close she could feel the steady rhythm of his heart and smell the sharp scent of sandalwood. She was not in the slightest concerned about being compromised, maids were not compromised and if they were, nobody cared.

"You must have been mistaken, Rufford," Lady Elizabeth said irritably. "There is no-one here."

"I could have sworn I saw him, he must have returned to the ball. No matter, I'll soon find him and get him here." There was a pause before Rufford added, "Do not forget our bargain Elizabeth. I have introduced you, it is up to you to secure a proposal, I shall in fact bet on you marrying him, against some considerable odds I might say, then you get Hampton and his money and from then on I want to know about all his business dealings, who he contacts, what he sells and more importantly, what he intends to buy. I had intended," he mused, "to win the bet, take Hampton's money, and see him humiliated, but this I think will be more profitable in the long term."

"Why? Do you intend to ruin him? I am hardly likely to provide you with the means to ruin my own husband, am I?" Lady Elizabeth asked, coolly.

"Of course not, dear Cousin, I merely wish to know so Hampton's investments work for me as well. He can do the work as befits his station in life and I shall take advantage of this knowledge to enrich the Rufford coffers. It is a victimless crime, if it is a crime at all," he replied smoothly.

"Cunning little bastard," Clara heard from above her. "Listen, Miss Clara, I am going back to the ball via this window. When I come back, I imagine the lovely Lady Elizabeth will try to compromise herself with me. When I call your name, make sure you come out and act as chaperone," he whispered, fishing in his pocket and handing over her cap before quietly unlatching the casement and stepping out.

Clara nodded, then turned her attention back to the couple in the room, "I shall expect you to demand Rufford III as a wedding gift which you will then return to me. I have it all planned. In any case," Rufford went on. "If he does not come up to snuff, we can always ensure you are a widow before too long."

"Really Rufford, how do you plan to do that? Hampton is a young man in his prime, not a gouty old earl," Lady Elizabeth drawled.

"Young men in their prime are often wont to do stupid things, especially when in their cups, particularly where a wager is concerned. If, for example, someone were to wager that he climbed onto the roof of Hampton Park and hoisted a flag, well, roofs are notoriously slippery…" he said vaguely.

Clara almost gasped out loud at her mistress' next words. "An interesting idea, Rufford. I shall give the matter some thought. It may be I come back to you if Hampton becomes tedious." There was a pause before Lady Elizabeth added, "You seem particularly keen to best this Mr. Hampton, Taylor, what has he done, I wonder, to make you quite so venomous?"

"I have my reasons, many reasons, not the least of which is his swindling me out of a particularly valuable piece of land which would have saved much of the Rufford fortune. Not to mention buying the Rufford emeralds and presenting them to his mistress who had at least the good sense to throw them at his head when he finished his affair with her. Apart from that, he is an upstart, a nobody, and here he is mixing with the cream of society who fawn on him as though he is some sort of god. I hate him and all he stands for." Clara could hear the venom in his voice.

"Then it would seem your scheme to rid us of him needs careful consideration."

"Of course, there will be additional payment to consider. I want those emeralds back."

"I do not doubt it. However, none of this will come to pass if you do not get Hampton here post haste."

As she heard the door click at Rufford's exit, Clara could hear Lady Elizabeth humming as she moved about the room, no doubt deciding on the best position for the charade she was about to play out. Clara could scarcely believe what she had just heard, Lady Elizabeth and her cousin had all but agreed to swindle Mr. Hampton and when he had served his purpose, murder him. She knew her mistress was a spoiled madam, but nothing had ever suggested she could be a ruthless killer. After tonight, she would have to find herself a new position. Of that, she was sure.

Clara's ears pricked up as she heard the door open once more. "Lady Elizabeth?" a familiar baritone said quietly. "Taylor Rufford suggested that you needed to see me as a matter of some urgency."

"Oh, Mr. Hampton, please come in. I am so distressed." Clara heard the tremor in the other woman's voice, one she frequently used on her father when he had refused her plea for more pin money. "I have lost the gold locket my father gave me with the likeness of my dear, departed grandmother in it. My father will be angry with me for losing it," she cried.

"Of course, my lady, but is it not more likely you lost the locket whilst dancing in the ballroom?" Clara detected just the slightest hint of irony in Mr. Hampton's voice.

"No, I definitely had it on when I came in. There was such a crush in the ballroom, I thought I would come in here for a few moments of quiet reflection with a book." Clara's eyebrows raised, Lady Elizabeth had only ever picked up a book to hurl it, as far as she knew.

"Yes, of course," Charlie said with irony which Lady Elizabeth missed. "It is always interesting to pick up a habit from one's youth."

"I think it may have dropped and rolled under the sofa," Lady Elizabeth suggested. "Would you mind?"

Clara peeked out carefully, worried about what Lady Elizabeth might do.

Charlie had bent down, keeping half an eye warily on the young woman behind him.

"No, my lady, I do not think your locket is here," he said as he rose.

"Oh no, what am I to do, sir?" Lady Elizabeth's eyes filled with tears. "I have little enough to remind me of dear grandmama," she sniffed.

"I am sorry to hear it."

"Now I shall have nothing and Papa will never forgive me," the wails got louder. "I shall of course never forgive myself," the tears were flowing freely as Elizabeth warmed to her theme.

She took a step towards Charlie, instead of taking her in his arms as she no doubt expected, he handed her a snowy white handkerchief.

"Mr. Hampton," she sobbed, "I suddenly feel quite faint. I believe I am about to swoon." She swayed towards him, instinctively he put his arms out to catch her. There was a flash of grey as Clara shot out from her hiding place and helped Charlie place her mistress on the sofa. The door crashed open and a small crowd led by Lord Morgan and Rufford entered. "I am certain she is in here..." Rufford said over his shoulder, then looked aghast as he saw Lady Elizabeth prone on the sofa with Clara administering hartshorn and Charlie standing several feet away.

"It's all right, Sir," Clara assured him, "My lady felt unwell and Mr. Hampton summoned me, she is feeling much better are you not my lady?"

Elizabeth's eyes glittered with malice as she replied, "Indeed, it is a miracle you were here, Blackburn, quite a miracle."

CHAPTER 7

*C*harlie reflected on the interesting night on the ride back to his home. Both encounters with Lady Elizabeth had been unpleasant, but the interlude between them with the maid had been as sweet as Lady Elizabeth had been bitter at the foiling of her plot.

He closed his eyes against the rocking carriage and pictured Clara's face devoid of the dreadful maid's cap. She was beautiful, quite stunningly beautiful, in fact. When he had been first observing her in profile, he had not appreciated her heart shaped face, the delicate curve of her cheek and generous mouth.

And then they'd been in the window, her huge green eyes filled with concern, her full breasts straining through the material of her gown, pressing against him. Her lips, looking as if they were made to be kissed made his blood surge like no woman had in what felt like an age.

It was illogical how drawn he was to a poor lady's maid working for a suitable lady, and he endeavored to put her out of his mind by the time he arrived home.

As he strode up the steps, his front door opened.

"Good evening, sir. I trust you had a pleasant evening." Pearson took his hat and cloak.

"I think it fair to say it was both entertaining and informative," Charlie replied, a slight frown creasing his brow as he considered Lady Elizabeth's plans, to say nothing of that snake Rufford. The wager had been for him to win the woman's hand without Rufford helping her to compromise herself, and while he thought about it, why was Rufford helping him anyway? He stood to lose the wager, something was not right and he intended to find out what it was.

"You have a visitor, sir." Pearson's normally smooth tone was hesitant.

Charlie raised his eyebrows. "At this time of night? Rather late for a social call."

"The gentleman insisted, sir. He is in the small library."

"I suspect I am going to get a somewhat unpleasant surprise when I go through that door, Pearson."

"A surprise, certainly, sir," Pearson agreed.

"At what point do you intend telling me who is in there?" He jerked his head towards the door.

Pearson took a steadying breath. "His Grace, the Duke of Wensley."

"What in the bloody hell is that old goat doing here?" Charlie kept his voice low but there was no mistaking his contempt. "How in hell did he get in?"

"The new young footman, sir, was unaware of your feelings on the matter of his grace and let him in, and as the duke has never attempted to visit before, it was not something we expected. By the time I was aware of the situation, his grace was ensconced in the small library," Pearson explained. "Should I dismiss the lad, sir?"

Charlie ran a hand through his dark hair. "No, Pearson, he is only young. We all make mistakes. Leave him as he is, just educate him on my feelings about unwanted and uninvited guests."

"Very generous, sir."

"I can assure you that generous is not what I am feeling now." Charlie turned the doorknob. "Go to bed, Pearson. I have a feeling that this may turn out to be a long night."

There were plenty of candles lit and a cheerful fire burning in the grate, and an old man sitting in a wingback chair by the fire, reading. At Charlie's entrance, he took off his spectacles and closed the book. The blue eyes, slightly faded with age, but still showing a keen intelligence, held his own. The duke still had a full head of hair, though it was now snowy white.

"Good evening, Charles," the old man greeted as though he greeted Charlie every evening.

"What do you want?" Charlie was not prepared to waste time in pleasantries he did not feel.

"Can a grandfather not visit his grandson without some ulterior motive?"

Charlie poured himself a generous measure of brandy before he sat in the opposite chair. "You rather gave up any claim to grandfather status when you cut my mother off without a penny," he stated coldly.

The old man's eyes clouded. "And that is something I must live with every waking hour. If I could turn back the clock I would, but I cannot."

Charlie looked at him steadily but said nothing. The sooner the old man was out of his house, the better. The duke took a breath. "I had to come here because you refused to answer my letters or speak with my lawyers."

"Yet you would not have gained admittance tonight were it not for an inexperienced footman," Charlie put in.

"Be that as it may, there are things we must discuss."

"I have nothing to say to you, and there is nothing you have to say to me that I wish to hear. So please feel free to take your leave, Your Grace." Charlie stood.

"Hear me out. If, when I have finished, there are to be no more words between us, then so be it. But at least listen to what I have to say," he paused. "Please," he added.

Charlie resumed his seat. "Very well, talk, but I doubt anything you say will change matters."

"That is a chance I must take." The older man took a sip of port before he began.

"When your mother came to me and told me she had married your father in secret, I confess I was furious. She had been the toast of her season, she could have had her pick of the eligible young men that year, including the heir to a dukedom, but she was always headstrong. She had fallen in love with Hampton, and that was that.

"I thought Hampton beneath her, it is no secret, and in my rage I made certain threats which, in the cold light of day, when I had had time to reflect, I had no intention of carrying out. By then it was too late, Annabelle had gone. I never saw her again." The duke paused for a moment to compose himself.

"Please believe me, Charles, I tried to find your mother, I never stopped trying, but it was as though she had vanished into thin air."

"They vanished into the slums of London," Charlie put in. "From which they would never escape."

"I know that now, but I searched and searched, you must believe me, I never stopped."

Charlie said nothing. He knew people could disappear into the rookeries of Clerkenwell. No-one there would reveal anything to anyone from the authorities, they all had their reasons for being there. They stuck together and looked after their own, no-one else would.

The old man wiped his eyes in a silent moment. "When I learned I had a grandson, I was overjoyed. I knew I could do nothing for my poor, dear Annabelle, but I could at least do something for her son."

"Annie," Charlie said.

"I beg your pardon?"

"Annie, everyone knew her as Annie," he explained. "I imagine Annabelle was a little too ton-ish for Clerkenwell," he steepled his fingers. "So how did you find out about me?"

"Almost by chance actually, one of my men was in a tavern, The something Cock."

"The Fighting Cock." Charlie knew it, he had been beaten enough when his step-mother had staggered out as he minded his younger brothers and sister in the street outside.

"The Fighting Cock, yes, when he heard a woman complaining about the three brats she was having to raise. Harry Hampton had only married her for someone to be a mother to his children, his wife had died birthing another, her words were 'rich women would have other women to have babies for them if they could, but she was getting rid of them.' When my man bought her a few drinks she was happy to tell him more of her story, Hampton didn't love her, he never had because he was still in love with his dead wife, but at least she had a roof over her head.

"At the end of the night, she took my man home, by which time he had summoned assistance and Hampton was brought to me. I had only seen him a handful of times but I knew him instantly. He confirmed that my dear Annabelle was dead and buried, not in the family vault as befits a Wensley, but in a pauper's grave in St. Giles. He also told me that your two younger brothers had gone into the navy, your little sister had died of a fever, and that you had been apprenticed to the bookseller.

"By the time I made contact, your brothers were both dead in battle and you had already moved on. I thought at one time, you too would be lost to me, but you returned and began to create a stir in the city. I watched from afar, hardly daring to contact you. Approaching the man was far more difficult than approaching the boy, but eventually I knew I must in order to tell you of your inheritance. Of course, by that time you did not wish to know."

"It is too late," Charlie stated flatly.

"It is never too late," the old man said fiercely. "Like it or no, you are my heir, my only living descendent and as such, one day you will follow me as Duke of Wensley."

"The hell I will. In any case, what about the law about passing on through the male line?"

"The only other male relative is a cousin who is older than I and has completely lost his wits, poor soul. The first duke was a canny fellow with three daughters and petitioned the king to allow his grandsons to inherit. That is how it works, you are my grandson, you will be the next duke." His tone softened. "Think of it as a gift to the grandchildren your mother never lived to see."

"Do not, sir, bring my mother into this..."

The discussion came to an abrupt end at the sound of raised voices in the hall.

"What the devil?" Charlie muttered as he opened the door and stepped into the passage.

"Sorry, sir," the young footman held a woman by the shoulders, "they pushed past me when I opened the door."

Belatedly, Charlie saw another, more richly dressed woman standing nearby. From behind him he heard a strangled gasp, "Therese? Is that you? Therese?" before his grandfather fell to the floor.

CHAPTER 8

*L*ady Elizabeth extended her hand, seemingly oblivious to the man on the floor. "Mr. Hampton, forgive the intrusion at this late hour, but as soon as my maid admitted she had not only been in Lord Sisson's library without leave, but had also engaged you in conversation, I dragged her here immediately to apologise." She paused. "Blackburn, attend to the gentleman on the floor so that we may hear ourselves speak," she added sharply.

Clara needed no second bidding as she extricated herself from the footman's grasp and they both knelt by the prostrate old man who was making increasingly weaker choking noises. Clara's nimble fingers were already working to release the knot and unwind his neckcloth. "It's not helping," she muttered. "Unfasten his waistcoat," she ordered the footman.

"I can't reach from here," he replied, rolling the duke onto his side to face him. Almost immediately, the old man's breathing became easier and his colour became paler.

"I shall, of course, dismiss her for her impertinence," Lady Elizabeth went on, utterly ignoring the struggle for life going on at her feet. "As my father always says, servants must know their place and if they do not, they must be taught it in a lesson they will never forget."

"Sir, what is going on?" Pearson ran down the hall, hastily donning his coat as he ran, "I was just about to retire when I heard the commotion. Is his grace all right?" he asked, seeing the old man on the floor. Lady Elizabeth's eyes narrowed as she finally took in the scene. "His grace?" she asked.

"The Duke of Wensley. Mr. Hampton's grandfather," Pearson supplied.

"Mr. Hampton is related to a duke?" Lady Elizabeth's tone was incredulous, "But he is so dismissive of the notion of titles."

Charlie looked up from where he was rolling up his jacket and gently placing it under his grandfather's head. "This is hardly the time nor place to discuss the matter of social status, my lady." He turned to the butler "Send for Doctor Wilson. Thank you," he added to the maid.

"I think the gentleman needs a blanket," Clara replied, "since his breathing eased, he had gone very pale and his skin is cold to the touch."

"You, what's your name?"

"Tomkins, sir."

"Right, Tomkins, get blankets and a warming brick." The young man set off down the corridor. "Do you think we should put him to bed?" he asked Clara.

"I think we should try and keep him warm until the doctor gets here," she replied, chafing the old man's hands to try and get them warm. "He'll know whether and how we should move the gentleman." She looked into his eyes and her breath caught; they were like molten silver, she could not look away, did not want to look away from the warmth she found there.

"Well, I shall leave you to your invalid," Lady Elizabeth's voice cut through the silence. "I was never very good with sick people and it seems that you have more than enough staff to cope. Come, Blackburn."

As Clara began to move her hand away, the duke clutched it and murmured. "No."

"I believe my grandfather wishes your maid to stay," Charlie spoke quietly.

Lady Elizabeth paused, pulling on one of her gloves, "Very well, I shall loan her to you for a few days." She turned to Clara. "You will remain here, Blackburn, until his grace is well enough to manage without you. I shall call on Mr. Hampton regularly to ensure you are working hard and being obedient and respectful."

"Are you quite sure this arrangement is proper, your ladyship? I should not like to think your maid's reputation will be compromised."

Charlie did not believe it at all but wanted to see Lady Elizabeth's reaction.

She smiled. "Maids cannot be compromised, Mr. Hampton, they are not the same as ladies. I was about to dismiss her anyway." She turned again to Clara. "However, if I hear from Mr. Hampton and his grace that you have acquitted yourself well, I shall consider reinstating you."

"You are more than kind, my lady," Clara said, knowing that Lady Elizabeth would never hear the sarcasm in her tone.

"That is settled then," Charlie said, glancing back at Clara. She felt her heart flutter again, just as it had in the library. Although it would be good to be away from Lady Elizabeth, and regain her employment, staying here with Mr. Hampton seemed like it might be dangerous in a different way altogether.

There was no point denying that her senses seemed to jangle whenever she thought of him. He was a handsome man, his dark hair flopped over his eyes in a way that made her want to touch it, his firm jaw was covered with a day's growth and his lips were often drawn back in a smile. He was a man of good humour, that much she had seen, but it was his eyes that fascinated her, she had never seen eyes change so much, cold and steely as he had regarded Lady Elizabeth and almost silver as he had looked at the duke. However, she must be under no illusion, he was a rich and powerful man, she was a maid, a nobody. All men like him would want would be a tumble between the sheets and then where would she be?

CHAPTER 9

*C*harlie stood by the open door. His grandfather was finally sleeping peacefully, having been given a sleeping draught by Dr Wilson who said he would call again in the morning. He did not think the duke was in danger but would know more at his next visit. For the moment, he recommended quiet and rest.

He watched as Clara tucked the sheets around the old man and tidied the pillows, talking softly to reassure him all the time, before sitting down in the chair next to the bed. She looked exhausted, even from his position in the doorway, he could see tiredness in her posture.

"When did you last eat?"

She jumped up at his voice, "I had something for breakfast, sir. Before the ball."

"That was hours ago, you must be starving."

"I'm fine, sir."

"Nonsense, you must eat. Come with me."

"I shouldn't leave his grace," she replied doubtfully.

"You will be no good to the duke if you faint from hunger," he pointed out.

Clara's stomach growled audibly. "I rest my case," he said, smiling. "I will get Tomkins to sit with my grandfather if that makes you feel you are not neglecting your duties," he added.

"It would, sir," she replied.

A few minutes later, she followed Charlie through the green baize door below stairs.

"Sit down, Miss Blackburn," Charlie ordered, gesturing to the large, well-scrubbed table in the centre of the room as he set about finding bread, cheese, and fruit. Thankfully, where were embers still glowing in the grate and the enough light was reflecting off the copper pans and pudding moulds. Charlie took pride in having a clean, stocked kitchen, having been without for most of his life. He set a laden platter before her.

"Thank you, sir."

Charlie noticed the widening of Clara's eyes as he sat down and began to help himself. He hoped she didn't feel ill at ease at a gentleman taking the liberty of dining with her.

"The food they serve at balls might be enough for ladies to pick at, but there's never enough of it," he explained. "I know you are hungry, Miss Blackburn," he said, pushing the platter towards her, "please, help yourself."

"It's just Blackburn, sir," she said quietly.

Charlie watched her face as thoughts flitted across it. She was most expressive, even unintentionally so. "Let me reassure you, Miss Blackburn, I know what it is to be poor. I was lucky; someone gave me a hand up for which I will always be grateful. But I never forget where I come from and I want you to know I would never mistreat or take advantage of any of my workers."

Clara looked at him for a moment before she smiled. "I am pleased to hear it, Mr. Hampton," she said, then she cut herself a slice of cheese.

Charlie's heart almost stopped in his chest. Her smile transformed her. Were she to be dressed in silks and satins, she would be the toast of the ton. In fact, he would like nothing better than to see her in something other than the hideous, stained grey gown she still wore. Actually, he corrected himself, he would rather see her wearing nothing at all, her titian hair spread on a pillow, so that he could run his fingers through it before he made love to her. He cleared his throat. Having just assured her he would behave properly, such thoughts were not helpful.

"Tell me about yourself, Miss Blackburn. How did you come to be working for Lady Elizabeth?"

Clara recounted her story, from being left at the foundling hospital, through her training as a lady's maid to the position with Lady Elizabeth.

"And you have no knowledge of who your parents were or where you came from?" he asked.

"No, sir." She paused for a moment before reaching for an apple and taking a bite. "The warden said my mother was a lady of some sort and when I was very little, gifts arrived from time to time, from my grandparents, I think. The warden said she would tell me all one day, but that day has yet to arrive."

"Are you not curious? Would you like to re-visit the warden and ask?"

Clara regarded him steadily, her fingers straying to the locket beneath her dress. "I do not think so, sir. What would be the point? My family gave me up, the gifts would suggest they knew where I was. If they had wanted to claim me, they surely would have done so."

"Perhaps there was some reason they could not," he suggested.

"Perhaps," she agreed. "But I was abandoned once, I should not want to be rejected a second time."

He nodded, his heart clenched in his chest. For some reason he did not understand, he did not like to think of this young woman alone and without protection. He was shocked to realise he wanted to take her in his arms and kiss her. It was more than mere lust, although he conceded his lust was not insignificant, for some reason he did not understand, he wanted to protect her from the cruelties of the world. God knew she had experienced more than her fair share of adversity in her young life, and he knew a fair share about adversity. Perhaps it was his own experience as a child that forged a bond between them. Yet she was not bitter or complaining as she had recounted her story without rancour, so unlike the women of the ton who complained if their bouquets didn't match their jewels. He quickly dismissed his lustful thoughts—no good could come of them for her or for him—but he could not help himself admiring her spirit.

Clara interrupted his reverie. "Thank you for the supper, sir, I had best get back to his grace." As she rose, Clara could not stifle a yawn. Charlie clicked his fingers. She'd surely been up almost a full twenty-four hours. "Miss Blackburn, what am I thinking? You must be exhausted. Come, you must rest, then you can be fresh for the duke in the morning."

"But sir...." Clara began.

"I will hear no protests. Tomkins can stay with my grandfather until morning. The doctor gave him a strong sedative so I do not expect he will need anything. Surely," he added, "it makes sense for you to be available when he is awake."

"If you say so, sir," Clara conceded.

"I do say so." He smiled. "Come, the guest room next to my grandfather's room is unused."

Clara stopped in her tracks. "I cannot sleep in a guest room, Mr. Hampton."

"Why not?"

"Because I am not a guest. It is not my place. I should sleep in the servants' quarters, not with my betters."

He closed the gap between them and placed a long finger under her chin, forcing her to look at him. "In my house, Miss Blackburn, you are a guest, one who has kindly offered to help nurse my grandfather. It would be churlish of me to offer you space in the servants' quarters. Quite apart from the fact that it is sensible is it not for you to sleep in the room next to the duke so that on future nights you are close by should he need anything."

Clara could not tear her eyes from his gaze. "It does sound sensible when you put it like that, but to be honest, Mr. Hampton, I am too tired to argue with you tonight."

"The matter is settled then. Follow me."

CHAPTER 10

*I*t took Clara a few moments to realise where she was, come morning. Last night, she had been too tired to do more than strip off her dress and stays and fall into bed. She looked at her surroundings. The room was large, much bigger than Lady Elizabeth's bedroom, with a silver and blue theme. Heavy velvet curtains hung at the windows, the same material was used as bed hangings, but these had been embroidered with silver thread. The walls were hung with pale blue watered silk wallpaper, contrasting beautifully with the dark mahogany furniture. A fire was already burning in the grate and someone had already brought in hot water which was steaming in the jug.

Unwilling to leave the warmth and comfort of the most luxurious bed she had ever slept in, or was ever likely to again, Clara's thoughts turned to the events of the previous night. Mr. Charles Hampton was quite unlike any man she had ever come across before. When he had come across her at the ball, he had treated her with the respect he would have shown to a lady. That thought brought to mind Lady Elizabeth and a frown to Clara's face. Although it was none of her business whether Lady Elizabeth married Mr. Hampton or some other rich man, she could not bear the thought of him having to live with her evil temper.

Clara suddenly sat up, remembering the conversation between Lady Elizabeth and her cousin, if Mr. Hampton was trapped into marrying

Lady Elizabeth, not only did they intend to take advantage of his hard work to enrich themselves, they had no conscience about killing him if he did not measure up. She knew she had only heard what amounted to an idle threat, just words really, but she felt she should warn him in some way. Lady Elizabeth was a selfish, spoiled, and willful young woman, but Clara did not think she would consider murder, but she shivered at the thought of Sir Taylor Rufford, there was something about him that made her flesh crawl, he was dangerous, of that she had no doubt. The question was, would Mr. Hampton believe what a lowly maid had to say?

Clara had already washed and was halfway into her dress when there was a knock at the door and a young woman entered, carrying several gowns.

"Oh, you're awake, miss." The maid placed the dresses on the bed and bobbed a curtsey. "The master sent these for you to wear while you're here," she explained.

Clara continued to put on her grey dress. "Well, you may tell Mr. Hampton," she paused, "What is your name?"

"Lily, Miss Clara."

"You may tell Mr. Hampton, Lily, that I am grateful for his generous offer, but as I am neither in his employment nor of any relation to him, I should feel more comfortable in my own gown."

"He said you might be difficult, miss."

"Did he indeed?" Clara could barely suppress a small smile.

"He said, if you were to refuse, to point out the stain on the front of your gown and suggest you wear this green one until your own can be laundered."

Clara looked down and found there was indeed a large mark where the doctor had spilled some of the sleeping draught he had been pouring into the cup she was holding. "Mr. Hampton seems to have thought of everything."

"Oh, he does, miss," Lily replied indicating the dress in her hands, "he said it was the plainest, simplest gown and probably the only one you would contemplate accepting."

Clara touched the stain, it was dark, sticky and beginning to harden. "Very well, I will wear the green gown temporarily," she conceded.

The gown felt wonderful, she could not deny. It was made of fine wool, with a high, fashionable waistline and long sleeves. The dark, rich green emphasized both her titian hair and her large, emerald eyes. The neckline was cut rather lower than she was either used to and was impractical, but she found a lace fichu and asked Lily to assist in tucking it in to make the dress respectable for a nurse. She gathered her hair into a tight chignon and secured it. "Is there a cap I might wear?"

Lily looked through the pile of clothing, "No, miss, but I could probably fashion something with this bit of lace and some pins if you like."

"That would be fine, Lily, and you don't need to address me as Miss. I'm Clara and just as much a servant here as you. I'm just here for a day or two to nurse his grace."

"I know, miss, but the master says you are his guest and are to be treated as such. Most definite about that he was," Lily replied, firmly.

Clara shook her head. Mr. Charles Hampton was more of a gentleman than the lords and viscounts she had encountered, who barely acknowledged her existence. She doubted that, even though she had chaperoned Lady Elizabeth many times, they would recognise her if they tripped over her.

"Your Mr. Hampton seems to be almost too good to be true," she murmured.

"Oh, he is, miss! Well, not too good to be true, I mean. But he's a good and kind master, I wouldn't want to work for any other."

"Well then, I must make sure I don't disappoint him," Clara moved to the door. "I had better see how the duke is fairing this morning."

The duke was awake, his eyes lit up when he saw Clara.

"I was beginning to think I had dreamed you. Come closer, girl."

Clara stood by the bed. "It is astonishing, you could almost be her."

"Who, Your Grace?"

"Therese. You are the spitting image of her. Of course, she would be an old woman now if she is still alive."

"Who is Therese, sir?" Clara asked, beginning to adjust the duke's pillows and see to the room.

The duke paused for a moment, lost in thought, "She was a girl I met in my youth, in Vienna actually. We spent the summer together, then circumstances came between us."

"Circumstances?"

"She was promised to another. I never saw her again." His flat tone was a sign he had said all he was going to on the matter, for the moment at least.

"What is your name, girl?"

"Blackburn, sir."

"No, your first name, the one your parents gave you."

"Clara, sir."

"Are you named for your mother?"

"I believe it is the name my mother gave me."

"You believe?"

"I was brought up as a foundling, sir."

"And have you never tried to find your parents?"

Clara smiled. How like his grandson he was. "No, sir. The parents of foundlings either cannot or will not take care of them. This is my life and I must make of it what I will."

The old man smiled. "Well said, young woman. You have spirit, another thing you have in common with Therese."

"I see your shaving things are ready, Your Grace," Clara said, changing the subject. Of course, she often thought of her parents and as all orphans do, wanted to know why they had abandoned her. Did they not love her? Was she someone who was not lovable? She quickly banished the thought, nothing good could come of thinking in that way. "Shall I call Tomkins to assist you?"

The duke frowned. "I sent him away, the boy was nervous, his hand shook so much I was in danger of him slitting my throat."

"You are a little intimidating, sir."

"Not to you apparently, young miss."

Clara laughed. "I am, or probably now rather was lady's maid to Lady Elizabeth Morgan. If that didn't scare me, nothing will."

"Then you can shave me."

Clara stopped laughing. "I can what?"

"Shave me, everything you need is there," he indicated the nightstand. "It's not difficult, just put on the soap with the brush and scrape it off with the blade."

"But I have never done it before."

"I do not imagine Lady Elizabeth needed much of a shave," he agreed. "Still, woman of spirit and so on, you should be able to cope. Just try not to chop off my nose."

"You are not inspiring me with confidence," Clara muttered as she picked up the brush.

Holding her breath, she applied the soap and drew the razor lightly across the old man's skin. She worked carefully and methodically, wiping the excess soap away gently with a snowy white towel, before handing the duke a mirror. He looked at his reflection from various angles before commenting, "Not bad, young Clara, you could make a fine valet one day."

CHAPTER 11

*C*harlie blinked his eyes to clear them of the image, almost unable to believe what he was seeing. Tomkins had, as instructed, informed him when his grandfather was awake. The last thing he expected to see was Clara helping with his toilette and, he noticed with some disdain, she seemed to know what she was doing. Perhaps this was not the first time she had helped a man with his morning ablutions. Perhaps his assumption of her innocence was entirely unfounded.

He waited until the razor was safely back on the nightstand before announcing his presence. "Good morning, Your Grace, Miss Blackburn, I trust you both slept well," he said in an unusually clipped tone. For some reason, he was irritated to find Clara so at ease with the old man.

"I did, but I shall soon be out of bed and out of your way," the duke replied.

"Not until Dr Wilson has seen you," Charlie heard himself saying. "It was quite a strange turn you had last night, so we must ensure you are well before you leave." Frankly, he couldn't give a damn about his grandfather, but if he left, Clara would leave and he found he didn't want that to happen, not just yet. She looked stunning in the dark, green gown, as he knew she would. He shook his head slightly, trying to reassert his usual cool logic that seemed to desert him whenever this woman was near. He liked to be completely in control and when Clara

Blackburn came into his mind, cool logic was replaced with warm desires.

"Ah, here is Tomkins with your breakfast Your Grace," Clara announced, cheerily. "I wonder if, sir, if I might have a word with Mr. Hampton, while you are eating?" she asked the duke.

The duke nodded, his attention already caught by what was under the silver cloche Tomkins was lifting from the tray.

"Perhaps you might join me for breakfast, Miss Blackburn?" Charlie asked, trying not to smile at the determined look on her face and imagining that he would enjoy finding out what put it there. Clara was silent as she followed him down the stairs.

The galleried landing opened onto a magnificent staircase, the walls were a pale lemon silk, a skylight at the top of the house allowed daylight to flood the area with light. A large chandelier would clearly do the same at night. Charlie stepped quickly down the staircase and opened a door. "I usually take breakfast in here, it is smaller and cosier than the formal dining room," he gestured for her to enter.

Even so, he must admit, the room was not small, the table could seat ten people with ease and beside the laden sideboard there were other small tables and beyond, a sofa in front of the white marble fireplace. Light came in through the two large windows which overlooked the garden.

"Please, Mr. Hampton, this has to stop," she said as he pulled out a chair for her.

"What does?"

"This treating me as a guest. I am not a guest. I am a servant. I know it, you know it, and every other servant here knows it," she began.

Charlie shrugged. "Why should it matter?"

Clara rolled her eyes. "Mr. Hampton, you're a man of the world, you know how it looks. The way you are treating me is going to make my life difficult. It's no use you or I pretending I am a genteel lady."

Charlie strolled over to the sideboard and began to pile a plate.

"And another thing," she went on, warming to her theme, "about the dresses. Women like me cannot accept or wear dresses like these. It makes me look like I am your courtesan."

Charlie looked up from his plate, his eyes bright with amusement. "Courtesan?" he could not help repeating before, seeing the look on Clara's face, he schooled his own into seriousness. "I really do not understand your concern. You came here with only one gown, which was stained. I, as your temporary employer, am obligated to provide you with something to wear while you are here. What possible objection could you have to that?"

"Well, I suppose it sounds reasonable when you put it like that," she conceded, "but they are hardly maids' outfits."

"My grandfather is a man of taste and refinement. One could not possibly expect him to look at you dressed in a dowdy fashion."

Astonishingly, Clara glared at him. His tone was reasonable, but she evidently knew he was dismissing her concerns.

"If you are concerned about it, let me assure you that the gowns were delivered first thing from Madame Flaubert's; Lily took measurements from your grey gown last night. They are all new and none of them worn by some previous mistress, if that is what you are thinking."

Clara blushed at his forthrightness. It was quite attractive to see.

"You will notice," he went on, greatly enjoying her pink cheeks, "there are no ball gowns such as a mistress might expect. Just two or three fairly simple day dresses." Simple they may be, but Madame Flaubert had managed to put a hefty price tag on them, not that he cared, it was just recompense for the seamstresses who must have laboured all night to complete them.

"Very well," Clara conceded. "There is, however, the issue of my name."

"I know your name. It is Clara." She did not give up easily, he had to give her that. She was most admirable in her strong manner and he felt himself rising against her, playing at her game, and enjoying himself immensely, though he took care not to let her see it.

"You cannot call me Clara, I must be addressed as Blackburn."

"No, I do not think so. Clara is a much nicer name."

"But it is not the done thing," she said sharply. "Servants are always addressed by their surnames, if they are addressed at all."

"I do not care what is or is not the done thing," he countered. "In my house you are not a servant, I think of you as a friend who has kindly offered to stay for a few days and look after my grandfather. While you are here, I shall call you Clara and, as we are friends, you will call me Charlie as we did in the library at the ball last night." He held up a hand to stop the protest forming on her lips. "That is the end of the matter, Clara."

"As you wish, sir," she said tightly

"Charlie," he insisted with poise.

"Charlie."

He grinned. "There that wasn't so bad was it, the Heavens did not fall in did they? Perhaps now we can eat."

The food was delicious, fluffy scrambled eggs and a variety of tomatoes and mushrooms that were surely a far cry from whatever porridge he was sure Lady Elizabeth deigned to give her servants. Charlie kept his eyes on his plate. All he knew was that he wanted to keep the woman across from him in his home for as long as possible. It was a puzzle.

The silence was broken by Pearson's entrance. "I apologise for interrupting your meal, sir, but Sir Taylor Rufford has arrived and requests to see you."

CHAPTER 12

Charlie had barely time to stand before Sir Taylor Rufford walked into the room.

"Sorry to disturb your breakfast, Hampton," Rufford drawled without the slightest hint that he was sorry at all. "But I happened to be passing on my way back from White's. London is agog with the news of your elevation," he stopped, suddenly noticing Clara who was doing her best to edge her way out of the room. "And who is this?" he asked, picking up his quizzing glass. "I do not believe I have had the pleasure."

"That is my grandfather's ward, fresh from the schoolroom, Rufford," Charlie improvised. Rufford would spread the news that Clara was his mistress all over London before luncheon if he wasn't careful, and the last thing he wanted was for Clara to be ruined before she had a chance in society, practically fresh from the orphanage as she was. He almost shook his head to dislodge the thought, but there it was, he wanted to present Clara to society and show them that accident of birth made no difference to what could be achieved. "She is far too young and innocent for you, Rufford."

He nodded to Clara who bobbed a curtsey and fled.

"Now, Rufford, what do you want?" Charlie had to tamp down the urge to beat Rufford to a pulp as his lascivious eyes followed Clara from the room.

"Comely little chit," Rufford commented. "Does she come with a dowry from the old duke?"

Charlie clenched his fists. "Not to you, now I ask once again, Rufford, what do you want?"

Rufford pulled out a chair and sat. "Well, Hampton, news that you are not only related to, but the heir to the Duke of Wensley has travelled fast."

"Courtesy of Lady Elizabeth Morgan, I imagine." It had to be, for apart from she and Clara, no-one else knew and Clara had been in his house all night.

Rufford inclined his head. "By the time you had retired for the night, news had already reached White's."

"People clearly have too much time on their hands."

"That is undoubtedly the case, of course, men of standing do not have to work for their daily crust," Rufford sneered.

The barb didn't cut Charlie, he'd heard it and worse before. "Perhaps they should."

"Be that as it may, this does rather complicate matters regarding our wager."

Charlie raised an eyebrow.

"You see, following her meeting with you at the ball, Lady Elizabeth was quite disillusioned at the prospect of marrying a man of no breeding. However, having now found that you are heir to a dukedom, Lady Elizabeth is quite determined to marry you.".

Charlie maintained his silence for in business negotiations he had learned the power of silence.

"The wager was intended for you to have to persuade a lady to marry you. It is hardly in the spirit of the wager if she is more than willing to fall into your bed. It alters the odds to, well nothing," Rufford explained as though it was the most reasonable idea in the world.

Charlie had no doubt Rufford thought himself clever, but he knew as well as anyone that Lady Elizabeth was nearing the end of her ability to marry well and that even his newly rich blood, dukedom or no, would be welcomed by her and her father as it would keep them in the life to which they were accustomed. He chose to play along with Rufford's scheme though, to see where it would lead.

"Then the wager would be defunct," Charlie's voice broke into his thoughts.

"Not entirely, if you recall, should you not marry Lady Elizabeth or some other woman of quality," he added as an afterthought, "you have to marry her maid." Rufford's eyes gleamed maliciously.

"I really cannot see why you are intent on pursuing this Rufford," Charlie drawled. "Surely the mere winnings of the bet are not enough to hold your interest. A man of your quality should have no worries or need to engage in such petty wagers, which are, even as you said, worth nothing."

"A wager is a wager, Hampton. And there were witnesses to it. Of course a gentleman never reneges on a bet or fails to pay his gambling debts. A man of quality has the honor of his word. Or is that something you would not know?" His lips pulled back in a semblance of a smile.

Charlie carefully unclenched his hands. The temptation to choke the life out of Rufford was almost irresistible. He had dealt with all manner of men in business, but never one so odious.

"It seems somewhat unfair does it not, on the maid, who has no idea that she is being wagered like a piece of horseflesh?"

Rufford shrugged. "She's just a maid. Once you've married her you can leave her on one of your estates. No-one will care. Besides, what woman low born or high could possibly object to becoming a duchess eventually? Even so," he added, "she might die in birth of a son if you're lucky—many women do. Then you'll be free. You can take a mistress, or a wife, whatever you wish, and have an heir with no need to cater to the demands of his maternal parentage."

Charlie's eyes narrowed. "I underestimated you, Rufford." Rufford inclined his head, a sly smile on his face. "It was not a compliment."

"I did not imagine it would be. Now," he said briskly. "I shall expect to hear of a wedding shortly or the whole of the ton will know you have reneged on your wager."

"I could just give you the £1,000 now," Charlie offered.

"You really think it's about the money, Hampton?" Rufford said, clearly humored. He steepled his fingers, "I admit at first it was. I won't deny £1,000 is a tidy sum and would go some way to paying off the more persistent of my creditors. But no, now that Elizabeth is out of the wager, though I suspect not out of the race to wed you, I find my satisfaction is not in the money at all. Would you like to know what it is?"

"I imagine you are about to tell me," Charlie replied.

He leaned forward his once handsome features twisted into a mask of rage. "It is your humiliation, Hampton. I despise you. I want to see that you and your kind never rise above their betters. Look what happened in France when the peasants took power. We must ensure that never happens here. You need to learn your place, Hampton."

Charlie never thought he would hear himself claiming the relationship he had spent years denying to himself. "I believe, as grandson to the Duke of Wensley, his heir in fact, I have already risen above my betters and certainly above you," he said with steel in his voice.

Rufford's eyes narrowed. "I do not know how you managed to trick the old man into believing you are his grandson, but I intend to find out and make it public. You won't be able to show your face within three hundred miles of London. Your reputation will be gone and your fortune will soon follow."

Charlie rose. "While I find your threats vaguely amusing, I am afraid I have important things to do. I was up late last night, and I am in much need of a rest, so I must bid you goodbye, Rufford. I should," he added, "be obliged if you did not call again. My house is free of vermin and I should like to keep it that way."

He rang the bell and Pearson arrived almost immediately. "Pearson, show Sir Rufford out and if he attempts to gain entry again, he will be an intruder. Shoot him."

"Very good, sir."

"As to the wager, it is defunct, I have no intention of offering for your cousin, nor her maid, nor any of the other women you no doubt suggested in order to muddy the waters of your plot with Lady Elizabeth to trap me into marriage. There will in fact be no marriage. Furthermore, should you ever come within a mile of me or my grandfather, it is you who will end up in the gutter where you belong," Charlie spoke quietly. Had Rufford known him he would have known he was at his most dangerous when he was quiet.

Rufford clamped his hat on his head. "Insult me if you will, but bear this in mind, Hampton. I always get what I want eventually."

"If you do not shift yourself from my home, what you will get is my boot up your arse," Charlie growled.

"Spoken like the street urchin you are," Rufford said over his shoulder as he headed for the door.

Charlie poured himself a cup of coffee. He had no time for the likes of Taylor Rufford, whom he considered to be a pompous fool. But there was no doubt that he wielded some degree of influence in who was accepted by London society and there was also no doubt that he would take great delight in destroying Charlie's reputation. He was respected now, he knew, but society was fickle as was the prince: he may be a favourite now, but he knew that could change in the blink of an eye, the wrong tone of voice or the wrong smile and he would be out of favour. A little innuendo here and a poisonous word there could damage him.

His thoughts turned to Clara. Marrying her wouldn't be a burden, of that he was sure. He enjoyed her company and he had a feeling she would be a responsive lover, in fact, just thinking about her naked and gasping in his bed made him harden instantly. He grinned to himself. They would be compatible in the bedroom and he would enjoy teaching her the pleasures of love-making.

He had been thinking of taking a wife, the discussion of that fact had led to the ridiculous wager. It was funny, he had no conscience about marrying someone such as Lady Elizabeth because she knew the rules, she would do her part and neither of them would be emotionally involved. Yet, his parents had married for love, would marrying Clara himself be such a bad idea? The thought caused him to stand still for a moment. Had he really just considered love? Such a fickly, damning emotion that was the antithesis of the logic he had used to build his new life. He walked briskly, his thoughts coming in a rush.

And yet, marrying her for a wager made while he was drunk? Could he do that to her? Would she ever forgive him if she found out and find out she would. Why was he even contemplating such a move when he barely knew the woman? Especially given his words on marriage to Rufford. He was being ridiculous. He sighed as he headed towards the library. His life was getting out of control, so was Clara's and she didn't even know it.

CHAPTER 13

It seemed he had only been at work for five minutes before Pearson rapped on the door. "What is it now, Pearson? I believe I have made it clear that I am not to be disturbed when I am working," he said testily.

"My apologies, sir, but Lady Elizabeth Morgan has called and wishes to speak with you on a matter of some importance."

"Can she not come back later?" Charlie gestured to the contracts on his desk.

"The lady was most persistent, sir." Pearson's tone was as neutral as ever, but even from his brief knowledge of the lady in question, 'most persistent' probably meant a full-blown tantrum, or at the very least, entailed tears and the stamping of feet.

"Very well, send her in." He knew that in order to win the battle, one must sometimes be prepared to lose a skirmish.

"Lady Elizabeth Morgan," Pearson announced as Elizabeth breezed in.

"Really, Mr. Hampton," she began, removing her gloves and bonnet and tossing them at Pearson, who beat a hasty retreat, "your butler is most disagreeable. I had to be quite forceful in order to get him to let me in to see you."

"Pearson is under strict orders never to admit visitors whilst I am working," Charlie explained.

"Well, that may do for ordinary people, but I expect an exception to be made for me." She settled herself on the sofa before the fire.

"I am sure you do," he replied mildly.

"After all," she went on without pausing for breath, "we are practically engaged."

This caught Charlie's full attention. "I beg your pardon."

"It is a well-known fact that you are looking for a wife, a woman of quality who is well versed in the ways of society. We danced together at the ball and were seen alone together. Society is already whispering about us. I am sure," she added purposefully, "you would agree that is enough. Were you not to propose now, my reputation would be besmirched and, as a gentleman, I cannot believe you would not act with honour."

"You seem to have everything planned," he replied, leaning his elbow on the marble mantelpiece. "Tell me Lady Morgan, how exactly one dance and a chaperoned meeting equate to the necessity for a proposal?"

"We were alone in the library. When I awoke from a swoon you were bending over me. Probably intent on having your wicked way."

Charlie almost laughed out loud. If ever there was a woman he did not want his wicked way with, she was sitting opposite him. "Your maid was present."

"She is just a maid and does not account for anything," Lady Morgan replied contemptuously.

"Your recollection would appear to be flawed, Lady Morgan, your maid was present and I was nowhere near you when the throng, led by your less-than-illustrious cousin coincidentally walked in as you fainted," Charlie replied, firmly.

"That is not the version I remember, nor is it the version I shall relate," she shot back, her eyes hard and her lips set in a thin, grim line. "Whom do you think society will believe, Rufford and me whose titles and breeding go back generations, or you? The newcomer with no breeding at all," she spat back.

"I do not think that is quite true, is it, Lady Morgan? Last night, until you realised I am the legitimate heir to the Duke of Wensley, you were keen enough for my money to hold your nose and marry me if you had to. But now, knowing something of my family connections I believe the stench of poverty has receded somewhat."

Lady Elizabeth regarded him coolly. "You are right, Mr. Hampton, I was prepared to marry you, it is what ton marriages are about. I provide the respectability and connections of belonging to one of the oldest families in England and you provide the money. As the only child of my father, my son would one day inherit the title Lord Morgan."

"I have my own connections, Lady Morgan, at the highest level and as for your title…" he left the sentence hanging.

"Very well," she snapped. "Since we are being honest, then you have to marry me because you compromised me. Nothing less will satisfy myself, my father, or society."

"I did nothing of the sort," Charlie replied quickly. "You intended to be found in a compromising situation and I admit, would have been, had it not been for your maid. She saved you from such an unfortunate scandal."

Lady Elizabeth's brows rose. "Blackburn? Of course, I remember. She was in the library with you, alone, something she will sorely regret when I have finished with her."

Charlie was instantly wary. On no account did he want Miss Blackburn, Clara, to fall back into the hands of this awful woman. "What do you mean?"

"Blackburn clearly thwarted my plans and she will be punished. Servants need to know their place and, when I am finished with her, not only will she be in no doubt she will be dismissed with no character."

"Do you know what happens to young women who lose their employment with no prospects of another place of work?" he asked, battling to maintain an even tone.

Lady Elizabeth shrugged. "She should have thought of that before she decided to thwart me," she replied.

"She will end up in the streets, possibly earning a few pence sewing or the like, but the chances are far more likely she will end up selling her body for sufficient food and drink to keep her alive. If she is lucky, she may last a year."

Lady Elizabeth shrugged again. "You are no gentleman to speak of such things to me. And she is no one of consequence for whom I should care what befalls her. In any case what happens to Blackburn when she is dismissed is neither my affair, nor would it be on my conscience."

"It most certainly would and should be, on both counts."

"Enough of this. I shall see Blackburn now, send for her if you please."

"I am afraid I cannot. She is out on an errand for the duke," he lied. He did not want Clara within a mile of this monster.

Lady Morgan rose, "Very well. Tell the little bitch she is dismissed. I shall send her belongings here, and woe betide her should I ever see her face again." He inclined his head, her last words were the only good to come out of her mouth. "Furthermore, Mr. Hampton, I fully intend that society knows you to be the scoundrel you are. I assure you when I have finished my reputation will emerge unscathed from this debacle, but you may well have to crawl back to the gutter from which you emerged."

She swept from the room.

CHAPTER 14

*C*harlie glanced at the decanter on the table beside the sofa, much as he felt like pouring himself a large glass of brandy, he would not. Down that road came ruin, as he knew from his father's example. Alcohol never solved problems, merely created more. Besides, the problem of Miss Blackburn was one of his own making and he would have to solve it.

He turned his attention to the sheaf of documents in front of him, work was what he turned to when he needed to focus, yet almost immediately Clara's visage came into his mind. Now that she had been cast aside by Lady Morgan, he would have to think what to do with her. He could not take the ridiculous wager seriously, if the others had bothered to listen they would have heard his refusal, but they weren't listening and, for all his connections, he knew that the one thing the ton took seriously was a gentleman's attitude to a wager. It did not matter how many creditors a man had, his gambling debts were always the first to be settled. He might bankrupt his grocer, tailor, or wine merchant, but he had to settle with his rich friends no matter how ridiculous the bet and they did not come more ridiculous than the one he had been forced into.

His cool logic exerted itself: the obvious and perhaps least troublesome idea was to find her another position. She was a trained lady's maid, after all, and although Lady Elizabeth had made it clear she would give no character, surely one of his friends' wives knew of someone who needed a good maid.

And yet...he knew in his heart he didn't want to see Clara return to life at the whim of a rich, spoiled woman who did not have the wit to know much beyond the signing of her own name. He took up his pen once again. Once again, the image of Clara came into his mind. She was witty, intelligent and courageous, why should she waste her talents fetching and carrying for some woman who, due to the accident of birth considered herself entitled to be waited on without gratitude or consideration for those she considered beneath her? Of course, not all the women of the ton were like that, the Duchess of Bainbridge and her sister-in-law, the Duchess of Whitney were women he held in the highest regard. But women of their calibre were few and far between and, he conceded, neither of them had taken a conventional route to becoming a duchess.

He could, of course, take the attitude that Miss Blackburn's predicament, of which she was still unaware, was mostly of her own making, and had he been born one of the ton no doubt he would have. She should not have ventured into the library at the Sisson Ball, everything that happened since had been as a result of that decision. On the other hand, she had saved him from being compromised by Lady Elizabeth and Sir Rufford, so he owed her a debt, a great debt. Coupled also with the fact that she had saved his grandfather and was nursing him with care and some affection.

These were the logical reasons he needed to help her, but he knew that none of them mattered a jot. Despite all the logical reasons, in truth, he simply did not want Clara to leave. He found he wanted to see her eyes gleam with delight when he made her laugh, he wanted to hear her laugh bubble up from deep within. He wanted to be the one to make her laugh, he wanted to spend time talking with her, not talking at her as he had noticed some men did with their wives. That thought caused his pen to still.

He shifted in his seat and swore softly as a blob of ink dropped onto the page, obliterating his note on the sale of a mine. His pen had been held aloft since he had begun to think of a solution to the problem of Clara. With a curse, he dried his pen and set it down. He sat back and closed his eyes. Certainly Clara was the only woman in a long time who had aroused interest in him, and arouse him she did, in every way. He had attempted to dismiss it as mere lust, the sort of feeling aroused in any red blooded man by a beautiful woman. He wanted her in his bed, there was no point in trying to deny it, but for the first time with a woman, he wanted to protect her, to keep her safe from harm, to make up for the harsh beginning she had faced in life. He knew what poverty looked and smelled like, but at least he had had a family who cared about him. It was only when his mother died his father had turned to drink, they had always been poor but his father's drinking had left them destitute.

Now that Lady Morgan had dismissed Clara due in part at least to him, he must take some responsibility, she would not fall into poverty, of that he was determined.

He would find a way to help Clara, he must put aside his personal feelings and think of what was best for her. If he was to make a rational decision, he could not allow himself to be emotionally involved, nor would he allow himself and Clara to be dragooned into a wedding for the sake of that damned bet, for though he would enjoy it, she would never forgive him and he would never forgive himself. Just as he took up his pen it occurred to him that although he could not marry her, there was no reason why he couldn't find her a wealthy husband. Though many of the ton needed not only a wife, but a wife with a sizeable dowry, some young lord with title but no money might be prepared to overlook a woman's lack of breeding for the right price. He began to scratch a few names on a clean sheet of paper.

He had just written three names when the door opened and Clara appeared, clutching a book.

"Oh, I am sorry, sir, I did not realise you were in here," she stammered. "His grace sent me to return this book and find something a little more exciting," she explained.

He rose and walked towards her, suddenly feeling his spirits lifting. "And what is it my grandfather has rejected?" he asked, taking the book from her. "*The Life and Times of a Sea Captain* by Rev. Walter Harrison-Blythe." He grimaced. "I rather suspect the good reverend has somewhat edited the more interesting parts since becoming a man of the church."

Clara laughed. "I agree, we only read the first four chapters, but if that was anything to go by, this book would bore young boys off joining the navy."

"Perhaps they have read it, that is why they are forced to take the king's shilling," he replied. "Now let us see what else we can find to amuse grandfather."

They perused the shelves. "You could try this, *Gulliver's Travels*," he reached a book from the top shelf. "It has been published a while but it always worth another read, and he cannot complain it is not exciting."

"Or this," Clara plucked a book from a lower shelf. As she ducked under his arm, he caught the scent of violets, that most innocent of flowers which sent thoughts that were entirely indecent scudding through his brain. "Faust? I am not sure I can approve that."

Clara arched an eyebrow, "Why not? I think his grace is old and wise enough to understand it, even if I have to read it in German."

Now it was Charlie's turn to raise an eyebrow. "You speak German?"

"Naturlich. Ich spreche Deutsch, Italiano, Francais et paulum Latine."

"But how?" He was perplexed, Clara was better educated it would appear, than the young men on his list, who had the benefit of education at the best schools and had spent three years at Oxford.

She shrugged. "At the foundling hospital, they found I had a talent for learning languages and sent me to the local vicar for lessons."

"You must have been his star pupil."

She grinned. "I don't know about that, but he was kind and I enjoyed having some time to learn."

"Well, whether you read it in German, English, French, or Italian, I am not sure the content is suitable for a young lady. Demons, the devil, and a man selling his soul."

"Oh, for goodness sake," she shot back. "I have known some ladies who would sell their souls for a new hat. Besides," she added, "if the devil himself pops up, I am quite sure my experience with Lady Elizabeth will be quite enough to ensure that I see him off."

Charlie laughed, mentally crossing off the first two names on his list of potential suitors. Clara, he decided, would have no trouble managing them, but he sincerely doubted they would be able to cope with her.

Suddenly, he became aware of her proximity, he was close enough to see her eyes were not one uniform colour, in amongst the green were little flecks of gold. He could see from the rapid rise and fall of her chest that she was aware of him too. He knew he should step back and let her go, but he could not. At that moment he wanted to kiss her, to taste her lips, to mold her body to his. Before he realised himself what he was doing, his hand reached out and cupped her face, his thumb traced the outline of her lips. Just one taste, one kiss, he promised himself as he lowered his lips to hers.

Clara stood rooted to the spot, willingly allowing him to take his leisure. His lips were warm and firm against hers, teasing and gentle at first but became more demanding as he gathered her to him and held her close against the hardness of his body. When she opened her mouth to him, he groaned and deepened the kiss. He had no idea how long they stood there, only that she was responding to him and wanting him as she pressed her body close to his.

The book she was holding slipped from her grasp and landed with a thud on the floor. Brought to his senses, Charlie stepped back, the spell broken.

"Clara...." he began.

"I must go, sir," she replied, swiftly picking up the book and almost running from the room.

Charlie rubbed his chin thoughtfully as he watched her leave. He would seek his grandfather's help immediately. Clara was proving to be a temptation and he was not sure it was a temptation he could or wanted to resist.

CHAPTER 15

"What do you think?" Charlie asked as he faced his grandfather who was now well enough to sit in the wing chair by the bed.

"Let me see the list."

Charlie handed over the piece of paper, since thinking up the scheme to marry Clara off, he had approached it as he would any business transaction. He had costings for dowry, dresses, accessories, bonnets, gloves, undergarments, slippers, and boots as well as dancing and drawing lessons. He had also allowed for the purchase of jewellery.

"I was thinking," he went on as the duke perused the paper in silence. "We would explain Clara's sudden emergence on the fact that she has been living quietly in the country since the death of her parents, but that you have persuaded her to have a season."

The old man looked up. "Very thorough planning. my boy. I can see you have a good head for business on you. There are one or two points we need to discuss, however."

Charlie met his grandfather's gaze. His blue eyes were slightly faded but there was no doubting the intelligence behind them.

"Even if you were to persuade Clara to go along with your scheme," the old man began, "which I very much doubt. None of these young men is remotely suitable."

Charlie reared back and said, "I assure you, sir, they are all from the top drawer of society."

"Of course, I should expect nothing less, but two of them are dissolute rakes who would go through Clara's money in two years and leave her rotting away in their crumbling stately piles in virtual poverty whilst doing so. This one," he went on, tapping the page, "already has half a dozen bastards, and this one is so feeble minded he could not take responsibility for a dog, let alone a wife."

"This still leaves three more, the Earl of Darton, the Earl of Ecclesfield, and Lord Goldthorpe," Charlie replied.

"Darton is a reckless fool who has somehow survived two duels and according to the law of averages, is unlikely to survive the third he will most certainly challenge. Though that might prove beneficial to Clara if she can get some allowance from the estate as his widow. Ecclesfield is a widower, twice Clara's age who, it is rumoured, pushed his late wife down the stairs when her dowry ran out. As for Goldthorpe, I do not like his silly face."

"You seem remarkably well informed," Charlie conceded.

"It is always best when putting one's own cards on the table, to have a fairly good idea what everyone else is holding."

"Then there is something else I should perhaps tell you, in the spirit of cards on the table." Charlie took a breath and recounted the story of the idiotic wager he had engaged in.

There was a moment's pause before it was broken by the old duke's rasping laughter. Charlie frowned not expecting this reaction. "I am somewhat surprised by your humour."

"I am laughing," his grandfather wheezed, "because for once in your young life you have made a foolish mistake from which you might learn. I am more than impressed by your business acumen, but it is reassuring to us lesser mortals to know that even you can make stupid mistakes." He became serious. "The question is, what are we to do now? Launching Clara into society when Rufford knows of the forfeit to marry the maid is going to be dashed difficult."

Charlie remembered his earlier clash with Rufford. "I do not think he will be an issue. He must have seen Clara a dozen times, yet when he saw her this morning, because she was not dressed as a maid, he had no idea who she was. Apart from Lady Morgan, I would wager that none in society would have any idea who Clara is, as a servant, she has been all but invisible. To be honest, out of context, I am not sure even Lady Elizabeth would know it was Clara."

"I have not had the pleasure of meeting this Lady Elizabeth, though from the expression on your face, I gather it may be less than pleasurable."

"Lady Elizabeth Morgan is a spoiled, selfish, unpleasant young woman," Charlie confirmed.

"I knew her grandfather. As I recall, he filled the family coffers and his son, Lady Elizabeth's father, made it his life's work to empty them. No wonder the young woman needs a wealthy husband."

"Well, I can assure you it will not be me," Charlie said decisively.

His grandfather steepled his fingers and closed his eyes in thought. "The way I see it," he began, "is that you have approached this as though Miss Blackburn, Clara has already agreed to your plan. Would I be right in thinking you have not yet mentioned it to her?"

Charlie shook his head. "No, but…"

"But nothing, my boy. One of the things I have learned about women over the years is that they do not like to have decisions about their future taken out of their hands." He held up a hand to stop Charlie's interruption. "Oh, they will go along with it, often because they have no choice," he continued, "but they have their ways of resisting which make our lives either difficult or damnably difficult. Whenever your grandmother and I had a disagreement, it always cost me an expensive trip to the jeweller." His eyes misted. "Sometimes, the price is greater than any jewel," he finished quietly.

Charlie nodded. In the few days he had known his grandfather, he had come to the conclusion that the old man both acknowledged his error with his daughter and had suffered the consequences for the rest of his life. There was always an air of melancholy behind the faded blue eyes, which, he noticed, were momentarily lifted when he was with Clara. It further occurred to Charlie that in contacting him, his grandfather was hoping not just for some kind of reconciliation, but to try to ensure that he did not make similar mistakes in his own life. His thoughts flitted back to Clara. She somehow managed to bring life and vivacity not just to his grandfather he noted, but to himself. In fact the whole household seemed lighter in the time she had been there. Contrary to her fears about his staff, they had taken to her as though she was one of their own. It was true, he acknowledged, that he actually felt lighter and happier when she was near. He dismissed the thought, telling himself he had been without a woman for too long time, that was all. Any woman with a pleasant face and an attractive personality would have the same effect, though even as he thought it he knew it to be a lie. No woman had ever aroused his interest or his body like the little maid.

"The question remains, what are we to do?" The duke's voice cut into his thoughts. "Now is not the time for wool gathering."

"What do you suggest?" Charlie's usual decisiveness seemed to have deserted him.

"Given your idea to find a suitable husband for Clara, I agree to your suggestion that I adopt her as my ward, your explanation of her previously growing up in the country would still apply. However, as she would be my ward, Clara will come and live with me. Should she continue to live here, tongues would wag and she would be ruined before your scheme could get underway. I can always send for my sister, your great Aunt Beatrice, to act as chaperone. She will jump at the chance as she has been bored to sobs since she retired to the country. Bea will also come in handy to teach Clara the ways of the ton she has not already learned."

"You seem to have thought of everything." Charlie was impressed by his grandfather's rapid plotting.

The duke laughed. "Your business acumen and attention to detail must have come from someone, my boy. I imagine there will be bumps on the road, but we have a workable plan. If Clara lives with me, it gives her respectability, but also means you may visit her as often or as little as you choose. It is ambitious, not to say risky, but I am sure between us we can pull it off. In the meantime, I shall give some thought to potential eligibles, I already have at least one name in mind."

"If we succeed, Clara's future will be secure," Charlie added.

"Now," the duke replied, "who is going to tell her?"

CHAPTER 16

Clara looked from one to the other. "Have you both completely lost your wits?" she burst out, completely forgetting she was addressing a duke and one of the richest men in the country. "I am a lady's maid, that is all I am. I have not been raised to be a lady. I would not know what to do or how I must behave."

"Let me assure you, Miss Blackburn, Clara, from what I have observed you already have the manners of a lady and, if I may say so, better manners that many women of high birth," the duke interrupted her. "But that is all beside the point, you are a fast study, you can learn all you need to know, and from what I have seen, it will not take you long."

"But I have no accomplishments. Lady Elizabeth spent many hours practising her drawing, singing and playing the pianoforte."

"That is why we shall engage tutors, these things can all be learned," Charlie put in.

"There is one other fairly large flaw in this ridiculous plan." Clara shook her head, still trying to comprehend the idea of turning her into a lady and more to the point, why? What possible reason could the duke and his grandson have for doing so? For their amusement? To prove that they had the money and power to do so? She was nothing to them, less than nothing, an orphaned servant girl who only happened to come into their orbit through the caprice of fate. The whole idea bordered on insanity. "Quite apart from any other consideration, there is the problem of Lady Elizabeth Morgan," she continued. "She is bound to recognise me. I shall be revealed as a fraud and you will be laughingstocks."

Charlie paused, considering her point. After some silence, during which Clara had a hope that this whole scheme would be discarded, he suddenly grinned, dashing her hopes. "I think it is fair to say, I can ensure that the threat from Lady Elizabeth is negated."

"How so?" asked the duke.

"I believe I own her father's mortgage and loans and if not, I shall by the end of the week. Should her ladyship prove to be difficult, I shall threaten to call them in."

"Is that not blackmail, sir?"

Charlie shrugged. "It is using one's knowledge to one's advantage. Frankly, I have little sympathy for Morgan or his daughter. He has made a virtue of spending more than his income and his failure to pay his creditors has no doubt put some merchants out of business. In my opinion, a spell in the Marshalsea would go some way to teaching him and his arrogant daughter a lesson both in economy and humility. I do not doubt that they would be above using any tactic to discredit me, were the boot to be on the other foot."

"It is true," the duke put in. "Morgan's estates were profitable, but since he inherited, he has done nothing to improve them. His tenants complain to my steward that the rents are too high for them to make a living while Morgan lives a life he cannot afford. The house of cards will come tumbling down sooner or later, regardless of anything Charlie does."

"There is one other thing," Charlie said then cleared his throat. "Lady Elizabeth herself called. It would seem that she is displeased with your foiling of her plan to compromise herself with me," he paused.

"And?" Clara prompted.

Charlie took a breath. "Well, to cut a long story short, Lady Elizabeth has terminated your employment."

"She sacked me?" Clara was barely surprised.

"Apparently so."

"Without a character?"

"Without a character," he confirmed.

That part did not come as a surprise at all. "I had meant to find a new position as soon as I could," she admitted. "I knew it was only a matter of time before I did something she could not countenance, at least it was something worthwhile and not for arranging her curls in the wrong way or something equally trivial."

"So you see," Charlie pressed home his advantage, "being in part responsible for you losing your position, it is only right and proper that I help you to find another."

Clara shook her head in exasperation. "Finding me a new position is one thing, Mr. Hampton. I imagine, given your friends, it would not be difficult, even without a character, but trying to present me to society is quite another. Are you not familiar with the saying about trying to make a silk purse from a sow's ear?"

"I cannot think of a prettier sow's ear." He grinned.

"But why are you doing this?"

Before Charlie could reply, the duke spoke. "Think of this as an experiment, Clara. The ton—and sadly at one time, many years ago I should have to count myself as one of their number in this—consider themselves as something different to ordinary mortals, that the accident of birth has somehow given them the right to rule, regardless of their competency or suitability to do so. If our little experiment is a success, you will prove that their sense of superiority is not only misplaced, but a sham."

"With respect, Your Grace, are you not still a member of the ton?" Clara looked at him steadily.

The old man smiled back at her. "And that proves my point, Miss Blackburn. You will be more than a match for the narrow mindedness and arrogance of society. However, I understand your concern of course, so let me add this: if at the end of a year, you have not found a suitable husband if that is what you wish, I shall give you a house and sufficient income for you to live in comfort and independence for the rest of your life. How does that sound?"

"It is very generous, Your Grace, but it still does not explain why you wish to do this."

The duke shot a glance at his grandson. "When I was younger than I am now, but old enough to know better, I did something which I have since regretted every day of my life, the details of which I will not go into now. But suffice it to say that the result of my narrow mindedness caused a great deal of suffering to too many people. Had I been prepared to see value in someone who was not from society, all this could and should have been avoided. Times are changing, and you, Miss Blackburn, are a part of that change. Through my folly, someone I loved dearly was cast down, I cannot undo that wrong, but please allow me the opportunity to help you to become the woman you should be."

"I do not know what to say, sir," Clara replied.

"Say yes, Clara," Charlie cut in.

"The idea is madness."

"I agree, but a little madness from time to time can be quite exhilarating," he grinned victoriously.

"There is a world of difference between exhilaration and fear," she shot back. "And I believe that while you might experience exhilaration, what I shall feel is fear. For one thing Lady Elizabeth…"

"I believe we have dealt with her," Charlie interrupted.

"…she is bound to recognise me immediately."

Charlie looked down at her, his eyes narrowing. "In all the time you worked for her, did she ever see you without a cap?"

Clara was horrified. "Never, Mr. Hampton. Lady Elizabeth and her parents were sticklers, if any of us appeared in less than perfect uniform or livery we were fined." Or beaten, though she did not mention that. "I believe she spent more time looking at our dress than she did at us," she finished. She suddenly clapped her hand to her mouth.

"What is it?" the duke asked.

"I had forgotten, quite forgotten. Lady Elizabeth cannot see so far, her father bought her some eyeglasses, but she refuses to wear them. I believe she struggles to see anything unless it is at the end of her nose," Clara explained.

"Then the problem is solved," Charlie exclaimed. "I doubt the woman even knows the colour of your hair, let alone your eyes. Once you are dressed as a lady, I doubt she will recognise you. She will probably think she knows you from a soiree or ball or some such. And, as I said, if she is a problem, I have the advantage."

"There is another flaw in your plan, Mr. Hampton, even if Lady Elizabeth does not recognise me, and I must say I am not convinced that she will not, she will, however, certainly remember my name."

"Then we must use a different name," the duke spoke. Both his voice and his eyes had more life than when he had arrived. "But something not too dissimilar," he added. "Clara must keep her first name, that is only sensible."

"Quite." Charlie agreed.

"I have it," the duke said. "You shall be Miss Clara Burns. It is not so dissimilar."

"Perfect, what do you say Clara? Are you willing to let Blackburn go and emerge re-born as Miss Clara Burns?"

"I…"

They were interrupted by the appearance of Pearson. "Begging your pardon, Your Grace, sir, miss. A small box has arrived for Miss Blackburn."

"I believe it will be your things from Lady Elizabeth," Charlie explained. "Would you like to go and unpack? We will talk later when you have had time to consider our proposal."

Clara was grateful for the reprieve, bobbed a quick curtsey, and fled.

CHAPTER 17

After her strange encounter with the duke and Mr. Hampton, Clara was glad of the small diversion of unpacking her meagre belongings from the small box. She shook out her best gown to try to remove the creases, to no avail. It would take a hot smoothing iron to make it in any way presentable and nothing would be able to disguise its shabbiness. Her second gown was even worse. She had never considered the state of her gowns before, the Morgans had provided her with clothing in their service and Lady Elizabeth's demands left little time for any kind of life outside her working hours, so it had not mattered much. Her breath stopped as she examined the gowns more closely, someone and she knew exactly who, had taken a pair of scissors to the skirts of both gowns and cut them. As she shook out the second gown, a note fluttered to the ground, she instantly recognised Lady Elizabeth's childish script.

> *Blackburn,*
>
> *Your employment is terminated with immediate effect. When your belongings were brought to me to check, I noticed a fragment of mirror and several pieces of lace and ribbon you have obviously stolen from my possession. I shall not call the watch to report these items as stolen. However, all outstanding wages will be forfeit and of course there is no question of a character reference.*

In the future, should I learn that you have managed to inveigle yourself into a position with a family of quality, you may rest assured that I shall have no compunction in revealing that you are both a liar and a thief.

Unfortunately, when your clothing was being packed, some of it was damaged.

Clara's knees almost gave way. She already knew she had lost her position and knew that Lady Elizabeth would withhold a character reference, but to be so vicious over a fragment of broken mirror and a few scraps of ribbon and lace she had salvaged when the other woman had discarded them was low, even for Lady Elizabeth. She sat on the edge of the bed, the letter still in her hand. Why would a woman who has so much be determined to take away everything from a woman who already had so little? Lady Elizabeth knew she was an orphan, she knew there was no loving family, however poor, to take her in until she could find some other work.

She considered her options, disregarding the uncomfortable conversation she had just left, perhaps a seamstress might take her on, a lady's maid is trained in delicate sewing and mending. Or, if that were not possible, she could probably find work as a laundry maid, though she only had experience of washing delicate ladies' things, which tended to be done of course by a lady's personal maid. The work of a regular laundry maid was frequently both hard and harsh, she knew that. Although faint, there was a small chance that she could return to the orphanage again, working with the warden for room and board and perhaps earning wages elsewhere.

Clara stood up and walked to the window where, in keeping with her mood, the rain was lashing down. She traced one of the droplets as it made its way down the glass. She would never again work as lady's maid to a lady of quality, Lady Elizabeth would see to that. Even those with new money would probably be reluctant to hire someone maligned as a liar and a thief, however false. She would have to move far away and work for a woman of much lower standing who might be prepared to take her on. Or, and this she conceded was the most likely outcome, she would end up as a maid of all work to a family who could barely afford a servant, where she would be expected to cook, clean, and serve for all the family. She had seen some of the girls from the foundling hospital who had become maids of all work, they had always looked exhausted and defeated.

Her finger stopped in its track as her mind returned to the earlier bizarre conversation. Her first instinct had been to reject the duke and Charlie's plan as ridiculous and unworkable, she still thought it was. But that was before she had read the letter, in the blink of an eye her circumstances and prospects had changed. Most of the doors open to her had been slammed shut. So what if she did as Charlie and his grandfather suggested and tried to pass herself off as a lady? What was the real harm? So what if they were found out? She had no doubt that the duke would survive, those with money and power always did, and Mr. Hampton would probably pretend the whole thing was a joke. Even if she was discovered, the duke had promised her a house and an income, so the outcome of their 'experiment' was less of a risk to her too. Why not? And if they did, by some miracle, pull it off, she would enjoy cocking a snook at Lady Elizabeth and her ilk, although it would be rather like poking a bear with a stick.

"Miss Blackburn? Clara? Are you quite well?" Charlie asked from by the door.

She turned to face him, startled at the sound of his voice. She saw his gaze take in the gowns, the lace, the mirror shards. "I am..." Her voice cracked.

He was at her side in an instant. "What? What is it that has distressed you?" he enquired.

Silently, she held out the note for him to read. It did not take him long. "Vindictive bitch," he growled, crumpling the note and pocketing it. "You are to think no more of this," he commanded.

She raised her eyes to his. "How can I? Lady Elizabeth has taken away any chance I had of working for a respectable family."

"It does not matter."

"Of course it matters, it is what I was trained to be, and I was good at it. I had hoped one day to rise to the position of housekeeper in a grand house, and that will never happen now," her eyes shimmered with unshed tears. "I wanted to have enough money, to be independent, you see," she explained, "so that I should not have to rely on the whim of someone else. I wanted to be a respected and respectable woman. I know I come from nothing, but I wanted to make something of myself, I thought I could, but..."

She felt Charlie gather her into his arms as the tears she had held in for so long began to fall. He gently stroked her back as sobs wracked her slender body, murmuring soft words of comfort as she wept, something she had not done for a very long time.

How long they stood there, she did not know. Eventually, Clara stepped back, sniffling. "I am sorry, Mr. Hampton, I should not have done that."

Charlie loosened his grip but did not entirely let her go. "Clara," he began, his eyes holding hers, "much as I would like, I cannot undo Lady Elizabeth's vindictiveness, but I think it is about time she was taught a lesson in humility, and you should be the one to teach her."

Clara's eyes widened. "I don't understand."

"I know you believe our plan to be hare-brained."

"To say the least."

"It is audacious I grant you that but think of the fun you can have taking down the snobbery of the so-called upper classes whose massive advantages spring only from being born in the right bed. Were they to have to make their own way in the world as you and I have, they would no doubt end up sitting on a dung heap with straw in their ears, eating turnips."

He was delighted to see Clara gave a watery giggle.

"And," he went on, "you have a tremendous advantage."

She raised an eyebrow. "And what is that?"

"You will be hiding in plain sight. No-one would imagine it possible that someone from what they consider to be the lower orders could or would be so audacious as to attempt what you are about to do. The idea would never occur to them." He paused. "What have you got to lose? Why not poke the bear?"

Clara paused for a moment. "I'll do it," she replied. "God help us."

CHAPTER 18

*C*harlie was sitting in the library, a book open on his lap, but his thoughts on the conversation he and his grandfather had had once Clara had left to unpack her meagre belongings.

"I believe there is a mystery to be solved concerning Miss Blackburn," the duke's voice cut into the silence. Charlie raised an eyebrow.

"What has she told you," the old man went on, "regarding her childhood?"

"That she was abandoned as a baby, left as a foundling."

"Did she tell you gifts had been sent to her and money to pay the vicar to tutor her?"

"I knew about the lessons, but not about the gifts, she merely said she knew she had a family somewhere but as they had abandoned her once, she did not want to risk rejection a second time. Clearly though," he added, "they must have been a family of some means. Perhaps a ruined lady?"

"Perhaps," the duke agreed. "Have you seen the locket she wears?"

Charlie shook his head.

"It is silver and has some specific markings, the like of which I believe I may have seen before."

"Did she say how she came by the locket?" Charlie was intrigued.

"Apparently it arrived with her when she was left at the orphanage.

The warden told her to come back when she reached her majority and she would tell her more."

"Curious."

"Curious indeed. I believe that while Clara is with me, being taught the finer points, I shall investigate and see what I can find out. It might be that Miss Blackburn is not who she thinks she is."

The whole situation was strange, but the plan was indeed moving forward. Charlie and the duke had already ordered a whole wardrobe for her, Lady Beatrice was on her way, visiting cards were at the printers, and tutors had been engaged. Clara would be leaving as soon as the carriage came to take her to the duke's home for her education. All he knew was that he was determined that Clara should and would have a better life, the life she deserved. She was more of a lady than those born to the rank and he was going to prove it.

Charles looked up as Clara entered the room. He said nothing for a moment, he could not, his breath had completely left his lungs. She was quite exquisite, the cut of the gown emphasized her narrow waist and the curve of her breasts. Her hair was glossy, the colour of ripe chestnuts but with highlights of burnished copper, the loose tendrils framed her delicate face and made him want to twirl one around his fingers and see if it was as silky as it looked. The green ribbon that had been woven through it brought out the colour of her magnificent, richly emerald eyes. She would certainly turn heads when she was launched into society, men would be trampling over each other to gain an introduction. And with the Duke of Wensley's sponsorship, offers of marriage would flood in, as he had planned. Oddly, the thought of that did not cheer him as it should.

"I came to say goodbye. The carriage will be here directly." Damnation, even her soft contralto voice was arousing.

He came round the desk to stand in front of her, close enough to see the anxiety in her eyes. "Clara," he said softly, "look at me." She met his gaze, but he could tell that she was nervous. "In a short time now, your life is going to change in ways you never imagined possible and you are going to relish every minute of it. I know at the moment you are feeling apprehensive, but you should not. You are a beautiful, good, and kind young woman and within days, men will be falling over themselves to propose to you."

Clara could not help but giggle. "I pity the poor housemaid who has to sweep them up."

Charlie laughed. Quite apart from her beauty, she was not vapid and devoid of personality as debutantes were trained to be, curated to reflect the interests of an eligible man. Life with her would be far from dull. He must ensure that whoever was chosen as her husband would appreciate her spirit and not try to crush it. Already his list of potential eligibles was getting dangerously short.

She held out her hand. "Well then, goodbye, Mr. Hampton."

"Charlie."

She cocked her head to one side. "I do not think so, Mr. Hampton. After all, I am now a lady, we have not properly been introduced." Her eyes sparkled as she teased.

He raised an eyebrow as he took her hand to kiss it before pulling her into his arms. "Consider this part of your education, Miss Burns. Young ladies who tease gentlemen may find that they are not gentlemen," he murmured as his lips took hers gently, until she opened her mouth and his tongue plunged inside, tasting her. He pulled her close, almost groaning as he felt her softness against his hard body. All he wanted to do in that moment was to sink into her softness and let it envelop him. He stilled for a moment when he realised that somehow her arms were around his neck, her fingers lightly caressing the nape of his neck. He almost jumped when her tongue touched his, she was kissing him back.

"God help me," he muttered, crushing her to him, his hands roamed her back and pert derriere. If there was ever a woman he wanted to make love to, here she was, in his arms, enticing him, arousing him in a way she had yet to realize was dangerous, stirring his heart and body into taking her, claiming her for himself. Yet he could not.

Charlie stepped back when he heard the door handle shift, releasing her as Pearson opened the door. "The carriage awaits, Miss Burns," he announced.

Clara drew a shaky breath. "Thank you, Pearson. And thank you for all the kindness you have shown me during my stay." She turned to Charlie and curtseyed. "Thank you for everything, Mr. Hampton, it has been most...instructive." She turned and left.

Charlie watched her leave with regret and rubbed his chin. "What have I done?" he murmured. "Have I unleashed an angel or a devil?" He could not help grinning a little, whatever Clara was, society was never going to be the same again.

CHAPTER 19

*C*lara sat in the carriage beside the duke, her hands demurely clasped in her lap, her face betraying nothing, but her thoughts were in a whirl. Twice now, Charlie Hampton had kissed her and each time her body had responded seemingly with a will of its own. She wanted more, she wanted to feel his hands on her skin, she wanted him to touch her where she almost ached for fulfilment, and she was quite sure these were not the thoughts or behaviour of a lady. Despite the plan, she knew that these desires were was what marked her as a wanton wench, nothing better than she should be, as she heard Lady Elizabeth's cook say when one of the maids left with a baby on the way and no ring on her finger.

"Are you feeling unwell my dear?" The duke's voice broke into her thoughts. "You seem somewhat...pre-occupied."

She smiled. "Just a little nervous," she admitted, which was true but was not what was entirely occupying her thoughts.

The duke patted her arm. "There is nothing to worry about my dear. Once Bea has taken you in hand you will be fit to be presented to the king. Indeed, it may be that the king is not fit to be presented to you." He chuckled. "In any case," he added, looking out of the window, "we have arrived, and by the look of the trunks being carried into the house, so has Bea."

Her duties as lady's maid had taken her into several London town houses, but nothing compared to the magnificence of Wensley House. It was the size of a small palace. "Oh my goodness," she exclaimed, taking in the elegant facade which must contain at least fifty windows.

"My grandfather, the first duke, re-modelled the house," the duke explained. "The other side has formal gardens and an entrance on to the river, something considered essential when the original house was built."

They entered through the large oak door into the marble entrance hall, where what seemed to Clara like an army of servants were assembled. "Good morning to you all," the duke addressed the gathering. "I am fully recovered and looking forward to being home again. This young lady is Miss Clara Burns who has recently become my ward and will be staying with us from now on." Clara could almost feel the curiosity as thirty pairs of eyes flicked in her direction. "That is all," the duke dismissed them. "Betts," he spoke to his butler, "I take it Lady Beatrice has arrived."

"Indeed she has, Your Grace. Her ladyship arrived earlier this morning and her luggage has just arrived."

"Very good, we shall have luncheon in the small dining room at one. Clara, this is Mrs. Betts, the housekeeper. Mrs. Betts, please show Miss Burns to her room."

"Certainly, Your Grace. Everything is prepared, Miss Burns' maid arrived earlier with the luggage," Mrs. Betts said with a curtsey.

"Good." The duke turned to Clara. "Take your time to explore and get used to your new home as I have no doubt my steward awaits me in the library, so I shall look forward to seeing you at luncheon."

Clara followed a silent Mrs. Betts through stairwells and hallways that turned her head. If ever Clara was glad to see a familiar face, it was as soon as she entered her new bedroom. Lily was folding the fine, new underwear and placing it in the rapidly filling drawer of the tallboy. "Oooh, miss, isn't it lovely?" she said as Clara sank down on the bed. "There's a dressing room through there," she pointed, "and there's even a special room just for bathing, imagine that."

Clara shook her head. "Imagine," she murmured.

"Now," Lily went on briskly, "Once you're ready I'm to take you down to Lady Beatrice before luncheon."

Clara's head snapped up. "Have you met Lady Beatrice? Already? I thought she only arrived this morning. What is she like?"

Lily grinned. "A whirlwind, miss."

Lily led Clara to a door and left her there to finish unpacking. As she prepared to knock, Clara patted her hair one last time, even though Lily had assured her that she looked 'perfect, miss, pretty as a picture'. She had just raised her hand when the door was flung open and a plump woman wearing a striking cerise gown and smiling broadly stood waiting on the other side.

"You must be Miss Burns, come in, come in, child. I want to know all about you. Someone who has charmed my dear brother Andrew must be very special indeed." She took Clara's hand and led her to the sofa. "Now, sit beside me and tell me all about yourself," she said as she settled her substantial frame on the sofa, picked up her little dog and patted the space next to her.

Clara held nothing back. If Lady Bea was to become part of the madcap scheme, she needed to know everything. Some time later, the older woman sat back against the cushions. "Well, my dear, your young life has certainly been eventful thus far, and," she added, her blue eyes twinkling, "I suspect it is about to get a whole lot more eventful in the near future."

"Are you sure, your ladyship, about your part in this?" Clara asked.

Lady Bea threw back her head in what was a most unladylike manner and laughed. "Oh, my dear, I would not miss this for the world. There are so many in society with an overdeveloped sense of their own importance and pride, most of whom have absolutely nothing at all to be proud about. Their antiquated views on breeding need challenging, and you, my dear, it seems to me, even after the briefest of conversations, are eminently well equipped to do it. Now, we must hurry to luncheon, Andrew is something of a stickler for punctuality."

Clara followed Lady Bea as she bustled out and sat at the table where it was indicated for her. The meal passed quickly, but Clara had little appetite and found listening to the brother and sister fascinating as the duke told Lady Bea of his recent reconciliation with his grandson.

"I am sure poor, dear Annabelle would be happy to know you are part of her son's life," Lady Bea said.

"It is early days, and I have much to do to win his trust completely, but I hope we may become closer," the duke replied.

"And your venture with Miss Burns should help."

The duke looked at Clara and smiled. "I am hoping that our little venture helps us all. Clara, your work will begin at once, as we have no time to lose."

The afternoon began with Clara's attempt at watercolours. Even to her untrained eye, it was horrendous.

"It is delightful, my dear," Lady Bea enthused when she inspected her work later. "The colours are vivid and the style is quite unique."

"You have absolutely no idea what it is meant to be, do you, Lady Bea?" Clara asked. "I don't blame you, your ladyship, I know what it is meant to be and I am struggling to see it."

"Ah well, practise makes perfect as they say."

"With respect, ma'am, I doubt poor Mr. Bennett will ever make an artist of me," she paused before turning the picture round. "Violets, it is supposed to be violets."

"Is it really?" Lady Bea stepped closer and took out her lorgnette. "Well, I suppose this style of art may become popular one day. Everything has its moment. Besides, each lady finds a skill for herself. Perhaps this will not do."

Clara tilted her head to one side, considering her work. "Well, when a painting of something that no-one knows what it is becomes considered to be art, then I shall call myself an artist."

"I think that is enough art for today," Lady Bea replied. "Now, away with you, child and dress for dinner, I believe my great-nephew is coming and I am looking forward to meeting him."

"So soon? But why is he coming?"

"I imagine he will want to know how you performed on your first day."

Clara quickly gathered up her art materials. "I think it best then that he does not see this."

"Probably wise," Lady Bea agreed with a smile.

Lily had already laid out a pale lemon watered silk gown for Clara. "How did the painting go, miss?"

"I do not think I shall be troubling the patrons of the Royal Academy now or at any time in the future," Clara replied. "I think it fair to say I am the most untalented person ever to hold a paintbrush and could not paint a picture worthy of looking at if my life depended on it."

"I'm sure it wasn't that bad, miss."

"I assure you those were Mr. Bennett's actual words," Clara grinned. "I think, unless the duke has some torment in mind for Mr. Bennett, I will leave watercolours to those who have a talent for it."

When Clara was ready with her hair drawn up into a loose chignon with two or three long ringlets curling over her shoulder, Lily presented her with a red velvet box. Inside was a magnificent set of pearls. "His grace sent these for you to wear tonight, he said they were for his daughter's twenty-first birthday, but he never got to give them to her. Would you like some help with the earrings Miss?"

"No thank you, Lily, I can manage." The pearls were magnificent, almost the size of birds' eggs. She would wear them tonight, she decided, and then would return them. Something this expensive should be worn by someone who was truly entitled to wear them. They were clearly intended to become a family heirloom one day.

She paused for a moment as that thought caused a shock to run through her body. These pearls would be passed down and the next woman to wear them would be Charlie's wife. Charlie was the duke's heir, of course he would marry and these pearls would belong to his lawful wife. The thought brought unexpected tears to her eyes. Her head told her that the woman who joined his life and shared his bed could never be her, but her heart wanted it.

She dashed the tears from her eyes—there was no point in wishing for something that could never be, she had learned that lesson a long time ago. She must concentrate on the moment; Fate had given her a wonderful opportunity and she would make the best of it. Perhaps at the end of the experiment she might still be able to call Charlie her friend, and if that was all there could ever be, she would be happy for that. She would have to be.

Charlie had already arrived and was sitting with his newly found great-aunt when Clara entered the drawing room. The duke looked up and smiled, "Ah, Clara, come in. You are looking lovely." His eyes lighted on the pearls. "They look wonderful, Clara. It is good to see them. Pearls always look better when they are worn."

"You are very kind, Your Grace," Clara replied. "But I shall return them to your safekeeping in the morning." The duke's smile slipped a fraction, prompting her to hastily say, "Oh, please do not think me ungrateful, sir. They are the most beautiful things I have ever seen, let alone have the privilege to wear. But they are a family heirloom and should really be worn by...," her words petered out.

"The next duchess?" Charlie put in. Clara nodded, feeling her cheeks redden.

"Well, in the meantime," Lady Bea broke the tension. "Andrew is perfectly correct, pearls need the warmth of human skin or they go dull.

So if you would do him the favour of wearing them, the future duchess I am sure will be very grateful. Whoever she is."

As he escorted her into the dining room Charlie remarked to Clara, "Grandfather is right, the pearls look wonderful, as do you."

"Thank you, Mr. Hampton," she replied, primly.

"You are welcome, Miss Burns." She could almost feel him grinning.

Throughout the meal, Clara began to relax as Lady Bea regaled them with tales of her brother as a boy. "I had no idea the aristocracy could be so wild and naughty," Clara laughed.

"You have not heard the worst of it my dear," the duke chuckled, "there are some tales that would even make Bea blush."

"I doubt it Andrew, as the widow of a general, I can assure you there is little mystery to me regarding men's thoughts or otherwise," Lady Bea replied, tartly.

"Words we would be well advised to remember," the duke said and winked at Charlie. He took a sip of wine before adding, "Now to the business of launching Clara into society. I assume by now, Bea, that you have formulated a plan."

"Of course. You don't think it was my dear husband, the general, who came up with every brilliant strategy, did you?"

"Never for a moment."

"In that case, I believe we shall introduce Clara to society in small steps. I have invited my god-daughters, Verity and Ella, to tea next week. They are charming girls, despite their odious father, and I am sure you will be the greatest of friends." She patted Clara's arm and smiled.

Clara shakily smiled back.

"Then, I thought we might have a small musicale or dinner here the following week and invite the eligibles before we throw a ball in a month's time."

"A ball?" Clara was alarmed.

"Of course, we must throw a ball in your honour, dear. People will expect it and you will have been to plenty of others by then, so everyone will know you. Frankly, if you are not engaged in six weeks, eight at the most, I shall not have done my job properly. Now, Andrew, that is my plan, the details we can add later."

"Splendid, splendid." Her brother raised his glass. "To the launching of Miss Clara Burns."

"She is not a ship, Andrew."

"But she, and you will be the talk of the season."

After the meal, Clara excused herself to a well-lit sitting room to practice another respectful talent, embroidery, which was going better than the last. She had some experience with mending and this was not so different.

She was sitting by the fire, her embroidery on her lap, when the door opened and Charlie strode in. She sprang to her feet. "I am sorry, Mr. Hampton, her ladyship retired almost as soon as we withdrew."

"Good, it gives me an opportunity to speak to you. Grandfather has also taken his leave. I think they both rather enjoyed the wine tonight. Are you all right? You seemed rather quiet during dinner."

"I am fine, just a little overwhelmed, I think. You all seem to think this little charade is going to pass without a hitch."

"Come and sit with me," he said and indicated the space next to him as he extended his long legs towards the fire. "Now, what specifically did my great-aunt say to worry you?"

"It is the balls," Clara replied. "I have never been to a ball—well—I have been to dozens, but we maids just stayed in the ladies' retiring room. I have never seen what actually goes on."

"A lot of drinking by the men, a huge amount of gossiping, a little flirting and dancing, obviously."

"That is the problem. I do not know how to dance."

"Of course you do."

"Well, country dances, reels, and jigs and things, but I do not know about quadrilles, gavottes, or waltzes."

"I'm sure Aunt Bea will have engaged plenty of tutors before your debut, but until then, we must do our due diligence to remedy your ignorance." He stood up and held out his hand. "Miss Burns, may I have the pleasure of this waltz?"

She stood up and curtseyed. "I believe you may." She smiled.

He stepped closer, one hand around her waist. "The thing about the waltz," he explained softly, his voice coming from very close to her ear, causing tingles down her neck. "Is that it was considered quite daring when it was introduced from Vienna." His voice was even softer as he drew her towards him. "All you need to do is count one-two-three and follow my lead. Do you think you can do that?"

"Yes," she replied, breathlessly. "Wait," she stopped. "How do I know when to start counting? I might be on one whilst you are on three."

"A fair point," he conceded. "You really need to just let your body feel the music. But to begin with," he continued, seeing the look of confusion in her eyes, "I shall start and we shall count together. Now, one-two-three …"

As they moved, Clara was acutely aware, not only of his hard body so close to hers, but his lips constantly brushing her ear. "Must we be so close?" she asked. "It can hardly be acceptable for young women to be held like this."

"That is the beauty of the waltz," he murmured, drawing her even closer. "Remember, one-two-three count with me."

By the time they had reached the windows, Clara had begun to relax slightly and enjoy herself. They stopped short of the heavy brocade drapes. "What do we do when we reach the boundary of the room?" she asked. "It is all very well, but I do not imagine they open the doors and the couples waltz outside and down the street in a merry line."

"Now we move on to lesson two," Charlie explained and before she had time to think, they had turned round and were waltzing back in the other direction. "Very good," Charlie's voice was low. "Now I am going to hum a tune so that you have an idea of putting your feet to the music."

They waltzed round the room twice before Clara stumbled. Charlie caught her and they collapsed onto the sofa, laughing. "I would say, Mr. Hampton, that your singing is probably even worse than my watercolour painting, so I do not feel that a career in the opera beckons for you nor an exhibition at the Royal Academy for me."

"I am hurt, Miss Burns. I have been told I have rather a fine baritone." He sang a verse of 'To a Young Lady with Lampreys'. Clara erupted into a fit of giggles. "I'm not sure," she gasped, "what is worse, your singing or the thought of the poor girl having to eat lampreys!"

Charlie shook his head. "Brutal, Miss Burns. Quite brutal, I am crushed," he finished, looking anything but.

"I will say, you are a better dance teacher." Clara's eyes danced with mischief. "You only stood on my foot twice."

"Impudent miss," he admonished her, grinning broadly. "It is a wonder I have any feet left at all with you galumphing about on them," he teased.

"Galumphing? Galumphing? I would remind you, sir, that I am now a lady and ladies never galumph," she shot back.

He laid a hand on his heart. "My apologies, I should never have accused you of such a heinous crime."

"Quite right."

"I must be punished of course."

"Of course," she laughed, then gasped as he slid to the floor and eased off her slipper.

"What are you doing?"

"My penance," he replied before taking one of her slender feet in his hands and gently rubbing it before bending his head and kissing her ankle. "Such delicate feet," he murmured before turning his attention to the other one.

She shivered, feeling warmth race up her leg to wet her centre. "Sir, Mr. Hampton, Charlie, I really don't think you should…"

"Then don't think lovely Clara, just feel." He moved once again beside her, twirling her ringlets between his fingers and tugging her gently towards him.

There was nothing gentle about his kiss. He demanded and she gave, willingly. He cupped her face so that she could not turn away, but she did not want to. She wanted this moment to last forever. When his hands drifted lower and slowly eased the bodice of her gown to expose her breasts, she felt no shame, only exquisite pleasure as he touched their already hardened peaks, first with his fingers and then as he bent his head and took them in his mouth.

"Oh, Charlie," she could scarcely breathe as sensation after sensation washed over her, her new undergarments becoming damp with her desires and need.

Just as suddenly as his passionate ministrations had begun, they ended. He sat back, his hands put her clothing to rights with speed that would have impressed a lady's maid. "I am sorry, Clara," his voice was husky with desire. "I apologise, that should not have happened."

"Why?" Clara's eyes were huge in her delicate face. "Is it because I am not really a lady? Because a real lady would not do the things I have just done?"

Charlie choked. "It is none of those things, Clara. You are a beautiful, unspoiled young woman and it is you who deserve better," he stood. "I had better go. Will you be all right?"

She nodded, wondering if she had made more than one mistake when agreeing to Charlie's plan.

CHAPTER 20

*C*lara's training continued apace, she would never be an artist, her watercolours had taught her that, but she was pleased to find she had what Mr. Antoine, her pianoforte teacher called a 'natural ear' for music. She could not read the manuscripts, but she found that if someone sang a melody, her fingers could, of their own volition find and harmonise the tune.

Her dancing lessons with Mr. Burrows were considerably much less exciting than the one she had experienced with Charlie. The thought of Charlie stilled her fingers over the keys. She had not seen him since their scene in the sitting room. He was avoiding her, she was sure of it and although she had not seen him physically, she could not seem to get his image out of her thoughts. Her fingers trailed idly over the keys as she brought to mind the way his eyes gleamed when he teased her, his deep baritone voice, and the way a wayward lock of dark hair flopped over his eyes when he leaned in to whisper in her ear. Her breath caught as she remembered the feel of his lips on her own and her breasts tightened at the memory of how he had touched her.

She straightened her spine, there was no point in mooning about Charlie Hampton, there was no future in it, the man was trying to marry her off to another man, for goodness sake. If he had wanted to marry her, no doubt he would have proposed it. She was pretty sure he would be happy enough to bed her, she was not an ignorant young lady after all, but that was all he would want, all she would ever be to him, and yet, a small voice persisted, if that was all he wanted, why hadn't he taken it when she had veritably offered him? She was, after all, only a servant.

Her reverie was interrupted as Lady Bea swept into the room. "Good, my dear, here you are. Now, make haste and change. Verity and Ella will be here for tea in an hour. This is your first test."

"But you said they were to come next week, your ladyship," Clara squeaked.

"Well, I probably did, but it is of no consequence. You must meet them soon and at least now you will not spend the next week working yourself up into a frazzle, so bad for the complexion. Wear the cream sprigged muslin with the pansies," she called after Clara's retreating form. "And do not run."

Half an hour later, Clara was sitting in the blue salon. The room was light and airy, the walls an eggshell blue with matching silk drapes. Various sofas, chairs, and tables were scattered around the room. Fires were burning in the two fireplaces, giving the room a cheerful warmth. Lady Bea looked up from her embroidery. "Do stop fidgeting, dear, a lady never fidgets." Clara clasped her hands tightly in her lap. "And do try to look less as though you are awaiting an execution, your own to be precise."

"I am a little nervous," Clara admitted, knowing that if she could not pass this test, the experiment would be over almost before it had begun.

"It is good to be a little nervous, Clara, it sharpens the mind, but once you have met Verity and Ella, you will be great friends, I am sure. They are charming girls. Their grandmother was a very dear friend of mine and I was honoured to be their godmother, though it has to be said that their father, the earl, is less to my taste, and since poor Leonora died, I have seen rather less of the girls than I should like. However, they are here now and I intend to make the most of our time together." Further conversation was cut short as Betts opened the door and announced, "Lady Ella and Lady Verity Grainger."

"Thank you, Betts, please bring tea," Lady Bea instructed. "Now, come in, girls and meet Miss Clara Burns, she is new to town."

Clara rose and curtseyed and within minutes was laughing as Verity and Ella were telling of their adventures in London.

"Of course, Papa only brought us to London because he could not think what else to do with us," Verity explained. "Part of the roof at Swallowfield fell down and is being repaired and it was not seemly to leave us there alone, especially as our companion, Miss Potter, declined to stay among the dirt and rubble and escaped to her sister."

"Fortunately, Papa is out a great deal so we are unable to irritate him too much," Ella said, adding, "do you have family, Miss Burns?"

"Clara is the duke's ward and as such has no other family to take care of her," Lady Bea put in quickly.

"I am so sorry, Miss Burns, I had not realised." Ella looked crestfallen.

"Do not trouble yourself, Lady Ella," Clara replied. "My parents were lost a long time ago, and please, call me Clara."

"Thank you, Clara, and we must be Verity and Ella." Verity smiled. "I hope we shall be great friends."

"I hope so, too," Clara smiled back, beginning to relax.

They were interrupted by Betts bringing in the tea. When he had finished placing it on the table he announced, "Mr. Hampton has arrived and wonders if he might be permitted to join you ladies for tea?"

"Mr. Charles Hampton?" Ella asked. "The newly discovered heir to the duke? Oh, how exciting. Please do let him join us." She looked at her godmother.

"Mr. Hampton does not usually ask permission for anything so he must be keen to meet you."

"Please show him in, Betts," Lady Bea ordered before looking sternly at the three girls. "And there is to be no nonsense from you," she said before adding, "I imagine there will be more than enough from him."

Charlie's arrival led to a great deal of laughter as he regaled them with stories of his travels.

"And did Mr. Hanowin truly have a diamond as big as a bird's egg?" Verity asked, her eyes wide.

"Indeed not, what Mr. Hanowin was trying to sell was a large piece of glass."

"And what happened when he was found out?" Clara asked.

"When he saw I had brought a diamond expert with me, he swallowed the thing."

"Oh my goodness," Ella exclaimed.

"Damn near killed himself, of course the thing got stuck, the diamond fellow and I had to thump his back quite ferociously."

"Oh, dear."

Charlie paused and took a sip of tea, then selected a sandwich and started eating it. "Mr. Hampton, you cannot leave the story hanging, what happened next? Did Mr. Hanowin survive? We are all agog," Clara demanded.

"Oh, he was as right as ninepence. The thing shot out of his mouth like a cork from a bottle, put a hole in a portrait of the king, though. Straight between the eyes, probably an act of treason actually."

"Mr. Hampton, it is a very interesting and entertaining story, but I am not sure whether or if any of it is true," Clara said with a laugh.

He grinned. "Well, as the saying goes, one should never let the truth get in the way of a good story. Now ladies, I have my landau outside, what say you to a drive around the park?"

"That would be wonderful Mr. Hampton. Papa never has time for such things," Ella said, her eyes shining.

"Then run and fetch your outdoor things." Lady Bea ordered, insisting on pelisses. "I do not want any of you catching your death of cold. Once the sun disappears behind a cloud you will thank me for this."

Within minutes, they were settled in Charlie's landau. Clara found herself sitting beside Charlie as the sisters opted to sit beside each other. She tried to ignore his presence against hers, but she felt as if her entire body was attuned to his warmth. Once in the park, their progress was inevitably slow as Charlie was greeted by a variety of friends and acquaintances, the first being the Lords Harper and Silcock. They trotted alongside. "So where have you been you slyboots?" Silcock poked Charlie with his riding crop. "Have not seen you in a dog's age."

"Business, Silcock, some of us have more to do than while away our lives at White's," Charlie replied.

"And what delightful business you seem to be involved in," Harper observed, raising his hat to the ladies. "Escorting such a bevy of beauty."

"Lady Ella, Lady Verity, may I introduce you to Lords Silcock and Harper," Charlie said graciously. "And this is my grandfather's ward, Miss Clara Burns."

"Charmed to meet you ladies," Silcock replied. "What say you we make our way towards the Serpentine? Perhaps we may all take a turn?"

Before Charlie could respond Lady Verity turned towards him, "Oh, may we Mr. Hampton, only if it is not inconvenient of course."

"How can I refuse?" Charlie smiled. Clara watched with a small amount of horror as Lords Harper and Silcock set off with the Grainger girls, leaving her to walk alone with Charlie.

"So," he nodded to the girls in front of them, "you appear to have passed your first test."

"They are lovely girls and I hope we may be friends, but I hardly think they will have scrutinised me as I suspect more sophisticated members of the ton will," she replied, keeping her eyes resolutely ahead.

"Perhaps so," he replied solemnly, "but the point is they do not suspect and nor will others."

Clara paused for a moment. "I just hope they will not feel disappointed should they find out the truth."

"Clara, no-one worth their salt would ever be disappointed with you if they take the trouble to get to know you and do not rush to judgement because of their small-minded prejudice."

"That is part of my concern, Charlie," she sighed. "I am not sure that they will trouble to try."

"The ton is notoriously fickle," he replied. "You will no doubt be much talked of for a week or so, then their voracious appetite for gossip and scandal will move on."

"It does not seem to have moved on from you," she shot back.

"That is because I consider it my pleasure, nay, my duty to give them something interesting to talk about." He grinned.

"You are quite incorrigible." She smiled back, poking him in the arm. Before she could retract her hand, he caught it and threaded it through his.

"Enough self doubt, Clara, think of how far you have come. From an abandoned baby in an orphanage, to a lady's maid, to a lady herself, not to mention a highly educated one at that. This was not the journey of a tender flower. You have courage and spirit. Let yourself be free to be who you are."

"My goodness, I doubt Marlborough gave a better speech on the eve of the Battle of Blenheim,"

"I rather have the feeling you are about to go into battle sooner than you anticipated," he replied, looking into the distance.

"Why?"

"Correct me if I am wrong, but is that not Lady Elizabeth on the arm of Sir Taylor Rufford?"

Clara looked to where he was looking. "Oh. my goodness, so it is, and I believe they have seen us," her voice rose in panic.

"Indeed. Well, Clara, here they come. Be calm, smile, and most importantly, do not forget to breathe." He squeezed her hand. "Don't forget Lady Elizabeth is quite an odious woman and if anyone needs taking down a peg or two, it is her."

Clara straightened her spine. "In that case, Charlie, be prepared to pick up some pegs."

CHAPTER 21

"Here we go," Charlie said softly as they approached.

Sir Taylor Rufford raised his hat politely. "Hampton," he greeted them coldly.

"Rufford," Charlie responded. "Lady Elizabeth," he bowed.

"Mr. Hampton," she said and gave the briefest of curtseys.

There was a pause before Rufford asked, "And this is?" looking down his long nose.

"The Duke of Wensley's ward," Charlie replied. "Sir Taylor Rufford and Lady Elizabeth Morgan, may I present Miss Clara Burns."

"Sir, my lady," Clara responded, bobbing them both a curtsey.

"Charming," Sir Rufford commented, as he bent over Clara's hand.

"And how is the duke?" Lady Elizabeth asked.

"Yes," put in Sir Rufford, "how is his grace? Restored to good health or are you closer to gaining your inheritance?" His voice held a sneer.

Clara felt Charlie tense beneath her fingers and squeezed his arm. "His grace is in good health, Sir Rufford, thank you for your concern," she put in quickly before Charlie could respond, flashing a brilliant smile. "We were a little concerned a few days ago, but all is now well," she finished.

"Ah, that reminds me, Mr. Hampton," Lady Elizabeth spoke, "the last time I saw you, I lent you my maid Blackburn to help nurse the poor duke. You may send her back now that your grandfather is recovered."

Clara's hand tightened instinctively. "I am sorry, Lady Elizabeth, but I was under the impression that you had dismissed the young woman. I believe her box of belongings was delivered along with a note that you no longer required her services."

Lady Elizabeth shrugged. "That was certainly my intention, however, the two girls I have employed since were completely hopeless. So I am prepared to take Blackburn back."

Charlie smiled. "I am sorry my lady, but Miss Blackburn is no longer either with myself or the duke."

"What do you mean?"

"When her belongings arrived along with her dismissal, Miss Blackburn left," he explained patiently adding, "neither the duke nor I having much need of a lady's maid."

"This is most irksome, have you no idea where she went?"

"Miss Blackburn appears to have vanished," Charlie said mildly. "London is full of young women therefore it would not be hard for her to disappear. Or perhaps she returned to her family?"

Lady Elizabeth's eyes narrowed. "She has no family, as you very well know. We got her from some sort of orphanage, that is why she was so cheap."

"Then I am afraid Miss Blackburn's whereabouts are lost to us. She may, of course, have found alternative employment, perhaps you might ask among your friends?" Charlie suggested, maintaining a polite mien.

Clara glanced nervously from Charlie to Lady Elizabeth. Surely if he wanted this scheme to succeed, he ought not to needle the one person who could truly ruin his plan.

"I doubt it, my note was most specific on that account," Lady Elizabeth snapped. "It really is most irritating. Though now I think on it, someone did call to ask about Blackburn's character. If the minx has found employment somewhere, I shall no doubt find out and put a stop to it."

"I believe good maids are hard to find," Clara said, curious to know whether Lady Elizabeth had any inkling of her identity. If so, she would know at once and be done with the scheme before it got too serious.

Lady Elizabeth glanced in her direction. "Indeed they are, Miss Burns, I had only just trained Blackburn to my standards, but there again I always felt she thought she was something above her station. No doubt when she has had enough of life outside of Morgan House she will come crawling back. Then she will understand the importance of obedience and loyalty." Lady Elizabeth's eyes flashed with anger before she quickly composed her features. "But no matter. What of you Miss Burns? I do not believe I have seen you at any events this season, though you seem familiar, perhaps our paths have crossed though we have not been introduced."

"No, I have only recently come to town," Clara replied. "The duke, my guardian, was insistent that I should experience something of society."

"How sweet," the young woman replied, leaning forward, "though I am surprised to find you being escorted by Mr. Hampton. Neither his parentage nor his manners are entirely top drawer. Be wary for your reputation, Miss Burns."

"Elizabeth," Sir Rufford interrupted, "we had better be on our way. We shall look forward to seeing you again Miss Burns, perhaps at the Govan Ball?"

"I do not believe I have received an invitation," Clara replied.

"You will, my dear, you will. The ton will want to know more about the mysterious ward of the duke and I hope to have the pleasure of a waltz with you before the evening is out," Sir Rufford said as he bent over her hand. "Come Elizabeth. Hampton," he nodded towards Charlie and the couple swept off.

Charlie's eyes narrowed to slits. "If that man comes within a mile of you at any function, I will take great pleasure in tearing his head off," he hissed.

Clara raised an eyebrow. "I may not be entirely au fait with social etiquette at balls, but I am fairly sure that is not on the list of dos."

Charlie turned to face her. "I mean it, Clara. Taylor Rufford is a vindictive, odious streak of malice. Have nothing to do with him."

Clara smiled. It was the first time in her life that someone cared enough about her to protect her, and sudden tears came inexplicably to her eyes.

Charlie looked down at her. "What is the matter, Clara? Why are you crying? Are you ill?" he asked anxiously.

"No, I am not crying. I never cry," she replied firmly, blinking away the tears. "I did all my crying years ago. It changes nothing and serves no purpose."

Charlie gazed at her silently for a few moments. "I think we must return to the carriage," was all he said. "I see Silcock and Harper returning.

The trip back was more silent than Clara had expected. Charlie did not seem interested in enjoying time with her, as well he shouldn't, she reminded herself. Modeling herself after him, she steeled herself upright and maintained a watch out of the window.

Upon their return, they were met by an eager Lady Bea who demanded a detailed report from the both of them about the outing.

"Well done my dear," Lady Bea said as she selected a slice of pound cake. "Verity and Ella so enjoyed your outing, and it seems you dealt very well with Rufford and Lady Elizabeth."

"I very much enjoyed meeting Verity and Ella," Clara replied. "Fortunately, Lady Elizabeth was so furious at the disappearance of her maid, she hardly paid any attention to me at all."

"Elizabeth Morgan is a spiteful cat, as is her mother before her. Should any man be unfortunate enough to have his proposal accepted, I imagine he would regret it before the honeymoon was over, possibly before the ink was dry on the marriage certificate."

"Lady Bea, you are quite incorrigible," Clara giggled.

"One of the advantages of getting older my dear, one can more or less say what one likes, even the truth. The disadvantage of growing older, sadly, is that no-one pays any heed."

"It would take a brave soul to ignore you, Lady Bea," Clara smiled.

"A brave man indeed," said the duke, smiling as he entered. "Now," he added, sitting in the wing chair, "tell me of your excursion."

When Clara finished her account for the second time, the duke steepled his fingers, "So, you survived your first skirmish with the enemy."

"I would not go so far as to describe Sir Rufford and Lady Elizabeth as actual enemies Your Grace."

"Well they are certainly not your friends," the duke commented.

"That I will concede." Clara remembered the murderous conversation she had heard in the library, the night of the Sisson ball. It was only a short time ago and yet it seemed like a lifetime. She should not forget how dangerous those two might really be, and she must remember to tell Charlie.

"Tell me, my dear," the duke said, leaning forward. "After you left the orphanage to take up your position with Lady Elizabeth, did the warden or anyone call on you, to see that you were fulfilling your duties properly, that sort of thing?"

Clara thought for a moment. "No, sir, in fact the warden was most specific, there was to be no contact until I came of age. She said she had enough work to do with the girls at the orphanage without having the bother of girls who had left."

"I see. And you have never returned?"

"I think the warden's message was quite clear."

"Indeed."

"Is it possible," Lady Bea suggested, "that the warden wanted to ensure that you girls settled into your new positions without being unsettled by visits?"

"Perhaps so," Clara replied. Unlikely, no-one ever really wanted orphans.

"Well in any case, that is all in the past and should remain there. You have a new life now and we must think about that," Lady Bea continued. "Now Andrew, I believe it is time for dinner."

CHAPTER 22

"You wanted to see me, Grandfather?" Charlie asked as he entered the duke's study.

The older man smiled, clearly enjoying being addressed informally as grandfather. "Yes, I do," he replied, indicating that Charlie sit opposite him.

Charlie checked his pocket watch. "We shall have to be quick, I promised Clara a ride in the park this morning."

The duke raised his eyebrows. "Does she ride? I did not think there was time or money spent on such things at an orphanage."

"Apparently an exception was made for Clara, one of the many puzzles that surround her," Charlie replied.

"It was the orphanage I wanted to speak with you about," the duke continued. "I paid a visit there a few days ago."

"You paid a visit?"

"Well, I sent a trusted employee, my man of business, Firth. I did not think it wise to go myself and raise suspicions, and given what he found out, it was a good thing indeed," he said, thoughtfully.

"Well?" Charlie could barely contain himself, his senses alert, he was uneasy. He was unusually concerned for Clara's well-being. Although he told himself it was only looking after his interests in their scheme, something told him it was more. He thought on the hurt Clara had suffered in the past, and he would make damned sure she would not suffer that hurt again. He would ensure he found her a husband who would treat her with love and respect. Hell, he would marry her himself if none of the men on his list came up to snuff. The thought stopped him in his tracks, once more he found himself contemplating marriage to Clara and each time the notion bounced into his consciousness, it seemed more and more attractive.

"It would seem that all the records for the years Clara was at the orphanage have disappeared."

"What do you mean?"

"Precisely what I say, the ledgers with the years from the time Clara was admitted to the year she left to take up employment at the Morgans, are missing."

Charlie frowned. "And is there an explanation for this?"

The duke shook his head. "Apparently no-one had noticed they were missing until Firth enquired.

Charlie shook his head. "How could it be that close to two decades of records could go missing without notice? It would seem either that someone took the ledgers because they did not want Clara to be found, or someone took them because they wanted to find her." He closed his eyes for a moment. "What of the warden? She would remember Clara would she not? She was the one to tell Clara to return when she was of age."

"Another interesting detail, the warden Firth spoke to is new, apparently the warden who knew Clara retired to live with her sister at the coast, I believe, for her health."

Charlie sighed exasperatedly. "So there is no-one at the orphanage who can tell us anything of Clara?"

"It would seem so, but," the duke paused.

"But?" Charlie prompted.

"Firth is a man of ingenuity, he spoke with one of the cooks, she remembered Clara very well. 'Something strange about the whole business,' she said. 'Never known an orphan who received gifts, she had a family somewhere, a rich family,' her final words to Firth were 'She weren't no proper orphan.'"

"This much we have already surmised from what Clara was told, she was the daughter of a gentlewoman," Charlie reminded the duke.

"It would seem though, from what the cook said, that many of the gifts came from abroad. Clara was never given any packaging, so she could not have known."

"Perhaps her mother moved abroad. It would not be the first time a woman in trouble did so."

"It is a possibility, but why remove all records of Clara from the orphanage?" the duke asked.

Charlie considered for a moment. "As I said, it would seem that someone did not want Clara to be found, the question is why."

"A further point," the duke spoke quietly, "we must proceed carefully. The cook let slip that Firth was not the only one enquiring about Clara."

Charlie leaned forward, his senses on full alert. "What?"

"A woman and a man called at the orphanage several weeks ago saying they were trying to find their long, lost sister who was kidnapped as a baby. They described the clothes Clara was wearing when she arrived, but more importantly, they also knew about the locket."

"But Clara was not given the locket until the day she left."

"Precisely."

"What information were they given? Were they told of Clara's position with Lady Elizabeth?"

"No, the cook apparently did not like the look of them and in her words she sent them away with a flea in their ear."

"Hell and damnation," Charlie stood up. "Something Lady Elizabeth said yesterday, it did not signify at the time."

"What?" asked his grandfather.

"She said someone had enquired about Clara, she thought it was for a reference and thankfully her spiteful nature meant she did not respond, but the point is, someone knows where Clara was."

"But how? The cook did not tell them."

"No, but a groom, kitchen maid, or someone at the orphanage could have, it is not difficult to loosen a tongue with coin."

There was a slight pause. "Do you believe Clara to be in danger?" the old man asked.

"At the moment, in all honesty, I could not say," Charlie replied. "All we know is that someone is looking for her, it may even be that her family is searching for her as circumstances may have changed and they can now take her back."

"I suspect that is not all you believe."

Charlie's eyes narrowed. "It seems to me that the records and the warden left together. This would suggest the warden suspected someone would come looking for Clara one day, and she felt it necessary to ensure that she was not found."

"And she made it difficult for them to find her. Then you do believe Clara to be in danger."

Charlie felt as though he had been punched in the stomach. The thought of Clara's life in danger terrified him, the fact that he did not know why or by whom almost caused him to be ill. He walked towards the door, "I will send a message to Pearson that should anyone enquire for Clara, no-one is to say anything. It may be that if they found out about the Morgans, they could trace Clara to me."

"And further, to me."

Charlie paused for a moment, his hand on the doorknob, gathering his thoughts. "It is entirely possible, but of course according to the story we put out Clara Blackburn disappeared. There is nothing to connect her with Clara Burns."

"Should we send her to the country for her safety until we find out more?" the duke asked.

"No, I think we proceed with our plan to hide Clara in plain sight. The gossip mill will alert us to strangers in our midst."

"Very well."

"I shall, however, ensure that a close but discreet watch is kept over her at all times."

"Do you think we should tell her what we have learned?"

Charlie considered the question. "Not yet, we do not know what the risk is and it is pointless to worry her unnecessarily."

"Does she not have a right to know?"

"Let us wait until we know a little more. Those who are looking for her may show their hand soon enough. We need to know whom we are dealing with and what they want with Clara."

"I knew from the beginning there was something strange yet familiar about that young woman, I just wish I could put my finger on it," the duke murmured.

"I have a feeling we may find out soon enough," Charlie replied grimly. "In the meantime though, we will proceed as though nothing has happened."

He had just left the duke when Clara came down the stairs. The sight almost took his breath away. She was wearing a midnight blue velvet riding habit with a jaunty little hat perched on her chestnut curls. The jacket was nipped in, emphasizing her trim waist and there was a white lace jabot at her throat. She had drawn up the skirt so that her black, polished boots were visible, Clara Burns was every inch a lady.

His mind flashed back to the sitting room, feeling her breasts which were now hidden from view, the thought of revealing them, and more, stirring in him that untoward desire once more. This was not part of the plan, though every time he saw Clara the plan seemed to go out of the window. He couldn't keep his hands off her, and yet he must. He knew he must. It was for the best. Especially now that he needed to watch her even more carefully.

Her eyes lit up when she saw him. "I am so looking forward to our ride, though I must confess to feeling a little nervous. It is a long time since I have been on a horse."

Charlie forced his features into a smile, silently acknowledging that he would be bereft if something untoward should happen to this woman who had crashed into his life such a short time ago. "I am sure it will come back, and I have a particularly gentle beast for you." He held out his arm. "Her name is Flame, let us go and meet her."

Two horses were waiting in the yard, Charlie's black stallion and a smaller, chestnut mare by his side. As Clara approached, the mare turned her head and whickered. "I think she likes you," Charlie said quietly.

"I hope so," she replied, gently patting the horse's neck. Charlie waited until she was safely in the saddle before mounting.

"We will take it gently so that you and Flame get used to each other," he said.

Clara smiled in reply, but he could see the tension in her eyes.

After a few minutes, Clara began to relax and enjoy herself. "I had forgotten how one's view of the world is different from atop a horse."

Charlie smiled back. "Indeed, the only better place would be on the wings of a bird."

"How wonderful that would be," she agreed, her eyes shining. "To be free like a bird and fly to the corners of the world."

"You would like to travel?" he asked. Young women, as far as he observed, seemed content with smaller horizons.

"Oh, I should and not just Europe. I should like to visit the pyramids in Egypt, the Great Wall of China, the Americas, and I should like to see lions in Africa."

"You sound like a friend of mine, Helen, Duchess of Bainbridge."

Clara's eyes widened. "The authoress? You know her?"

"She is the woman who changed my life," he replied.

"How?" she asked.

"By giving me a chance. Like you, I came from nothing."

"But your grandfather…." she began.

"I knew nothing of him almost until the same time I met you. It was Helen who started me on the road to success, something I shall never forget."

"My goodness," Clara murmured.

Charlie wheeled his horse round so that he could face her. "You have more in common with Helen than you realise. As a child, she was brought up by her aunt who hated her. But, like you, she rose above it like a lily to the surface of the pond. I believe you and she will become great friends. Now," he added, "Flame is in need of a little speed."

CHAPTER 23

*T*hey had barely taken a few strides when Charlie's eyes narrowed, "Damnation, I believe that bloody pair is following me," he muttered.

"Who?" Clara asked, her eyes following his gaze. "Oh, no," she murmured.

"Exactly," he ground out as Lady Elizabeth and Sir Taylor Rufford rode towards them.

"Could we pretend we have not seen them and take another path?" Clara asked.

Charlie turned to her. "Unfortunately not, being polite to people one does not like lies at the heart of social interaction amongst the ton. Half of them despise the other half because they have too much money and no brains and the other half despise them because they have the brains and no money. Poor titled men must marry rich women whom they cannot stand in order to produce the all-important heir, and so the merry-go-round continues."

"You really do not paint a very attractive picture, Mr. Hampton. It makes me wonder why I am to be launched into this maelstrom of derision and hate? Would I not be better marrying a chimney sweep that I love? It would be a poorer life only in terms of money."

Charlie could not help but smile. "You cannot live on love. Marrying a man of means will give you a home and one day, children. Is that not what all women want?" Even as he spoke the words, he doubted them. Was what he and the duke were doing for Clara or themselves? Were they passing her off to society to prove a point to society, or was it really to ensure that she had some security in her life? The men they thought of for her all seemed upstanding and kind, but who knew what happened behind closed doors? The thought brought him up short; he did not want to think of another man touching Clara's hair, kissing her breasts, or making love to her perfectly luscious body. Yet somehow worse would be if she ended up shackled in a marriage with no affection.

"Yet missing from your list is love, affection, and a little happiness," she replied.

"But why only a little happiness?" he countered.

"I do not believe we are entitled to be happy all of the time, but we are surely entitled to a little happiness from time to time to sustain us," she responded. "Now I believe we must both pin smiles on our faces, for this, I fear, is not to be one of those times." She smiled as Lady Elizabeth and her cousin approached.

"Lord, Mr. Hampton, I do believe you are stalking me," Lady Elizabeth flashed Charlie a dazzling smile.

"A similar thought occurred to me my lady," he replied, nodding his head in a bow. Perhaps she had not given up on snaring him after all.

"And I see you have your grandfather's charming young ward with you, Miss…?"

"Burns," Clara replied.

Charlie thought satisfied that it was a good sign if Lady Elizabeth had not remembered her, she clearly made no connection between Miss Burns and her missing maid.

"Perhaps we might ride together for a while," Sir Rufford suggested. "As Miss Burns has only just come up to town, she should learn some of society's ways from those who are at the centre of it."

"Perhaps she should learn what to expect," Charlie agreed enigmatically. His hands tightened on his reins as he fought the urge to drag Rufford from his horse and punch him.

"So Miss Burns, are you to attend the ball given by Lord and Lady Frazer? It is always a grand affair…" Rufford's voice faded as he and Clara rode in front.

"Quite an attractive young woman, Miss Burns," Lady Elizabeth's voice sounded harsh in his ear. "Do tell, how did she come to be the duke's ward?"

"She is an orphan as her parents died when she was a baby," he replied, which was, as far as he knew, the truth. "Her grandmother who died recently was a friend of my grandfather's," he lied.

"What an interesting story. How sweet of your grandfather to take her on at his age." Her words were kind, but her sly smile was not.

"Indeed."

"Of course, there are those in society who might raise their eyebrows at a young woman living with a very old man. Miss Burns really must ensure that she takes care of her reputation," she persisted.

"Fortunately, my grandfather's sister, Lady Beatrice is there to chaperone."

"I am glad to hear it. Unfortunately, that does not..." she paused for dramatic effect, "but I must not say more."

"Oh, please do, my lady."

"Well, it hardly seems polite to point it out, but if Miss Burns is to retain her so far blameless reputation, I fear she must avoid certain individuals."

"Such as Rufford?" Charlie could not resist. "I quite agree."

"No." Lady Elizabeth shook her head, causing her curls to bounce. "Of course not, Taylor is a highly regarded member of the ton."

By himself, Charlie thought, sourly.

"I mean to say," she continued, "Miss Burns really must avoid, well...you." She delivered the final word with a dazzling smile.

"Indeed?" Charlie raised an eyebrow. "And what damage pray do you imagine a humble soul such as myself can possibly inflict on the ward of a duke?"

"Come, come, Mr. Hampton, you are neither humble nor naive, but you are extremely well known as a libertine. If Miss Burns continues to associate herself with you, then her reputation will be in tatters. All it would take," she continued with a malicious gleam in her eye, "is a little word or a disparaging comment or two from concerned parties and her season would be over before it had begun."

She was right, the poisonous tongues of the ton had ruined the marriage chances of many a young girl.

"And what would you suggest?" he asked, knowing already what the response would be.

"Miss Burns needs a friend amongst the ton. Someone who can make the right introductions. Lady Beatrice is, of course, an acceptable, though somewhat eccentric, chaperone, but her influence among people of fashion waned a generation ago, if indeed she had any influence at all."

"And you would be prepared to serve this function, to be Miss Burn's friend?"

Lady Elizabeth smiled, reminding Charlie of a picture he had seen in a book of a crocodile with an antelope in its mouth. "Taylor and I are perhaps the only people who could ensure that Miss Burns takes her rightful place in society." She paused, her eyes searching Charlie's face before adding, "You may not appreciate it, Mr. Hampton, but Taylor and I have been at the centre of society for several years. We know anyone who is anyone. For a consideration, if we approve of an individual, their path into society is assured."

"And if you do not?" Charlie could not resist asking.

"They will never get beyond the furthest reaches. It is quite simple. Taylor and I decide who is to be admitted to the club, as it were."

Charlie leaned towards her. "I had not realised your influence was so great," he spoke softly, "but let me make this clear, my lady, if I hear that you or your odious cousin have said or done anything which may jeopardise Miss Burns' entrance into society, I will personally ensure that the two of you are never able to show your faces in London again. Do I make myself clear?"

"Perfectly," she spat back, her eyes as cold as chips of ice. "But I would warn you, Mr. Hampton, something about this business of the duke's mysterious ward and your connection with her does not ring true with me. So I shall find out, and when I do, I shall reveal to the whole of London society what it is, and then we shall see what society does to those who try to fool them." She wheeled her horse around. "Good day," she said sharply.

"Good riddance," Charlie muttered under his breath. He could not seem to help himself goading Lady Elizabeth even though he knew it was unwise, especially now she seemed to have suspicions.

He watched as her horse trotted smartly towards Clara and Rufford, anyone else observing would have seen a cordial leave-taking as they all nodded to each other and Clara turned her horse towards him alone. She smiled as she approached. Now that she had found her confidence, he could see that she sat a horse well. He had often considered women to be superior riders, judging the skill involved in remaining in a side-saddle to be far more challenging than riding astride. They returned to the yard in silence, he looking forward to being away from prying eyes and ears to discuss the ride with her.

In a second, his world was turned upside down. Flame suddenly reared, spooked by something he had not seen. Clara was on the ground with Flame's hooves dangerously close. He raced towards her, praying to a God he was not sure he believed in and dragged her from under the horse's hooves as they crashed to the ground where her head had been. The groom arrived at the same time and managed to calm the terrified horse. Charlie cradled Clara in his arms, her face was as white as chalk and her eyes were closed. "Clara, my darling, speak to me," he pleaded, his mouth close to her ear. "Come back to me, Clara."

Her eyes opened, but he could see she was not entirely focused. "I don't understand," she murmured. "What happened?"

"Flame reared and threw you. Are you all right? Are you in pain? Tell me what hurts."

She managed a weak smile. "My dignity mostly," she replied, trying to get up.

"Stay still while I check nothing is broken," he commanded, running his hands lightly over her body.

"Are you mad?" she protested. "This is a public place. You know it's not proper."

"Proper be damned," he replied. "Injuries trump proper every time."

"What are you doing?" she asked as he scooped her into his arms. "I am taking you home, I do not think anything is broken, but we shall send for the physician to make sure." He turned to the groom, "Take the horse back and tell his grace to summon his doctor, Miss Burns will remain with me."

"I am perfectly able to walk," Clara protested as he strode towards his house with her in his arms. "In any case, I should get straight back in the saddle after a fall."

"I do not doubt it Clara, but for once in your life, let someone take care of you."

She opened her mouth to speak but thought the better of it. She could feel the steady rhythm of Charlie's heart through his shirt and the hardness of his muscles as he carried her through the door. Letting someone take care of her was not a concept she was familiar with.

"Lean on me," he commanded as he mounted the steps.

CHAPTER 24

*T*ruth to tell she had not wanted the moment to end. With his strong arms around her, she felt that someone cared what happened to her, that she was not entirely alone. For the first time in her life, she had people who cared. It was a bittersweet moment because she knew it could not last. Soon their adventure would be over and they would go their separate ways, she to the cottage she had been promised and he to marry some lady of the ton, and that would be that. She could not fall in love with Charlie Hampton, she would not fall in love with Charlie Hampton. The problem was, she already had.

It did not take long for a doctor to be summoned, and Charlie had insisted that she remain on the couch beside him as he watched over her.

"I am perfectly well, sir," Clara addressed the doctor, who had insisted that she be taken to her bed, "and if I could get up, I should feel a lot better," she finished on a smile, hoping to persuade him.

He looked over the pince-nez on his nose. "I think I must be the judge of that, young lady, your pulse is a little fast and you have a slight fever."

Clara was not in the least surprised, every time she thought of Charlie Hampton her pulse raced. She could still feel his warmth and strength of his arms as he carried her. All she had wanted to do was press herself against his hard body. She had almost cried out when he had run his hands over her to determine the extent of her injuries. She wanted to feel those strong, capable hands on her without layers of fabric between them. She wanted to feel his hands on her, skin to skin, even now, just thinking about it caused her nipples to tighten and a fluttering in her belly. It was madness, she knew it was, but she could not help it.

Ever since she had met him, Charlie Hampton had shown her nothing but kindness, he had treated her—a maid, an orphan, a no-one —with the greatest respect. If they had met at another time, before he had made his money or before he found he was the grandson of a duke, then something might have come of it. Nothing could come of it now, the chasm between them was too wide.

"…beef tea and a drop of this at night." The doctor's words cut into her thoughts. He placed his hat on. "Good day, Miss Burns. No long-term damage I believe, nothing that a few days rest won't cure."

"Miss, what are you doing?" Lily cried when she returned from seeing the doctor out.

"I think it is fairly obvious," Clara replied, easing her arm into her gown. "If you would just deal with the fastenings please."

"But the doctor said…"

"The doctor is more used to dealing with society ladies who take to their beds if their bonnet strings are too tight. You and I, Lily, know that women like us do not take to our beds at the drop of a hat."

"Or a drop from a horse, if all's said."

The two women giggled. "No doubt the doctor will present his grace with a ridiculous bill which has more to do with his own self importance than anything else," Clara continued as Lily quickly laced her gown and started to repair the damage to her hair. Once it was done, she went to the library.

At the door she paused at the rumble of voices. "I think, Your Grace, I have the reason why Flame reared," came the groom's voice, sounding upset.

"Go on lad, spit it out," the duke responded.

"When I got back, I rubbed her down as usual and there was an injury on her hind quarters, a small cut as though she was hit by a sharp stone."

"Wait a minute," Charlie's voice cut in. "Are you saying that someone deliberately threw a stone to make the horse rear?"

"Given the depth of the wound, sir, I would say so," the groom replied. "I would go even further," he added. "For the stone to leave a mark like this, I would say that it had been sharpened and would have come from a slingshot or some such."

"But why would anyone want to injure a horse?" Clara asked, stepping into the room. "It does not make any sense."

"Some people are cruel, miss," the groom responded. "Boys who tied puppies' tails together as children sometimes progress to other things, and I did see a group of lads near the trees as we rode by."

"Thank you, Brown, you may go," the duke commanded.

"I still do not understand," Clara repeated, sitting down on the sofa. "Why would anyone want to hurt Flame? She's the gentlest horse anyone could want."

Charlie and the duke exchanged glances. "It may be that Flame was not the intended target," Charlie said gently.

"What do you mean?"

"It is possible that Flame was not the target at all. You were."

Clara's eyes widened. "Me?" she squeaked. "But that makes even less sense. Why would anyone want to attack me? I am a nobody, no-one would have anything to gain by attacking me."

"That we do not yet know, Clara," the duke sighed. "But there are things about your past that do not seem to add up to the fact that you are the simple orphan you think yourself to be."

"This is not news," Clara shrugged. "I always assumed I was the unwanted child of a lady. The gifts and the extra lessons I received suggested I had a family of some means somewhere. But I was too much of an embarrassment for them to acknowledge me. That is the end of the story."

"Exactly," the duke replied. "But it would appear that is not quite the end of the story."

Clara smoothed her skirts. "Sir, my family clearly knew where I was, but chose to leave me at the orphanage. Does that not tell you something?"

"It does," he replied.

"Good, because it tells me that I was and remain unwanted by them." She could feel the tears pricking her eyes and she blinked, she would not cry, she had not cried over this since she was a small child and she would not cry now.

"Clara," Charlie said softly, and she met his eyes, though hers were brimming. He looked as she felt: that he longed to pull her into his arms. She could think of nothing better. For all her bravery and feistiness, underneath she was a frightened and vulnerable young woman. Clearly awake of his grandfather's presence, he settled for taking her small hand in his large one. "Could it be possible that there is another reason for your family's neglect of you?"

"I don't think so," her voice trembled.

"Clara," the old man took up the story. "It is my belief that there is something about the circumstances of your birth that threatened something or someone."

Clara looked from the duke to his grandson. "And do you believe this too?"

Charlie looked into her emerald eyes. "I believe it is a possibility."

"On the evidence of some naughty boys flinging stones at a horse?"

The duke and Charlie exchanged a look. They clearly knew more than they were willing for her to know. Charlie smiled forcedly and said, "You are right of course, perhaps we are reading too much into too little. Now perhaps you should go and change if you feel well enough to go to the theatre?"

Clara jumped to her feet. "I am quite well, thank you and looking forward to seeing Mr. Sheridan's comedy. It will put this nonsense about danger into perspective I am sure." At the door she turned and added, "There is no possible reason why anyone should want to harm me, as a lady's maid I was all but invisible and apart from yourselves and a very few others no-one has the slightest idea who I am. Furthermore, I am not some delicate hothouse flower, I am quite capable of taking care of myself."

CHAPTER 25

There was a moment of silence before the duke commented with a chuckle, "It seems we have unleashed quite a firebrand."

"Indeed," Charlie replied thoughtfully, "The question is how are we to keep her safe, preferably without her knowing the need for it?"

"There is one way," the duke began. "Though I am not entirely sure you will agree."

"What?" Charlie asked.

"Marry her."

"I beg your pardon."

"It is the ideal solution both to assuring Clara's safety and the question of finding a suitable husband. Which I frankly doubt is possible, given your lengthy criteria. In fact, the only man who would appear to measure up in any way would be—well, you."

Charlie strode over to the side table and poured himself a generous measure of brandy which he downed in one swallow, before pouring another and returning to his seat. He could not deny the thought had occurred to him even before the mystery surrounding her had emerged.

"Marry Clara," he murmured.

"You have the men to provide a guard, your house is like a fortress, and you will be on hand all the time to ensure that nothing is neglected. Besides," he added, his old eyes twinkling, "I should like to dandle a great-grandchild or two on my lap before I die."

Charlie spluttered over his brandy.

"I see the notion is not distasteful to you," his grandfather continued.

"It is not," Charlie admitted. "But is it enough on which to base a marriage?"

"Marriages have been based on much less."

Charlie nodded, a short while ago he had been contemplating such a match. "But were they happy?" he asked, not sure whether he was asking his grandfather or himself.

"Your grandmother and I were not a love match. Our fathers arranged the match when we were infants. In fact, we had only met a handful of times as adults before we were married. At the wedding breakfast, your grandmother said to me, 'Andrew, we are now man and wife and if we are not to spend a lifetime making each other miserable, we must become friends,' and we did. Your grandmother was wise beyond her years. She knew that from friendship, love could grow, and it did. I loved her not only until the day she died—I love her still. Had she not died giving birth to Annabelle's brother who died with her, things would have been very different, but," he added, looking at Charlie, "my consolation is that I have a grandson with whom I am reconciled." Charlie could see the tears in the faded blue eyes.

Charlie swirled the amber liquid in his glass. "I am not sure Clara would accept," he murmured.

"Then you must woo her," the duke replied, briskly. "And quickly. The moment she makes her debut young blades will be around her like flies around a honeypot."

It was true, Rufford had already shown an interest in her potential dowry, if nothing else. He was the first, but he would not be the last, of that Charlie had no doubt, Impoverished lords and undesirables of all kinds would fall out of the woodwork, each hoping to have access to her money and her bed. He could think of at least three who would be prepared to ruin her in order to get their hands on her dowry.

He put his glass down, he was not about to let that happen. Clara deserved better, he was not sure he was much better but he was better than fortune hunters, libertines and cads.

"Where are you going?" his grandfather asked.

Charlie paused, his hand on the doorknob. "To get a special licence, by this time next week, I expect to be a married man."

· · ·

Charlie arrived at the theatre shortly after his great-aunt. He accompanied her through the throngs to his grandfather's private box.

"I am quite looking forward to this," Lady Bea announced, settling her substantial frame into the gilt chair in the duke's box. "I have not seen 'The School for Scandal' since '77 with Frances Abington and Jane Pope. Of course, in those days everyone wanted to know on whom Sheridan had based his characters."

"And do you know?" the duke enquired.

"I was considerably younger than I am now, and in any case I should not tell you even if I did. Though I will say this," she added, with a gleam in her eye. "One or two society ladies of my acquaintance were certainly more- tight lipped afterwards."

"Do you know the play?" Charlie leaned towards Clara.

"This is the first time I have been to the theatre," she admitted looking around at the red velvet curtains and sparkling chandeliers and listening to the low murmur of the audience as they waited expectantly for the curtains to part. "There is enough drama here for me to observe without the play."

Charlie looked around, he had not considered this, it was interesting to see life through Clara's eyes. He patronised the theatre regularly partly because he enjoyed it, and partly he admitted because it was the done thing. There were times when he sat mentally writing contracts if a play was particularly tedious.

"Why do you rich people choose to sit in boxes with a poor view of the stage, when surely a better view could be had from over there in the circle?" Clara asked.

"Ah," the duke replied. "Part of the experience of going to the theatre is not only to see, but to be seen. The theatre box gives us privacy to watch the performance or not as the case may be, but also to be seen at the important points. One has to patronise the arts and be seen doing so.

"Take Lady Campion. She is well known as a great patroness of the arts. Or should I say artists," the duke pointed to a handsome woman in the opposite box. "Her town house had to have rooms added to accommodate her paintings."

"All portraits of herself," Lady Bea sniffed. "And if what I hear is true, the artists are treated to bed and board until the painting is complete, then another artist is engaged."

"You are beginning to sound like one of Sheridan's characters Bea," the duke put in.

"My mistake, Andrew, perhaps Lady Campion's explanation that she is striving for perfection is true after all."

Clara looked puzzled. "I don't understand."

Charlie grinned. "You will." He could not help but watch her as the performance unfolded. He loved the way she threw back her head and laughed with abandon. Not only did he enjoy hearing her laugh, but her elegant profile enchanted him. She was looking particularly lovely this evening in a gown of pale green embroidered at the neck, waist, and hem with russet leaves and flowers. The colours suited her perfectly, enhancing both her vivid eyes and hair. No-one looking at her for the first time would have any notion that until a few days ago, she was working as a maid. The ton put so much value on breeding, yet like much else about them, it was only skin deep.

As the audience applauded the end of the first act, the duke turned to Charlie. "Would you arrange some refreshments? Bea and I should like to visit the Dowager Duchess of Leyburn in her box. We spent many hours with her as children and neither of us has seen her in years." He turned to Clara. "You do not mind my dear do you?"

Clara smiled. "Of course not, there is an entire theatre full of people to chaperone me and I shall enjoy watching them."

Lady Bea tugged the curtain. "There my dear, now you can see without most of the crowd being able to see you."

CHAPTER 26

*C*harlie did not leave until Clara was able to assure him that she could quite manage herself in a private box without issue. She was sure no one would bother to look her way, let alone come call on her in the duke's box, after all, so few people had any idea of who she was.

Once alone, she peered over the side, entranced by the sight of bobbing feathers and glittering jewels as men and women greeted each other across the auditorium. The hubbub of chatter rose and fell, punctuated by the occasional peal of laughter. She did not hear the quiet click of the door and almost dropped her fan as a pair of hands came round her face and covered her eyes. "Guess who," a voice whispered hoarsely, close to her ear.

"Charlie," she giggled. "That is not how a gentleman is supposed to behave."

Within seconds, she was hauled out of her seat and slammed against the rear wall. "Forget Charlie Hampton," Taylor Rufford hissed as he pressed his body close to hers. "He is a nobody, an upstart. You, my beauty, should not waste your time consorting with the likes of him."

"Sir Rufford," she stammered, "please let me go."

"I will, my dear. Of course I will, once you have consented to marry me."

"What?" Clara's eyes were wide, "I barely know you, sir."

He shook his head. "It is of no consequence for you will get to know me when we are wed."

"I don't understand, sir," she continued, desperately hoping the duke or Charlie would appear. "We have met a handful of times, less than a handful, why on earth would you even contemplate marrying me?"

"You are the ward of a duke and although not, I believe, an heiress, you come with a reasonable dowry. Believe me my dear, you will not get a better offer. I am prepared to take you on, but I doubt any other man of quality would." He stepped back but kept a firm hold on her shoulders.

"His Grace…" she began.

His lips thinned. "If you are thinking that the duke would allow his only heir to marry you, you are more stupid than I thought. He does not need your dowry. He will not marry you—bed you, yes of course, and probably already has—but he will set his sights much higher. He needs, in short, to marry a woman of breeding."

"Given your apparent distaste for me, I wonder that you are prepared to demean yourself and align yourself with one so low," she shot back. The shock had gone and was replaced by anger.

"You are the ward of a duke and come with a sizeable dowry which are your two best assets. Though," he paused, twisting a curl around his fingers and pulling her towards him, rubbing his body against hers in a lascivious manner. "I find I am far from repulsed at the thought of bedding you." His voice lowered. "I shall enjoy teaching you how to please me between the sheets. I can teach you far more than Hampton can, and erase whatever he has shown you. By the time I have finished with you, you will be able to please and pleasure every gentleman in London, and I might just loan you out so that I can watch." He laughed softly.

"You are despicable," she hissed. "I would not marry you if you were covered in gold and the last man on earth. For all your fine clothes and I presume at times, your fancy manners you are nothing but a charlatan, a bully, and…" The slap echoed around her head and she tasted blood. She stared at him in shock, unable to believe he had struck her. The hand that had slapped her grasped her throat. "I can see I shall also have to teach you some manners, Miss Burns. Here is lesson one: I always get what I want." His other arm grabbed her around the waist and he lowered his head, laughing softly as she struggled. "There is no point, Miss Burns, should the good duke enter as I hope he does, you are already ruined and the wedding date is as good as set."

His kiss was a travesty, he ground her lips against her teeth and forced his tongue into her mouth. Clara stilled for a moment and as he relaxed, she bit his lip and brought up her knee with as much force as she could muster.

"Don't you ever come near me again, Sir Taylor Rufford," her voice dripped with contempt, "because if you do, I swear your days of pleasure will be well and truly over."

He attempted to straighten up. "You little bitch," he gasped. "You will live to regret this for I will destroy you."

"I doubt it," she shot back. "Now get out and crawl back under whatever rock you came from."

As the door clicked shut, Clara sank to the floor, her legs could no longer support her, the confrontation with Sir Rufford having drained her of all energies. Below, she could hear the buzz of a thousand conversations. She did not know how long she sat there, she did not hear the door open, nor did she register Charlie until he was kneeling before her.

"Clara, what has happened? Are you ill?" Her face was as white as chalk. At the sound of his voice, she raised her eyes to look at him. He took her hands in his and chafed them to try and get some warmth into her frozen fingers, his eyes seeking hers as if desperate.

"Clara, you are obviously unwell, I am going to see if I can find a physician," he said, worriedly.

"No," her voice was firm but low. "Do not leave me, I am not ill."

"Then what..." He broke off, his fingers gently brushing aside her hair, and he gasped.

With that, she knew that Sir Rufford had left his mark on her, visible on her body. She looked down, feeling as if she could see the bruises rising from under her sleeves.

"Clara what the hell happened?" he demanded.

"I'm fine," she replied, standing up.

"Clearly you are not." He took her arm gently. "And that," he added, "is not an answer to my question."

"Very well," she sighed. "I will tell you on the condition that you do not do anything rash."

He looked at her, that sentence alone told him that whatever had happened was serious. "Very well," he agreed.

"Do I have your word?" she persisted.

"You have my word," he said solemnly.

"I had a visit from Sir Taylor Rufford," she began.

"That bastard was here? In this box?" he exploded.

"Nothing rash, remember?" she reminded him. Charlie subsided.

"He did me the honour of proposing marriage and was a little put out when I refused."

"My God…" His eyes narrowed. "Did he try to force himself on you? Because if he did…"

"He did try to kiss me, but I am of the opinion that he would be reluctant to consider it again," she responded with a rueful smile.

"And why is that?"

"I bit his lip and kneed him in the…well, where I am pretty sure a gentleman would prefer not to be kneed."

"You kneed him in the ba…er crown jewels?" Charlie could not keep the amusement from his voice. "That would explain why I caught a glimpse of him in the foyer walking in a most peculiar manner."

"I sincerely hope he is doing that for some time."

Charlie scooped up her shawl and gently placed it round her shoulders. "Come, I am taking you home."

"But what about the duke and Lady Bea?"

"I will send a message."

"But…"

"No buts, you have experienced an ordeal and are still in shock. I blame myself for leaving you here unattended. Do not argue with me Clara, let me take care of you."

CHAPTER 27

Charlie watched as Clara settled herself on the squabs, no, not settled, she huddled. He could almost see her withdrawing into herself. Damn Taylor Rufford to hell. He certainly would not do anything rash, when he moved against the odious little creep, it would be considered and planned. And immensely effective. He had promised nothing rash and nothing rash it would be.

Clara stared out of the window, seeing nothing, barely aware of her surroundings as they passed through the streets of London. She almost jumped when Charlie moved to sit next to her and took her in his arms. "You are shaking and cold," he explained. Though in all honesty he just wanted to hold her close.

"Thank you," she said quietly, gratefully accepting the warmth and comfort he offered. "I have mixed with footmen and stableboys all my life," she said, "yet none of them treated me with the contempt Sir Rufford seemed to think was acceptable."

"Rufford is a complete knave and deserves to be called out," Charlie ground out.

She raised her head to look at him. "A duel? He is not worth the risk to your health or reputation, to say nothing of your liberty should you be found out. Oh," she added, as if suddenly remembering something, "you remember the night we met, at the ball where Lady Elizabeth was trying to get herself caught alone with you?"

He nodded. "I do."

"When you had gone, I overheard them talking, well sort of arguing really. When you were married, Lady Elizabeth was to pass on details of your business transactions to Sir Rufford so that he could make similar investments and ride on your coat tails so to speak. You would do the work and he would gain the benefit."

"I believe I did in fact hear this," Charlie replied.

"But there is more, he suggested that if you became a bore, then there were ways of removing you and allowing Lady Elizabeth to inherit your money."

"Are you suggesting Rufford was planning to murder me?"

"I think he was planning an accident of some sort."

"Bloody hell."

"Apparently," she went on, "they would persuade you to take on a ridiculous wager when you were in your cups, such as hoisting a flag from your chimney pot or some such nonsense and ensuring that you came down head first. I believe," she added, "that young gentlemen are apt to make such insane wagers when drunk."

"It has been known," he replied, drily. Much like the wager that found them in their current situation.

"Well Lady Elizabeth did not greet the prospect with unbounded joy."

"I am pleased to hear it."

"She said she would come back to Sir Rufford when she had thought about it."

"Good God. I know Elizabeth Morgan is a spoiled, pampered hussy, but this is a revelation. I pity the poor fool she eventually inveigles into marriage."

"I imagine if she could, she would move straight into widowhood with the convenience of her husband's money without the inconvenience of the actual husband." Clara grinned.

Charlie felt some of the tension leave her body, his breath caught in his throat as she smiled up at him. He brushed back a stray curl, it was a mistake, once he felt the silkiness of her cheek and caught the subtle scent of vanilla and roses, he stroked her jaw before gently pulling her towards him. "I want very much to kiss you Clara." His voice was low and he could feel her body tense and shiver against him. His lips found hers, gently exploring her mouth then he trailed a series of whisper light kisses down her slender throat before returning his attention to her mouth gently teasing her lips with his tongue until she opened for him. With a soft groan he gathered her to him, pressing her soft body against his hardness willing her to feel the sincerity in his soul and wishing to erase the pain and memory of Rufford's body near hers.

Eventually, he broke the kiss as his conscience roared into life. "I am so sorry Clara, that should not have happened, but I want you to know that I would never do anything to hurt you."

"I think I know that, Charlie," she whispered.

"What are you thinking?" he asked gently, curious at the expressions that flitted across her lovely face.

"I am wondering," she replied softly, "what good deed I must have done to be rewarded with meeting my guardian angel. You have taken me from a maid and made me into what you saw I could be, welcoming me into your home and giving me safety and security far beyond what I could have wished for or achieved myself."

"I am not your guardian Clara, and I am certainly not an angel," he whispered, tracing her delicate ear with his tongue and trailing kisses down her throat until he reached the swell of her breasts. He looked up. "At this moment, all I want to do is remove every stitch of clothing and make love to you. I want to pleasure you so that you cling to me, I want to hear you cry my name. These are not the thoughts of an angel."

She looked at him through heavy lidded eyes. "Then perhaps I do not need an angel," she whispered. "Perhaps I need only to be desired by a man, a man such as you."

"My God, Clara." His voice was thick with desire as he crushed her to him. This time his kiss was not gentle, but fierce and demanding, full of pent-up longing and need. She welcomed him, matching passion with passion, desire with desire. She almost cried out with frustration when Charlie drew back.

"Know that I want you, Clara, as much as any man has ever wanted a woman," he began, before tenderly tucking an errant curl behind her ear. "But not like this. Before all is completely lost, there are things that need to be said, things I must tell you." His conscience had managed to perforate his brain, though his hand continued to caress her leg until her lidded eyes told him that he must restrain himself. There was so much he had kept from her, things which could change her life, things she had a right, needed to know. And yet, he knew he could not tell her about the wager, he was afraid that would be something she would not forgive. He sighed; he would face that another time.

Clara shook her head. "I do not think I understand."

"Then let us go inside and I will attempt to explain," he replied as the carriage slowed to a stop and the door was opened by a footman. "Things are more complicated than you are aware."

"If you say so," she replied, giving him her hand as she stepped down. "Quite how much more complicated than you trying to pass me off as a lady, I struggle to imagine."

Within minutes they were ensconced in the green drawing room, the curtains had been drawn and a fire lit. Several candelabras lent an air of intimacy and soft glow, reflected in the large gilt mirrors on each wall. Earlier generations of Wensleys looked down on them impassively, their lofty portraits a sign of the history, wealth and prestige of the family Charlie belonged to. He strode to the walnut table and poured two glasses of brandy.

"Goodness," Clara commented, taking the glass, "if brandy is needed you must have something very serious to say."

Charlie took a sip, welcoming its fiery warmth as it slipped down his throat. He set the glass aside and took a seat opposite her. "Clara," he began, "you remember the night my grandfather was taken ill?"

She nodded.

"That night he called you Therese."

"I remember."

"He said you reminded him of a young woman he had known in his youth."

"He was having some sort of attack, these things can do odd things to the brain," she replied. "People see things that are not there."

"Perhaps, but he also commented on the locket you wear."

Clara's fingers flew to the locket. "What about it? I did not steal it if that is what you are going to say."

He smiled, taking her glass and setting it down before taking her small hands in his. "Of course not. You told the duke that you had been given the locket by the warden at the orphanage and it was left with you when you were taken there as a babe in arms."

"Go on."

"Grandfather recognised the markings, not as a pattern as you had thought but as a language he had come across in his youthful travels."

"What language?" She sat forward.

"That, I do not know." Clara's disappointment was palpable.

"However, grandfather was intrigued and decided to investigate further. He sent a trusted man to the orphanage, but the warden has retired."

Clara smiled., "Mrs. Gowman was always a fair woman, I hope she enjoys her retirement."

"Indeed, but that is not the point of the story. It transpired that all the records of your attendance at the orphanage had been removed."

Clara's eyes widened. "But why?"

"That is an interesting question to which I do not currently have an answer. It seems that the duke is not the only one curious about you. A man and woman were at the orphanage and at the Morgans enquiring about you."

"Could they be my family come to find me after all this time?" Her eyes shone with hope.

"It is possible," he conceded. "But it is also possible that you represent some sort of threat to someone."

Clara laughed. "That is ridiculous, what kind of threat could I possibly be? To anyone?"

"The fact that great pains were taken to hide you and hide the evidence of your whereabouts would suggest you are not quite the simple orphan you think yourself to be."

"Then how should we find out?"

He paused, knowing that his reply could change Clara's life completely. "We have managed to track down Mrs. Gowman who seems to be the only link with your past," he paused once more. "It would seem that we shall be taking a trip to Lyme Regis."

CHAPTER 28

*T*he trip was arranged with amazing haste, such was the combined wealth and power of the duke and Charlie. At breakfast, the following day, the duke announced, "I have a small estate just along the bay from Lyme, at Charmouth. I shall send word directly to have it made ready for us. By the time we are packed and travelled, it should be prepared for our arrival."

"Have you sent word to Mrs. Gowman letting her know we are coming?" Clara asked.

Charlie and his grandfather exchanged glances, it was Charlie who spoke, "We thought it best to give no prior warning of our intentions. Given the fact that others appear to be searching for you, we cannot risk word of your whereabouts leaking out."

Clara frowned. "But if, as you say these people already know about the orphanage and my service to Lady Elizabeth, surely they can trace me to you."

The duke smiled. "Fortunately, they are looking for a lady's maid called Blackburn. They do not know about the beautiful Miss Clara Burns, the Duke of Wensley's ward, newly arrived in town who dazzled at the theatre last night."

"I beg your pardon?"

"See." He handed her *The Review*. "It is all in here, and a little light relief from the doom and gloom in *The Times*." He winked before adding, "it belongs to Lady Bea, of course."

"Of course," Clara replied, her eyes dancing, "Really," she exclaimed a moment later, "have people nothing better to do than write this nonsense?"

"In any case," Charlie interrupted, "should anyone call at my house looking for Blackburn, they will be told that she left without a trace. My employees are extremely loyal to me and it would appear also to you." He turned to Clara. "You made quite an impression on them in the short time you were there."

"Enough of this," Lady Bea put in, whilst spooning a generous amount of marmalade onto her plate, "Clara, you must go and select the gowns you wish your maid to pack. A trip to Lyme and a mystery to solve! When I came to be chaperone to young Clara, I had no idea it would be so diverting! And," she looked at the duke, "as you are so sniffy about my copy of *The Review* you might put it down and take up your unopened copy of *The Times*."

Clara hastily finished eating and went to alert Lily about the impending trip, only to find that she need not have been concerned.

Lily had already laid out a selection of gowns, spencers, pelisses, bonnets, gloves and shawls on the bed, with a collection of shoes, boots and slippers on the floor.

"My goodness," Clara exclaimed, "I only found out about our visit a few minutes ago."

"Servants' hall, miss," Lily giggled. "What's said in the dining room is known by us all before the table is cleared."

Clara laughed. "I remember the servant grapevine being long and fast flowing."

"Exactly, miss." Lily's face fell. "Though no-one would ever breathe a word to anyone outside of the house, miss. Loyalty, miss, that's the thing his grace and Mr. Hampton both prize above anything else."

"Of course, Lily, I would never doubt it for a moment. Now, shall we pack?"

"You'll need to cover all eventualities, it being the sea-side and all. I ain't never seen the sea, but it's big and wet so you'll need those sturdy boots."

"From what I understand, Lily, when one ventures into the sea, one does not wear boots at all."

Lily looked horrified. "What? No boots? Well I never."

"In fact, I might try the new craze for sea bathing," Clara could not help adding.

"What? All of you? In the sea? Oh, miss." Lily squeaked.

"It is quite the thing," Clara continued. "Apparently it has great health-giving properties."

"Well you won't catch me doing that, Miss Clara. I heard that drinking the waters in Bath was bad enough, but bathing in the sea? Madness. If the good Lord had intended us to be in the sea, he would have stopped creation at the fish, that's what I say, and you'll catch your death of cold."

"Well, we shall see," Clara said as she picked up a gown.

Early the next morning, Clara wriggled in her seat. The duke's carriage was luxurious, but even so, one could only sit still for so long and the constant motion made her feel slightly queasy.

"Are you all right my dear?" The duke's voice broke into her thoughts. "You are looking a little pale."

"I am fine, I am not used to sitting still for so long," she explained.

"No, I do not suppose that your previous life left much time for relaxation."

"No indeed," she laughed, but kind as the duke had been to her, and she had seen what a good employer he was, the duke would never truly understand the lifestyle of his servants. In fact, he was only probably familiar with the few upper servants, the ones he saw, he would have no idea of the army below stairs apart from their maintenance. He would never have come across the housemaids who rose before dawn to ensure that the fire-grates were cleaned and the fires lit and, she would wager, he had never spoken to the scullery maids who washed the pots and pans. But he paid his servants well and they had an afternoon off each week.

"Well, we shall soon be at The Lamb in Hartley Row. I have taken rooms for the night," he interrupted her reverie.

"Thank heavens for that," Lady Bea put in, waking from a nap. "Travelling is both fatiguing and boring."

"Tomorrow, we shall be in Dorchester where we shall meet up with my grandson. Fortunately, there has been only little rain and the road is tolerably passable."

When they arrived at the sizeable coaching inn, Lady Bea decided she must lie down. "To get the wrinkles out of my bones."

Clara found Hartley Row charming, the wide street and neat thatched cottages seemed so clean after London. She could not help but be surprised at the variety of shops selling goods she thought would only be available in the bigger towns, she enjoyed strolling down the High Street with the duke filling in the time before dinner and looking at the butchers, bakers, shoemakers, bookshop, and haberdashery.

"It is peaceful here," she mused.

"Unless you happen to be near the blacksmith's," the duke replied.

"Indeed," she agreed. They had spent a few minutes watching the blacksmith as he hammered a horse-shoe into shape on his anvil. The ducks on the nearby pond protested loudly each time the hammer fell.

"Come," the old man said, leading Clara down the narrow lane beyond the newly built Baptist Church and past Causeway Farm. "Look, they are playing cricket." They watched for a while as the youths of the village thwacked the hard leather ball with a stout wooden bat. A great shout went up as the ball was hit in their direction, the young man running to catch it tripped and sprawled on the grass. Without thinking, Clara stepped forwards and caught the ball to much cheering and teasing of the unfortunate young man.

"Well done, my dear." The duke grinned as she held out the ball to the red-faced young man. "I should think you would want her on your team."

"Indeed so, your 'onour. Not many lasses can catch a cricket ball, an' she be a darn sight prettier than ol' 'enry. You got a place on our team any time you likes, miss."

"Thank you." Clara smiled, handing back the ball, "I shall consider your offer."

"How did you come to know of this place, Your Grace?" Clara asked as they took the short walk back to The Lamb.

"Charlie told me of it. His business interests have meant much travelling and this is a stop he makes if he is traveling to see his ships in Portsmouth or Southampton."

"Well, I think it is delightful."

The duke cocked his head to one side. "I think you will enjoy Dorchester and Lyme too, possibly even more."

"Why?"

"We shall be reunited with Charlie."

Charlie stood by the door of The George and watched the coach draw to a stop. He was sure that his grandfather had taken the time to calm Clara. While she had packed, Charlie had told the duke all that he had related to Clara and all that he had gathered about Rufford's attack.

His grandfather was worried about what Rufford might do, though Charlie was sure that once he returned to town to leverage the man's debt, Rufford would either slink away or quiet down. The old man was quite sure that Charlie needed to tell Clara about the wager quickly or risk having her reject his eventual proposal. Despite that, he did send Charlie ahead and made sure that the old orphanage warden's home was under surveillance by trusted souls in case she attempted to leave without providing them answers.

CHAPTER 29

a s the coach drew to a stop, Charlie was already standing at the door of The George, with a large grin on his face. "Welcome to Dorchester," he said as he helped Clara down. Then he leaned closer adding softly, "I have missed you." His thumbs gently rubbed her knuckles sending a dart of awareness jolting through her body.

"It has only been two days," she replied before adding "but I missed you as well." It was true, she had missed his ready smile and easy company, the way he could make her laugh and how he made her feel she could accomplish anything. She also missed the way his dark hair flopped over his eyes and how he used his hands to emphasise a point he was making. She remembered how good it had felt when he had taken her in his arms and, she admitted, she wanted to feel it again, and more. She wanted to feel his lips on hers and his body next to hers, heartbeat to heartbeat, skin to skin.

"Come, Clara," Lady Bea's voice broke into her thoughts, "there is time to freshen up before dinner is brought to us, and I am gasping for tea."

"And after dinner, there is to be dancing," the duke announced. "As luck would have it, we have arrived during the sheep fair and there is to be an assembly tonight here, at The George."

"Should we be announcing our presence here, Andrew?" Lady Bea asked. "I thought that is why we took a more circuitous route from London, so that no-one would be aware of our destination."

"You are right, Bea, but were someone to have been following us I would have been informed. Besides," he added with a twinkle in his eye, "we are not so old that we do not remember enjoying an evening dancing. Surely we can indulge the young folk tonight."

"Very well," his sister conceded. "Now make haste all of you, I, for one, am famished."

"It was ever thus," the duke commented as he escorted Lady Bea into the inn.

After tea, Lady Bea announced that she would 'rest her eyes' for a short time. Clara tried to read, but her attention quickly wandered. It was, after all, her first trip out of London and she wanted to see and experience everything. Setting her book aside, she quietly left the older woman gently snoring and made her way down the stairs. As soon as she entered the main room, she saw Charlie at a table with several papers laid out in front of him. Seemingly sensing her presence, he looked up and smiled. "And where might you be going?" he asked.

"I thought I might go for a short walk," she replied, tying her bonnet strings.

He rose. "Then please permit me to accompany you."

"You really do not need to trouble yourself," she replied. "I am perfectly capable of walking by myself. I have, in fact been doing so in London since I was a child."

"It is no trouble, and I am sure you are quite experienced," he replied as he gathered the papers and placed them in a leather document bag. "However, there are good reasons. Firstly, I should welcome the diversion, secondly, much as you are familiar with the streets of London, you do not know Dorchester and thirdly, young ladies of society, such as you are becoming, do not wander about on their own."

"Ridiculous nonsense," Clara sniffed. "Young ladies are not puppy dogs who need to be on a leash in case they dash off."

Charlie's eyes gleamed with humour. "Indeed not, but that is how it is and perhaps one day these social rules will be well and truly broken, but for today, we must be satisfied merely to bend them a little. Now, if you would wait for me here, I need to return these documents to my room."

Clara watched as he disappeared, his long legs making short work of the stairs and in less than a minute, he was back, offering his arm.

"May I say," he began as they stepped outside, "that you are looking very lovely today." Clara looked down, the pale lemon sprigged muslin with tiny green leaves embroidered at the waist and hem was one of her favourite gowns. When she wore it with the matching dark green pelisse and bonnet, she felt confident and warm.

"Thank you, Mr. Hampton," she replied. "Though for the life of me I cannot understand why wealthy women have to change their clothes so often. Even as a maid, when I had to dress Lady Elizabeth, I had not considered the amount of time it takes. Do you know, they change five times a day, there are morning dresses, afternoon dresses, riding habits, ball gowns, there are even special dresses for drinking tea," she rolled her eyes. "I would wager," she went on, "that gentlemen do not have to faff around changing all day, they have more important things to do. I thought it was bad enough when I was a lady's maid having barely one thing to wear every day, but it is just as bad, if not worse actually having to do the changing all the time. No wonder Lady Elizabeth was always so bad tempered."

Charlie laughed. "I had not really considered the matter, though now that I know, I shall certainly take far more notice of what ladies wear, given the trouble they go to."

They walked down the steep High Street. Charlie could not help commenting on some of the women he saw. "Do you think that is a special gown just for shopping? Does one have to have a special gown for buying vegetables? Or fish? Or perhaps a gown for buying other gowns?"

"You are incorrigible," Clara replied, but could not help chuckling. "I cannot help noticing how many fine new houses there are," she commented as they strolled down South Walks.

"There was a bad fire here a few years ago. Consequently, houses are no longer permitted to have thatched roofs," Charlie explained. "It is true of many towns and cities, building is flourishing," he added.

"Is that a trade you have interests in?" Clara asked.

He looked down at her with interest. "You are the first woman I believe who has shown the slightest curiosity about my business. Most of them," he added, "have shown interest only in the money it can generate."

"That is because women, well, young ladies at any rate, are only encouraged to fill their heads with fluff. If they show the slightest sign of actually possessing, let alone using a brain, they are generally despised as bluestockings and placed firmly at the back of the shelf," she admonished him. "The ladies' retiring room," she continued in response to his quizzical look, "was quite the place to learn what young ladies really think. They are forced to lead quite shallow lives and many of them become shallow as a result."

"That certainly explains much about ladies of society, if you ask me. It is astonishing that you and Helen are so much more educated and worldly even though you lived in a much smaller corner of the world. Anyway, since you ask, I have an interest in several building businesses in Bath, Liverpool and London as well as in the city of New York," Charlie replied.

"In America?" her eyes widened.

"Indeed, it is a young and vast country and there are many opportunities there. The thing about business," he went on, "is to diversify."

"To not put all your eggs in one basket?" she asked.

"Exactly, so that if one area is not performing well, other areas take up the slack, so to speak."

"Well," she responded, looking around, "business certainly seems to be thriving here in Dorchester."

"For the moment."

She looked up at him. "What do you mean?"

"All this," he gestured, "is built on the profits from wool, raising sheep, spinning, and weaving. Even small landowners can make profits, but things are changing."

"I do not understand," she replied. "Surely people will still raise sheep and wool is always required is it not?"

"Two things are changing rapidly," he explained, sounding quite surprised by her interest. "Have you heard of Manchester?" he asked.

"The town in the north of England?"

He nodded. "Exciting things are happening there. Instead of small weavers working in their own cottages, great factories are being built for weaving."

"Can they not build these factories here, in Dorchester?"

"These factories are powered by new steam engines. Lancashire and Yorkshire have an abundance of the two things needed to make steam, coal and water. It rains a lot in Manchester," he grinned.

"Which runs into the rivers?"

"Exactly."

"Surely there are rivers in Dorset."

"Indeed there are, but no coal."

"So Dorset will not be able to compete with the factories in the north," Clara murmured.

"No. The factories can produce yarn and cloth extremely quickly and engineers are developing new machinery all the time. We are at the beginning of a new and exciting era."

"What is the other thing? You said factories, what is the other thing that means changes are coming?" she asked.

"Trade," he said. "Goods are now coming from all over the world. If we just consider fabrics, cotton comes to England to be woven, silk from the east. There are new techniques for dyeing and printing. People no longer rely on wool for much of their clothing and because factories produce things more cheaply. Soon, maids will be able to afford almost the same cloth as their mistresses, though perhaps not the same styles."

"I cannot imagine Lady Elizabeth being very happy with that," Clara said.

"The Lady Elizabeths of this world will soon have to learn to be as useful and productive as their maids," he replied, surprising her by dropping a light kiss on her nose. "Now, we had better return to The George before Lady Bea notices you are gone.

CHAPTER 30

*L*ady Bea had certainly noticed Clara's absence. "You simply cannot go cavorting around the countryside with Mr. Hampton," she admonished, though added, "no matter how handsome he might be."

"We were just walking, in the full view of the whole of Dorchester," Clara replied. "And he was giving me a valuable lesson in business."

"Well, in that case, very good," the older woman replied. "Frankly, I despair at the lack of education young girls receive about anything sensible. Embroidery and flower arranging are all very well but useless if one allows one's husband to drink or gamble away his inheritance, and yours. A word of advice my dear, always ensure that you have some money hidden away from your husband. My dearly departed was a wonderful husband but had the brains of a peagoose when it came to money. Fortunately, I was able to manage the situation so that he could not invest it in ridiculous hare-brained schemes that were never going to work."

"Goodness, my lady, when I have sufficient funds, I shall come to you to learn how to manage them," Clara replied with a smile.

"You do that, young miss, there is more to being a society hostess than people imagine, and keeping a firm hold on the purse strings is one of them. Society is littered with foolish men and women who had no idea of how much they had until they lost it through bad management and in some cases what can only be described as sheer stupidity."

"You do not seem to have a very high opinion of society, my lady."

"Oh, many of them are all right, but it is a good thing some of them were born into wealth for they could barely master eating with a knife and fork, let alone earning sufficient to put food on the table. Now, enough of this talk, I hear the fiddlers tuning up. I imagine tonight will be more entertaining than an evening in Almacks."

Lady Bea was quite right. The large room was already crowded when they made their entrance. Garlands of flowers and greenery had been hung from the rafters and a small stage for the musicians had been set up at one end of the room. The rich silks, satins, and brocades of the local gentry contrasted with the more muted wool tones of the squires' and farmers' wives, but all were arrayed in as much finery as they could muster. Charlie and his grandfather were already in the room, talking to a couple they introduced as Sir David and Lady Caunce, the largest landowner in the area.

"A pleasure to entertain you and your party, Your Grace," Lady Caunce said, adding, "but next time you are in the area, you must allow us to extend our hospitality."

"I understand you have an estate close to Lyme…" Sir David's voice grew quieter as the four older people turned towards an alcove where chairs had been put out.

"Would you care to dance, Miss Burns?" Charlie asked, holding out his hand. They had missed the traditional opening minuet, but the second set was announced so six couples were forming. "Thank goodness it is not the waltz," Clara murmured as they took their places.

"As your sometime dancing teacher, I am crushed, Miss Burns," Charlie replied with a laugh.

"Do you imagine the waltz will have made it to Dorchester?" Clara asked.

"We shall see," he replied with a gleam in his eye.

There was no opportunity to reply as the country dances were both quick and intricate, with many changes of partner and Clara was relieved when she was finally reunited with Charlie. "I do not think my toes will ever be the same again," she grumbled good naturedly as they made their way to sit. "Squire Milton's son is not the most graceful of dancers."

"And built like a brick outhouse," Charlie agreed, causing Clara to giggle. "Neither does he seem to know his left from his right. You may have noticed that when he changed partners, he always managed to turn the wrong way, hence there was an unseemly tussle with the next gentleman who complained Milton had taken his partner."

"I did observe something of the sort, it reminded me of a session at Gentleman Jackson's," Charlie replied. Clara laughed again. It was so easy to be in his company, if only it could go on forever. How she longed to be in his arms, to feel his kiss and to be loved by him, to hear his voice in the morning, to laugh at his jokes and share his plans. It could never be, she knew that. Despite the fact that he was the first man to see her as a desirable woman of value, once their trip to Lyme was over, he would concentrate on his plan to find her a husband, and he would find himself a convenient wife. She had taken him into her heart, as dangerous and foolish as it may be, and she would always love him, even knowing that he could never love her or wed her. Now that he would one day become a duke, he had even more responsibilities, she would never be more than a footnote in his life.

"What deep and meaningful thoughts you must be having," Charlie's baritone broke into her reverie as familiar, jaunty music began to play. He stood. "Come Clara, it would seem that the waltz has indeed travelled to Dorchester."

CHAPTER 31

*A*s he took her in his arms, it took all of Charlie's willpower not to drag her close and cover her eminently kissable lips with his own. He had been aching to hold her since she had stepped from his grandfather's coach. His need for her was growing and he was beginning to get used to the almost constant state of arousal whenever he thought of her, which was frequently. He wanted to make love to her, but it was more than that he acknowledged, he wanted her by his side, to talk to her and listen to her views, to have a family—something he had never thought about much before other than to have someone to pass on his wealth to, perhaps because he had not met Clara.

He realised now that he did not want a cold, arranged ton marriage that fit all the coldly calculated, rational boxes that surrounded him. He wanted what he remembered his parents had before his mother died and his father found consolation at the bottom of a bottle. He had judged his father harshly, he now understood, his father had not been able to recover from his mother's death. Now he had Clara, he understood how devastated he would be should he lose her, and he did not even truly have her yet.

He smiled down at her. "Try not to count out loud," he advised, tightening his hold as she startled at the sound of his voice.

"Just do not do anything extravagant," she replied, her brow furrowed in concentration.

"Of course not," he replied smoothly, "nothing that will overwhelm you." Clara looked ready to panic as he led her in a series of unfamiliar turns but relaxed into his arms as she realized that he was holding her so tightly that she could only follow his lead.

"You wretch," she said, her eyes dancing as she rose from the customary deep curtsey at the end.

"It is always good to challenge oneself, Clara," he replied. "Think how boring life would be if we merely repeated what we know and never tried anything new."

"I hardly think you can accuse me of that," she shot back. "My life has been turned upside down in a small number of weeks. I am surprised that my hair has not turned white."

He laughed. God it felt good, not just holding her in his arms, but just being with her. "Come," he said, "I feel the need for a little air."

The yard behind the inn was crowded with stable lads as a late coach arrived, so they strolled through the quiet streets until they found a small square. "There is a bench," he pointed out. "Shall we sit for a minute?"

They sat in silence for a little while. "It always makes me feel so small and insignificant," Clara ventured.

"What do you mean?" he asked.

"Look up," she replied. "Look at all those stars like candles scattered across the night sky. I sometimes wonder what they look like and what we look like to them. They seem so far away and here we are, two tiny insignificant dots in some grand scheme of things."

He took her hands in his and drew her gently towards him. "Dots we may be, but believe me, Clara, you are not, nor could you ever be insignificant." His lips met hers in a gentle kiss.

He drew back but kept her hands in his. "Clara, much as I would like to kiss you all night, there is something I need to say to you." He paused, smiling at her look of puzzlement. "I know we have only known each other for a short time, but I would be honoured if you would consent to become my wife."

Clara's eyebrows shot up. "I beg your pardon?"

"I want you to marry me," he clarified, almost as surprised at himself as she was. He had agreed with his grandfather to marry Clara, but he had not intended to propose when they had left the inn. Another thought popped unbidden into his head, that carrying on a pretense that the marriage was all as a matter of convenience would be patently false, that he was eager to have her by his side, in his bed, full with his children, and growing old beside him.

"Why?"

The single syllable surprised him.

"Why?" she repeated. "You could have any woman in the ton, even without the dukedom you will one day inherit. People like you do not marry people like me."

"Clara, look at me."

She raised her head and he could see her eyes brimming with unshed tears. "I have not led a conventional life, Clara, my circumstances as a child would not be recognised by the ton and until a few months ago, I had no knowledge of my grandfather, let alone who he is."

"I don't understand." A single tear strayed down her cheek until he stopped it with his finger.

"It means that I don't feel the need to obey the ridiculous rules of society. Things are changing Clara and we will be part of that change. A man's status should not depend on his parentage, nor should a woman's. I want to be part of this new world of ideas and I want to do it with you by my side."

"But I thought you wanted to find a husband for me."

"And I have," he smiled.

"A suitable husband."

"I can think of no-one more suited to being with you."

"But what of your plan? To prove to the ton that the circumstances of one's birth should not determine forever one's place in society."

"Plans can be changed," he deftly batted aside her concerns.

"And the duke? What will he say?"

"He will be ecstatic at the prospect of seeing my heirs quickly born."

"But what about…" she stopped. "I mean to say," she went on, "that as far as I know, nearly every gentleman takes at least one mistress. I would ask only that you do it so that I do not know."

He reared back. "I have no intention of taking a mistress," he replied. "Neither now nor at any time in the future." It was true, he realised. He didn't want another woman, he just wanted Clara safe and secure in his protection. "I am quite confident that you will satisfy any needs I have, be they physical or companionable, without any desire to turn elsewhere."

"Then I shall marry you," she replied shakily.

The kiss was a taste of the passion they would share, as they each gave and received pleasure in equal measure. "Come," Charlie said, tucking her hand in the crook of his arm. "Let us go and tell Grandfather." He frowned slightly, there was still the undisclosed matter of the wager, but he would tell her of it one day and they would laugh about it. He was sure.

CHAPTER 32

For some reason, the duke did not seem entirely surprised when Clara spoke to him. "I am delighted, my dear," he said and kissed her on both cheeks.

"But what of the plan and the expense you have already undertaken?" Clara began.

"Neither Charlie nor I are in need of funds. As for the ball, we shall make it your wedding ball."

"You seem remarkably sanguine about your grandson marrying so far beneath him."

The duke took both her hands in his. "If I have learned anything in this long life, it is that love is no respecter of persons." He held up a hand when Clara began to speak. "Charlie's mother fell in love with someone I considered to be unsuitable. I lost her and it took many years for me to find Charlie. I will not make the same foolish mistake again. Besides," he added, his eyes twinkling, "it will remain to be seen whether it is you who will be marrying beneath your station."

"Well, I think it is marvellous news," Lady Bea trilled. "I so love a good wedding, but there is so much to arrange, the gown, the flowers, to say nothing of the wedding breakfast. We must send out invitations, St. Paul's I think, of course, nearly all the ton will expect an invitation. Still I imagine we shall manage it within the year."

Charlie looked up from his breakfast. "A year? I do not think so,

Aunt. It does not take me that long to negotiate business in the New World and that includes twelve weeks at sea."

"But…"

"No buts, Aunt. Clara and I will be married as soon as we return to London." He turned to Clara. "If that is what you wish, my love. By all means, we can have the wedding Lady Bea is planning. I only want to make you happy. But," he added softly so that only she could hear, "I do not think I can wait two months, let alone a year."

She felt the heat of her blush fill her body. He had not mentioned love in his proposal, but there was certainly plenty of passion and friendship between them. "I too do not wish to wait," she whispered. "Just a small wedding somewhere private. I have a feeling that once the match is known, it will become something of a circus. Perhaps we can keep it to ourselves as long as possible."

"Then it is settled. As soon as we return to London it will be a small, private ceremony at Wensley House," the duke announced.

"But what about the banns?" Clara asked.

"No need for banns," the old man chuckled. "Charlie already has a special licence."

Clara's eyebrows shot up. "You must have been very confident of my answer, or did you have one ready in case you needed to propose to some woman in a hurry?"

Charlie shot his grandfather a look before taking her hand. "It is true, I cannot deny it, Clara. I decided I wanted to ask you when we were in London but then events overtook us." He gripped her hand tighter and looked deep into her eyes. "Know this, Clara, there is and never has been any woman I have wanted to marry, only you."

"Are you sure? Truly?"

"I truly am," he promised. "That is all. Though I need to tell you about…"

"Come along, if we do not set off now, we shall never make it before nightfall," Lady Bea interrupted. "You can finish your declaration of love later."

Charlie mentally crossed his fingers, perhaps Clara would never hear about the wager. Clara smiled at him; a declaration of love was something she felt she would never hear.

They arrived at Charmouth House just as the sun was going down. "Oh, it is lovely." Clara's eyes gleamed as she glimpsed the sun glittering on the myriad windows as they rounded the curve of the drive.

"It was built as a hunting lodge," the duke explained. "My great-grandfather rebuilt it and my grandfather added the servants' wing and enclosed the parkland. My grandmother designed the gardens. They also collected most of the furniture and paintings on their travels abroad, quite a thing back then, long before young men went on the Grand Tour."

"I have not been here since I was a girl," Lady Bea exclaimed.

"I think you will find little has changed," the duke replied. "Now let us go inside, I have ordered an early dinner. We have an early start to go into Lyme."

Clara retired early, but barely slept. She did know what, if anything, Mrs. Gowman could tell her. As ever, her fingers felt for her locket, the faint markings familiar for the short time she'd had it, but just still visible. She had always wondered about her family, as every orphan did, perhaps they had been looking for her since they had left her. She knew she was hoping against hope, but perhaps she had been somehow given away by mistake, perhaps it had all been an awful nightmare that was about to come to an end. She might find out the truth about the gifts and lessons she had received in her time at the orphanage.

When she heard the hall clock strike three in the morning, Clara decided to go in search of a book; perhaps if she read for a while it would quieten her mind and tire her eyes so that she could sleep for a few hours at least. Candles still burned in their sconces as she perused the library shelves for something to read. "Nothing too exciting," she murmured to herself. "Perhaps some sermons might do the trick. Ah, the Rev. Johnson's 'Sermons on Avoiding the Fires of Hell' is sure to make me weary."

"I imagine the good reverend will put you to sleep by the end of the first page," a deep voice came from behind her. She spun and jumped in surprise and fear.

"Mr. Hampton...Charlie," she squeaked. "I did not realise there was anyone here."

He was sitting on a chesterfield by the dying embers, a book open on his lap and a glass of brandy dangling from his fingers. He had removed his jacket and waistcoat and sat in his buckskins, his right ankle atop his left knee. His neckcloth lay at his feet and the top buttons of his shirt were undone, revealing a dusting of dark hair at the base of his throat.

"I think, as an engaged couple we might dispense with the formalities, Clara. Come sweet one," he beckoned. "Sit beside me."

He had almost stopped breathing when Clara had entered the room in her fine lawn nightrail which offered him a spectacular view. Her waist was narrow, even without the restriction of stays, her breasts were outlined against the sheer material, ripe for touching, his mouth went dry at the thought of them in his hands or mouth. His eyes drifted lower to the promise of the dark shadow between her legs. God, if he continued on this train of thought he would be in serious danger of losing control, something he had never done and he would not do now he told himself firmly, even if it killed him. He would never take what Clara was not willing to give, even though his experience told him he could probably succeed in seducing her. Although she was probably not as naive as gently brought up young women, she was inexperienced, and that could be her undoing.

He closed his eyes momentarily, gathering what shreds of control he had left. "So, what brings you to the delights of the good reverend?" he kept his tone light, as he indicated the book she clasped in her hands.

"I could not sleep," she admitted. "The thought of finding some answers about my past has disquieted me I think."

"Are you worried about what you might hear?"

She nodded. "I know it is childish of me and foolish, but I cannot help hoping that I have a family somewhere. That I was left at the orphanage by mistake but for some reason my family could not come back to claim me."

He took her hands. "Clara we have to face the possibility that we may find nothing from this Mrs. Gowman."

"I know, my head tells me so, but my heart cannot refrain from hoping. For some answers at least."

He tenderly brushed a stray tendril from her face. "Whatever we find, be it something or be it nothing, know that I will be by your side. Always."

"Oh, Charlie," she sighed, her eyes filling with tears as she brushed them away. "I do not know what has come over me, I swear I am not usually such a watering pot."

He smiled. "It is understandable, love, this is an emotional journey." His fingers grazed her cheek. "Good God, you are frozen. Come here." He drew her onto his lap and covered them both with a comforter.

"Charlie," Clara gasped, "even for an engaged couple I do not believe this is considered proper behaviour."

"Proper behaviour be damned," he replied, drawing her closer. "Neither you nor I were brought up to follow society's rules, which seem to be made to make men and women miserable in each others' company. Were I still a street boy, we would have been caught in a much worse situation by now and would have been wed for months. Besides, I have no intention of allowing my affianced bride to freeze to death."

Clara snuggled close, there was nowhere else she wanted to be in the world than here. She rested her head on his chest, feeling the steady beat of his heart. Whatever happened tomorrow or in the future, Charlie would keep her safe. She turned the thought round in her mind. She had never expected to have someone to take care of her, she had been taught that she must look out for herself, she suddenly felt at peace.

"Stop wriggling, woman," Charlie breathed into her ear, "or you will begin something neither you nor I may be able to stop."

She raised her head to face him, suddenly aware of his arousal beneath her. "Mr. Hampton," she replied, looking as innocent as she could, "what on earth do you mean?"

"This," he murmured, as his lips caught hers in one drugging kiss after another. She almost cried out when he raised his head. "Clara, we have to stop."

"What if I do not want to stop?" she asked, her eyes glazed with passion.

"You do not know what you are asking."

"Oh, I do, Charlie," she replied, taking his hand and kissing each finger. He needed no further invitation, he eased her nightrail from her shoulders, pausing to gaze at her creamy, pert breasts before lowering his head and suckling first one and then the other, smiling as he heard her hiss of pleasure.

Without taking his mouth from its delightful work, he stroked first her calf then her thigh, and she gasped as his questing fingers found the soft tangle of curls that covered her most intimate place. He quickly found the small nub he knew would give her the greatest pleasure and stroked it in tiny circles until she was helpless with need, her legs quivering, unsure of whether to open to him or keep him close.

———

"Come, Clara, come for me, give yourself up to it," he whispered, his fingers slipping inside her. God she was tight and wet. It took every ounce of self-control he had not to release the fall of his trousers and plunge into her again and again, giving them both the release that her body was begging for him to give to her. But he would not yet, though it very well might kill him or drive him insane. When they were safely married, he would make her his completely and as frequently as they both could manage; judging by tonight, they would both have a great deal of pleasure.

As she came on his exploring fingers, he covered her mouth with his, catching her cries. He had never known a woman to be so responsive.

"Oh, Charlie," Clara murmured when she could finally speak.

"I know love, I know," he replied, still tracing circles on her soft skin. "And when we are married, it will be even better."

"Even better than that?" she asked, a wicked gleam in her eye.

"Oh, I can assure you, love, when we are both naked and in my bed, or study, or on a rug in front of the fire, with no thought for who might hear us or interrupt, there will be more, much, much more, but for now that must be enough."

"But should I not do something for you? It seems unfair that you have given me pleasure without taking pleasure yourself."

"God give me strength." He kissed her nose. "I took great pleasure in attending to your need, my sweet, but there will be other nights, many other nights when we will take pleasure in each other. But for now, that must be enough or I shall go quietly mad. Come, let me escort you to your room. Try to get some rest, we have a difficult day ahead of us tomorrow."

CHAPTER 33

"The woman has what?" the duke's voice bounced around the breakfast room, almost causing the teacups to rattle on their saucers.

"Disappeared, Your Grace," the unfortunate servant twisted the brim of his hat uncomfortably in his hands.

"How, may I ask," the duke demanded, "was that possible?"

The man twisted his hat once more, "The woman left her house and went to the dress-maker. I followed her as I have done many times and waited across the street so that I had a clear view of the door."

"And then what happened?" Clara asked.

The man turned to her. "Well miss, ladies, as you know sometimes take quite a while at the dressmaker's. I could see through the window the woman looking at bolts of cloth. Then she went further inside and there was no sign of her."

"Did you not think of going in and seeking her?" the duke asked.

"Your instructions were that I was to be discreet, Your Grace."

"Of course," Clara said in a voice that was considerably calmer than she was feeling. "When did you discover that the woman had gone?"

For the first time, the servant allowed himself a brief smile. "I paid a lad sixpence to go in and tell the woman there was an urgent message for her waiting at home."

"And? Get on with it, man," the duke demanded.

"The dressmaker told the boy that the woman was taking tea with her and would be home directly when she had finished the fitting for her gown. It seemed a reasonable explanation at the time."

"And in the meantime, our lady vanished," Charlie mused.

"I can only assume, sir, that the lady made her escape through a door at the back and made her way to either The Royal Lion or The Mariners Inn and boarded a coach."

"In which case she could be on her way to London, Bath, Bristol, Southampton, or New York for all we know. It would seem that our time here has been wasted," the duke said. "We may as well return to London and consider what we might do."

"No," Clara exclaimed. "Please, let us try in Lyme." She turned to the servant, "I believe you said that Mrs. Gowman shared her house with another woman?"

"Yes, miss."

"Then could we not try to speak with her?" she pleaded with the duke. "She may know something."

"Very well," the duke sighed. "Having come all this way, we might as well try."

The journey to Lyme was rather subdued, each occupant in the coach was absorbed in their own thoughts. Clara's mind was full of questions. Did Mrs. Gowman somehow know she was coming? And if so, why had she left in such a hurry? Was she in some sort of trouble? Or was it that she had noticed she was being followed and panicked? None of it made any sense. She was so preoccupied, that her first glimpse of the sea almost passed her by, but she could not help but marvel as the sun glinted on the waves.

"When our business is done, whatever the outcome, shall you like to take a turn along the beach?" Charlie asked.

"I should like that very much."

Before long, the coach had stopped outside a row of neat cottages painted in a variety of white, pink, and blue.

"I suggest you wait in the coach. my dear, while we question the woman," the duke suggested.

"I would like to come with you, if you don't mind, Your Grace," Clara replied. "This is, after all, about my life and besides, I believe she might be more willing to talk if I am present. You and Mr. Hampton might seem rather intimidating."

Charlie looked at his grandfather. "Clara may have a point," he conceded.

"Very well," the duke replied, raising his cane to rap on the door.

It was not long before they heard footsteps and the door was opened. An older, plump woman in a grey dress and apron with white hair escaping from her lace cap stood before them. The duke raised his hat. "Good morning, I am the Duke of Wensely, and we are enquiring after a Mrs. Gowman who was once warden of an orphanage in London and whom we are given to believe is residing here."

The woman's eyes flicked towards Clara. "Are you Miss Clara?" she asked.

"Yes," Clara could scarcely breathe.

"You'd better all come in," the woman said, holding the door open.

"I am Bettina Tovey," the woman announced when they were all seated and tea had been brought into the small but comfortably furnished sitting room. "Mrs. Gowman is not here, but I suspect you already know that."

The duke nodded. "Do you know where she is?" he asked.

Mrs. Tovey shook her head. "She told me she was going away, but it was better, safer, if I did not know where."

"Is Mrs. Gowman in some sort of danger?" Clara's eyes were wide. "This all sounds terribly mysterious."

"Mrs. Gowman is well able of looking out for herself, but she knew this day would come. Might I ask, Miss Clara, do you by any chance own a silver locket?"

Clara's fingers automatically reached for it, she slid it over her head and handed it to the older woman. "Mrs. Gowman gave it to me the day I left," she explained. "I believe it came from my family. The markings are a little faint," she added.

There was a pause while Mrs. Tovey examined the locket, and Clara could hardly breathe.

"It is as Mrs. Gowman described it. Please excuse me for a moment."

"Are you all right, Clara?" Charlie asked when the older woman had left the room. "You look very pale."

"I am just nervous," Clara replied.

"Of course," the duke put in. "Anyone would be. Who knows, we may be about to discover something highly significant about the circumstances of your birth and why you were given to the orphanage."

"Or about my family," Clara replied, her eyes gleaming.

"Of course, we may learn nothing at all," Charlie said. "I am hoping against hope that you find the answers you desperately want, Clara, but we must face the possibility that this might all have been for naught."

"I understand," Clara responded. "I know the chance is remote, but it is still a chance." Her heart felt as though it would leap out of her chest as the door opened. She watched as Mrs. Tovey carefully placed two boxes on the small table, one was a small wooden box with pewter decoration and brass hinges and lock with a key hanging from a faded red ribbon. The other was a black jewel case with a small gold crown engraved on the lid.

"Mrs. Gowman left these to give to you when you arrived." Mrs. Tovey held out the jewel box. "I do not know whether they will contain anything that will answer your questions, but Mrs. Gowman was adamant that you and only you should be the one to open them."

The duke leaned forward. "Is there someone else who has tried to claim them?"

"Not that I know, but it was made clear to me that I must only give them to a woman matching Miss Clara's description and who had the locket."

Clara's fingers shook as she carefully unclasped the box and lifted the lid. Her eyes widened. "It is the same!" she exclaimed, holding up a veritable replica of the silver locket, yet this was of gold, the markings picked out in diamonds. It was clear this locket was of the finest quality. Perhaps there would be portraits of her parents, a lock of hair, anything to give her a clue as to where she came from. She handed it to Charlie. "Open it for me please, I can't bear to look."

There was a moment of silence as three pairs of eyes followed Charlie's fingers. "I am afraid there is nothing in it," he said, his voice gentle. "I am so sorry."

Clara bit her lip to stop the sob that threatened to escape. She had been so sure she would find an answer. How cruel fate was to raise her hopes and dash them.

"What about the other box?" the duke asked quickly. "Perhaps there is something in there."

Clara turned the key and opened the box. It was lined with a rich, red velvet, there were two small compartments with drawers and a larger space at the bottom. All of them were empty.

"Come, Clara," Charlie murmured and placed his arm around her narrow shoulders. "Let us go home. It has been a long morning and there is much to think about. I know you were hoping for more, but the discovery of the new locket gives us something to investigate further. A piece like this is something a jeweller would no doubt remember not only making, but who he made it for. We have another lead, please do not despair."

"That is true, Clara," the duke put in. "As soon as we are back in London, I will have my best man investigate its origins. We may not have made the progress we were hoping for but have no doubt we have made some progress."

Clara turned to Mrs. Tovey. "May I ask, ma'am? What is Mrs. Gowman to you?"

Mrs. Tovey paused for a moment. "Mrs. Gowman and I grew up together, but circumstances beyond our control and which I do not wish to go into meant that we were apart for many years. I was delighted when she was able to join me here, she is one of my dearest friends."

"And will she come back?" Clara asked.

"I expect, all things being equal that she will. When she is ready." She leaned forward and patted Clara's hand. "The truth is near, my dear, do not give up hope and never doubt yourself. You will find what you are looking for."

"I believe you are right," Clara replied, even though she did not in all honesty feel it.

As they bade their fare-wells Charlie took Clara's hand and tucked it through his arm, "I know the last thing you feel like now is a walk, but I promised you a walk along the beach and a bit of fresh air will do wonders to blow away the cobwebs."

Leaving the duke happily reading his newspaper in the carriage, they made their way down the steep lane towards the beach. Charlie did his best to elicit a smile from her, "I imagine Grandfather is, at this moment, examining the locket for further clues and tipping the box this way and that to see if there is a secret compartment.

Clara paused mid-step. "Do you suppose there might be?"

"I meant it as a jest, but I suppose it is possible."

"My background seems to be one mystery after another," Clara murmured.

"Well try to forget about it for a few moments and enjoy your first walk on the beach."

They walked in silence for a while, the only sounds being the gentle swishing of the waves and the skirl of the seagulls as they wheeled and dived overhead. From time to time, Clara stopped to pick up a shell and examine it.

"What are those?" she pointed to what looked like gypsy caravans near the water's edge.

"Bathing machines," Charlie explained. "Those I think are for ladies who wish to immerse themselves completely in the sea. It is supposed to be good for one's health."

"Do they not risk drowning?"

"There are attendants to ensure that they do not, too many drownings would be bad for business." He laughed.

"Have you ever done this?"

"Not here, recently anyway. I don't find the English waters particularly inviting, but yes I have swum in the sea, one day I will teach you if you wish, personally I prefer to do it…"

"Where?"

"Where it is warm enough to do it with you…naked."

CHAPTER 34

*B*ack in London, Lady Bea's primary focus was on successfully launching Clara into society before her wedding. It had been decided that the wedding would be a small, private affair at Charlie's House with only the duke and Lady Bea present, along with Charlie's friends Harper and Silcock. Although Clara would have enjoyed having Cook from the orphanage attend, it was decided that more secrecy was perhaps needed. The ball would take place in the evening when the marriage would be formally announced.

"I imagine it will create something of a stir," Lady Bea remarked, drawing the thread through her embroidery.

"I imagine it will," Clara replied.

"It is something of a distraction, but before that, we have many functions to attend," Lady Bea indicated the pile of invitations on the mantle-piece.

Clara rose and leafed through them, "At Homes, Musicales, Concerts, Routs, and at least one ball," she murmured. "Do we have to go to all of them?"

"Of course." Lady Bea snipped the thread. "There is only one thing worse than being invited to all these functions and that is not being invited. Besides, Verity and Ella are very much looking forward to seeing you again." She selected another thread. "I sense there is a problem from the frown on your face."

Clara carefully composed her features. "Oh, of course I should like to see Verity and Ella, it is just that I also might see Lady Elizabeth."

"I do not think we need to trouble ourselves with that minx. If she has not realised yet who you are, I doubt she will."

"I hope you are right." Clara picked up her embroidery.

The invitation to tea with Lady Ella and Lady Verity was willingly accepted, she could hardly wait to tell them at least some of the details of her trip to the coast, though the visit to Mrs. Tovey was to remain a secret for the time being. She dressed with care in a new gown of the palest, fine green wool embroidered with leaves picked out in a darker green around the waist and hem. The days had begun to get colder, so she decided to wear the matching green pelisse. By the time they set off, the early morning frost had cleared and the sky was a clear blue. The Grainger house was only two streets away, so Clara decided to walk and, much to her surprise, so did Lady Bea. "What? Did you think I would let you face this alone? Besides, I shall keep that old reprobate of an earl out of your hair my dear," she said, fastening her bonnet, picking up her cane, and taking Lily's arm.

There were one or two other girls Clara recognised as they entered, but she was dismayed to find Lady Elizabeth sitting at the small dressing table in the retiring room when she stopped to tidy her hair.

"Ah, Miss Burns," Lady Elizabeth began, though her attention was focused on the maid who was attempting to dress her hair. "Not like that, you idiot girl," she snapped. "If you pull any tighter you, will pull it out! Ladies' maids," she continued in a softer tone to Clara, "are so damnably difficult to train and this one," she indicated the young woman, who was close to tears, "has not the slightest idea of how to dress hair."

"Indeed," Clara agreed, her eyes sparkling with amusement, "a good ladies' maid is to be treasured," she replied, knowing that irony would go completely over Lady Elizabeth's head. She grinned at Lily who stifled a giggle.

"Come, sit beside me," Lady Elizabeth patted the padded stool. "Perhaps your maid might repair the damage that stupid girl has done?"

"Of course."

"Go and attend to the hem of my pelisse," she ordered. "There are some specks of mud which I do not expect to see when I am ready to depart." Clara had never seen a girl with more relief on her face as she fled the room.

"Lily, would you please attend to Lady Elizabeth," Clara instructed Lily with an apologetic smile.

"You call your servants by their given names?" Lady Elizabeth raised an aristocratic eyebrow.

"I do."

"Then let me give you some advice, Miss Burns. It may be acceptable in the country where you have grown up, but here in town, one refers to one's servants by their surnames if one needs to refer to them by name at all. I doubt my father has ever known and certainly never used any servant's name." She laughed. "The thing is," she went on," servants in town tend to be far more uppity and need to learn their place. Believe me, I speak from experience." She peered into the mirror.

"How so?"

"I had a maid a while ago. Quite a good one, I trained her myself and she certainly could dress hair, I will say that for her. Had her for years. But what happened? One day she flounced off without so much as a by your leave."

"Was she unhappy?" Clara could not resist asking.

"I doubt it. What could she have to be unhappy about? She was fed, clothed, and had a roof over her head. Servants are not like us in any case. They have no understanding of the refinements of our class."

"And she just upped and left you say?" Clara could not help pressing.

Lady Elizabeth studied herself in the mirror before replying. "Blackburn had disgraced herself at a ball by sneaking into the library rather than confining herself to the ladies' retiring room or below stairs. Not only that, she had the temerity to approach a gentleman who was in there. In fact, said gentleman was Mr. Hampton, though his gentlemanly credentials at that time were somewhat dubious. It is only since his relationship with the duke emerged that he has been considered entirely top drawer. Be gentle with the pearls, girl," she snapped at Lily who was placing pearl decorated pins into her curls. "They are worth more that you will earn in your lifetime."

"Perhaps, Lily, that might be the last pin. I am sure her ladyship would not have her hair overdressed for tea," Clara interjected.

"Certainly," Lily replied, "if that is to your liking, my lady? There are five pins left, shall I place the spare ones in your reticule, my lady?"

Lady Elizabeth gave a slight nod, barely able to contain her irritation. Lily counted the pins in. She smiled brightly at Clara. "Shall I attend to your hair now, Miss Burns?"

"Just tidy it please, Lily." Clara smiled back.

"One really does not need to say 'please' to servants, Miss Burns. One gives an order and they obey and that is the end of the matter. I can see that I shall have to educate you in these matters if you are to enter society well here in town."

"You were telling me of the night your maid disgraced herself," Clara intervened with false interest.

"Well, when I discovered Blackburn, had engaged in conversation with Mr. Hampton, I took her straight to his house to apologise. And this is where," she added with a smug grin, "I learned the most interesting titbit of gossip of the year first. The Duke of Wensley was there and was taken ill. During the commotion, it was then that it emerged that Mr. Hamton is in fact his grandson and heir. A secret that had been well kept I can tell you."

"But what has this to do with your maid?"

"I lent her to help nurse the old man. It should come as no surprise, even to someone as green as you, that regardless of Mr. Hampton's considerable wealth, now that he is an heir to a dukedom, his eligibility is at the very least, doubled. I realised that with Blackburn acting as the duke's nurse, I should have greater access to Mr. Hampton." She suddenly frowned, an expression with which Clara was wholly familiar. "That is, until the stupid girl ran off."

"But what would cause her to run off?"

Lady Elizabeth patted her hair and studied her reflection from right to left.

"I neither know nor care. I sent her things on. She would trouble to sell anything, I made sure of that and, should she try to gain employment elsewhere among the ton, she will find every door slammed in her face."

"You would not give her a character?"

"Not only that, I should take great delight in revealing that she is a thief."

"She stole something? How shocking. Was it a piece of jewellery or clothing? An antique perhaps, or money?"

"Not exactly. I found a piece of mirror among her possessions, but it is enough."

Clara rose to move away. "Perhaps that is why she left," she said. "With no prospect of work as a lady's maid to a good family, she may have chosen to try her luck elsewhere, in one of the industrial cities of the north with a family in trade."

"She can ply her trade among the sailors with the other whores at the docks for all I care," Lady Elizabeth huffed. "Now, be a dear and pass the pot of rouge."

As Clara stood behind and reached over, she heard the other woman's hissed intake of breath.

"Is everything all right, my lady?" she asked.

A sly smile spread over Lady Elizabeth's features. "I rather think it is, Miss Burns, I rather think it is."

CHAPTER 35

"*L*ady Beatrice was just telling us of your trip to Lyme Regis," Lady Ella said as she handed Clara a cup of tea. "How exciting."

"Oh, it was," Clara replied. "I had never seen the sea and his grace was good enough to indulge me."

"Of course Brighton is the place," Lady Elizabeth opined, taking a tiny bite of seed cake. "The Marine Pavillion is quite spectacular and I believe the prince intends to enlarge it further, according to my father at any rate, who is of course a close confidant of the prince."

"I hear there are quite scandalous goings on there," Lady Verity said.

"I should be more surprised should there not," Lady Bea sniffed. "That man attracts scandal as flowers attract bees, and I am not entirely convinced that he is a suitable topic for young ladies at tea."

"Then tell us about your life in the country, Miss Burns," Lady Elizabeth turned to Clara. "For we know next to nothing about you and it is always interesting to learn about a new friend," she smiled, but it did not reach her eyes.

"I hardly know where to begin."

"Begin at the beginning, who were your parents?"

Was Clara imagining it or was Lady Elizabeth's tone sharper than usual?

"Clara's parents were distant cousins of ours," Lady Bea put in.

"When Wensley heard of their untimely deaths, he did not hesitate to do his Christian duty, and, I might add, it has been a pleasure." She looked warmly at Clara.

"And did you not go to school?" Lady Elizabeth persisted. "I imagine the duke would have been only too grateful to send a child to school, I know my parents were, and there are so few good schools for young ladies. Everyone seems to know everyone, it is quite astounding that our paths have only recently crossed."

"I received my education from the local vicar," Clara said confidently. This answer was more or less truthful, unlike Lady Bea's. "He instructed me in Latin, French, Italian, a little Greek and German, as well as some Science and Mathematics."

"I loved mathematics," Lady Ella spoke. "The logic and patterns of numbers are infinitely fascinating."

"Much to the chagrin of our father," Lady Verity said, "who constantly told Ella that being able to manage her pin money was all she needed to know and further study of mathematics would give her wrinkles."

"Thank goodness I too had a willing teacher in the vicar," Clara conceded.

"Well, I hated mathematics," Lady Elizabeth announced. "All those horrid columns of numbers would never add up. Such a bore."

"But how will you know if your tradesmen are dealing honestly with you if you do not check your accounts?"

Again, Lady Elizabeth smiled slyly. "One has people to do that sort of thing. True ladies never have to bother whether the books will balance, their fathers or husbands will ensure that they do."

"Though it would be a very foolish man indeed who let his wife or daughter's spending run away from him, would it not, my dear?" Lady Bea smiled back at Lady Elizabeth. "For believe you me, down that road runs ruin and debtors' prison," she added for good measure.

Lady Elizabeth paled slightly. "You have the right of it, ma'am, perhaps I should have paid more attention to my lessons. However, being the duke's ward, I imagine, leaves you little concern regarding income." She smoothed an imaginary wrinkle from her skirts. "Tell me, Miss Burns, I do not believe I caught which of his grace's estates you were raised on."

"Clara was raised on the duke's Yorkshire estate. He is the Duke of

Wensley after all," Lady Bea said before Clara could even draw breath. Tall tales seemed to trip off her tongue with ease.

"Strange," Lady Elizabeth murmured, delicately taking a sip of tea. "You do not appear to have the accent of one raised in the north."

"Of course she does not," Lay Bea replied tartly, "neither do you have the accent of one from Essex, though I believe that is where your father's primary estate is located is it not?"

"You are correct of course," the younger woman replied through gritted teeth.

"Lady Elizabeth," Verity put in. "I believe you are to play and sing at the Countess of Durham's musicale tomorrow evening. Have you decided on your repertoire?"

Clara was relieved that attention was shifted from her, she knew from experience that Lady Elizabth's favourite topic of conversation was Lady Elizabeth and had been alarmed by her sudden interest in her own background.

"Indeed, I have," the young woman replied. "I shall sing an aria or two from one of Handel's oratorios and play some Bach. The pieces are quite demanding but not beyond my ability. And yourself, Lady Verity, shall you not delight us with your playing?"

"I am afraid not," Verity said with humour. "I have neither the skill to play nor the patience to practise and improve. Ella plays like an angel, though only in private."

"Of course, with your disfigurement I quite see why you would not wish to draw attention to yourself." Lady Elizabeth's words were said with a sympathetic tone, but Clara could see that her barbs had wounded, the burn scars would never go away and although Lady Ella's hair hid them for the most part, she could see that they had affected her deeply.

"I have never understood the fact that on a man, a scar is viewed as a mark of honour, yet on a woman it must be covered, as though we are not permitted an imperfection. See," Clara drew her hair back to reveal a heart shaped birthmark the size of a strawberry just below her left ear. "To hear Mrs. Gowman, my...governess, one would think I looked like a pirate, so insistent was she that it had to be covered at all times."

"It is true that gentlemen demand perfection," Lady Elizabeth conceded.

"However imperfect they themselves might be," Lady Bea commented, to which they all laughed.

"I believe," she went on, "that it is only in the human race that it is the female who must attract a mate. In the feathered world, it is the cocks who are dressed to impress a mate and build a nest to her satisfaction."

"Whereas we must squeeze ourselves into the most ridiculous fashions, eat like birds, and do nothing remotely interesting to attract a husband," Lady Verity complained.

"And we are taught to be dutiful, obedient, and boring, with the result that we bore our husbands and ourselves within the year," Lady Ella added.

Lady Elizabeth shrugged. "But once we have done our duty and provided one heir, preferably a second just to be sure, we are free to live our own lives. So long as we are discreet, in my opinion it is a small price to pay for a lifetime of comfort, gowns, and jewels."

"But what of love?" Clara could not help but ask, even though she had heard Lady Elizabeth's opinion on the matter long ago.

"One might fall in love with one's husband I suppose, but generally one marries for wealth, position and security which most husbands are willing to provide in exchange for an heir. Of course, it is important for our fathers to choose well."

"Our fathers rarely seem to take our feelings on the matter into consideration," Lady Verity said with feeling. "Poor Sarah Packenham was married off to a man older than her father so that their estates might be joined."

"And Alice Walsh was made to marry Lord Tiverton even though he ruined her in order to get his hands on her fortune," Ella added. "He ran through the money in a year and sold her house from under her."

Lady Elizabeth turned once again to Clara. "But what of you, Miss Burns? Has the duke already begun to find you a suitable husband. Or at least someone prepared to take you off his hands?"

Clara blushed, but not for the insult. Her suitable husband had been found and was eager to have her come into his hands.

Once again, Lady Bea came to her rescue. "I believe my brother is considering the matter, though rest assured, Lady Elizabeth, Clara will not be forced to marry anyone who does not suit or could not love. Now," she rose, "we must be going, Clara and I have promised to call in on Her Majesty, the Queen."

CHAPTER 36

Charlie paused in the doorway of the morning room, entranced. Clara sat curled up on the window seat in a gown of pale green muslin, decorated at the waist and hem with dark green ribbons, some of which were also threaded through her chestnut curls. She looked like a sensuous wood nymph. On her lap lay the wooden box on which her fingers absently traced the pattern, though he could see her attention was not engaged. He frowned, always attuned to her, he instinctively knew that something troubled her, he also knew that she would be reluctant to reveal what it was.

"Good morning, Clara." He smiled as his deep voice made her jump.

"Mr. Hampton."

"Charlie. We are alone, in any case what is the point of our forenames if we rarely use them?" he smiled to lighten the mood.

"Charlie, then. You startled me, I did not hear you come in." She smiled but he could see it was her polite, social smile, not the one he wanted.

He sat beside her on the window seat and cupped her face before dropping a light kiss on her lips. "I have been longing to do that for days."

She rolled her eyes. "I very much doubt it since I saw you yesterday and I seem to recall there were kisses in the library, the glass house, and the drawing room just before Lady Bea came in."

He laughed. "What can I say? Guilty as charged, though I am not in the slightest repentant." He kissed her again, this time until she was breathless.

"Now, when I came in just now, you looked as though you had received a message from the prophet of doom inviting you to attend your own funeral. What is it that troubles you?"

She looked at him, her eyes like the cool depths of an emerald pool. "Yesterday, Lady Bea and I went to tea with the Grainger girls."

"Thus far I see no reason for alarm, unless old Earl Grainger's cook still makes rock cakes that taste exactly like actual rocks."

"Lady Elizabeth was there."

"I see. An unpleasant experience I have no doubt, but hardly presaging an imminent visit from the four horsemen of the apocalypse."

"She knows."

He paused, his eyes narrowed. "She knows what? From my experience I would say that the aforementioned lady barely knows how to spell her name."

"Oh Charlie, do not be obtuse. I am sure Lady Elizabeth knows who I am and what I was."

"What makes you so sure? You have seen her several times and she has not shown the slightest inkling."

Clara looked at him, drinking in his potent masculinity. He was, as ever, dressed in muted colours. He did not need to dress in the bright silks of the ton, he stood out from the crowd anyway. His midnight blue jacket contrasted with the sparkling white of his neckcloth, his cream waistcoat covered his strong abdomen, and Charlie Hampton had no need of the corsets she knew some gentlemen of the ton wore. His long, muscled legs stretched his buff trousers as they disappeared into his highly polished hessians. Clara wanted to catch this moment and keep it in her memory forever, because she knew that once Lady Elizabeth spoke, it was unlikely that she would ever see Charlie Hampton again, her adventure would be over. She would break their engagement, even though it was not public, and she knew that Charlie would survive the scandal only if she was no longer a part of his life. She could not bear to think of him becoming a social outcast because of his association with her. Regardless of his words regarding his lack of interest in the rules of society, there would be damage to his reputation and she could not bear to think that she was the cause. It would break her heart, she realised, but she would have to learn to live with that.

"She saw me, standing behind her in the mirror," she continued.

Charlie shook his head. "I do not understand. What does that signify?"

Clara sighed. "Lady Elizabeth was in the retiring room when I arrived. Her maid was attempting to dress her hair. Eventually, Lily was asked to repair the damage."

Charlie raised his eyebrows. "I think you are going to have to go into more detail, my love. Forgive me, but the goings on in a ladies' retiring room are something of a mystery."

"I should hope so," she replied with a ghost of a smile.

"Please," he prompted, "continue."

"We chatted for a while, then, as I stood, she asked me to pass her the pot of rouge and I am sure that is when she knew."

"Because?"

"Oh, Charlie, because as her maid I had done precisely that a hundred times," she said.

"And you think that because she saw you in that context she realised who you were?"

"Exactly."

"You could be mistaken," he tried to reassure her. "It is possible that you are reading more into this because you are sensitive to it, whereas Lady Elizabther has no real reason to doubt who you say you are."

Clara shook her head. "She definitely knows. When we were at tea, she was constantly asking questions about my parents, my education, my relationship with his grace, anything to try and catch me out."

"But if as you believe, she has some inkling as to who you are, why did she not reveal it?"

Clara arched an eyebrow. "Charlie Hampton, for someone as intelligent as you, I am surprised that you do not understand how devious people like Lady Elizabeth can be. She will be waiting to make her suspicions public at a time that will cause the most embarrassment of course."

He nodded slowly. "Of course."

"It will be at the Christmas Ball," she murmured.

"What?"

"Lady Elizabeth will reveal all at the Christmas Ball," she explained. "It is the perfect opportunity, my launch into society, everyone has been invited." Clara bit her lip. "And there is nothing we can do to stop her."

He took her by the shoulders. "She can say what she likes, by then you will be my wife," he said firmly.

"Oh Charlie," she replied quietly, "don't you see? I cannot possibly marry you now. Everyone would know that you tainted yourself by being married to someone like me."

She pressed a finger to his lips. "You know it is so Charlie, the ton will forgive you almost anything, especially as one day you will be a duke. But they do not forgive those who marry beneath their class."

"Devil take it, Clara," he burst out. "Do you think I care about any of that? I had no dealings with society until I was a wealthy man and I do not care a fig for their hypocritical rules. They accept me or they do not, I care not, and because they know I do not care about them, they have no power over me, and they will have no power over you either."

He stalked to the door, turned the key, and pocketed it.

"What are you doing?" Clara asked, nervously licking her lips.

"I am going to prove to you once and for all that we belong together. We were made for each other. Lady Elizabeth can do her worst, but I will not lose you. Society can go hang. I will marry you, Clara, and that is all that matters."

CHAPTER 37

The box dropped to the floor with a crash as Clara stood to face him. "Sometimes I think you are quite mad, Charlie Hampton," she said as he walked slowly towards her, loosening his neckcloth as he walked.

"Perhaps I am," he replied, "but it is because you make me so. Ever since we met you have dominated my thoughts to the point that I struggle to concentrate on business, but that is nothing compared to the nights, where you have tormented my dreams, always just too far away from me to touch."

"I am not too far away from you now," she said softly.

"No, you are not." His arms went around her, drawing her to him as his mouth came down on hers. He poured everything he had into that kiss, hoping that she would understand the depth of his feelings for her which he struggled to put into words. He may not have a silver tongue, but he could show her with his body that she was not only desired, she was loved. There was no denying it, somewhere along the line he had fallen deeply and irrevocably in love with Clara and of all the women that he knew he could have, there would only ever be one he wanted to spend the rest of his life with.

Of their own volition, Clara's arms seemed to wind themselves around his neck, her fingers burrowing into the soft hair at the nape of his neck. Whatever happened, whatever the consequences of Lady Elizabeth's words, she would have this moment, even if it had to last her for the rest of her life. When his tongue traced along her lips, she instinctively opened them to let him in, moaning softly as his tongue touched hers. "Clara," he murmured, moving slightly to kiss the sensitive spot beneath her ear, "you are so beautiful, I cannot wait to make you my wife."

"Oh, Charlie," she sighed, her whole body attuned to his, "I have told you...."

"Shh sweeting." He placed a long finger on her lips, "Do not speak, just feel how good this is. How good we are. You have no idea how rare this is."

Clara gasped as his fingers dipped down her bodice and gently stroked what he found there. In an instant, the tips of her breasts hardened under his touch.

It did not take him long to work her bodice down so that her breasts were exposed to his gaze. "So beautiful," he murmured, lowering his head to first one and then the other, teasing and laving with his mouth and stroking with his fingers. Clara could scarcely breathe, all her thoughts were centred on the wonderful things Charlie was doing to her and her body's response, from the tautness of her nipples to the tightness in her stomach and beyond to the sensations in the centre of her femininity.

Suddenly, Charlie looked up, his blue eyes holding hers, "Do you trust me, Clara?"

"I think so," she replied, softly, breathlessly.

"I would never do anything to hurt you, believe me."

"I know."

"When we are married, I vow that I will protect you from whatever the world throws at us."

"Charlie, we have been through this," she protested.

"Trust me, Clara."

He carried her to the sofa and gently laid her on it, kneeling in front of her. "The world has not been kind to you, Clara, but from now on, you will have someone to protect you. You will never have to worry again and I promise you that you will have everything you desire."

She looked at him from lowered eyes, her eyelashes fanning her cheeks. "There is one thing I desire now," she whispered.

"Tell me."

"I desire you to make love to me, here. Now."

There was a silence as he rocked back on his knees.

"Now you think I am no doubt a lightskirt, no better than I should be," she said, turning her head so that she could not see the look of disgust she expected to see on his face.

Stretching out a hand, he turned her towards him. "I think nothing of the kind," he reassured. "In fact, I am delighted that you are not some missish prude who regards a sexual relationship as a duty to be endured. Believe me, Clara, when I say that making love with you will be exciting, stimulating and I believe, deeply, deeply satisfying," he groaned, "for both of us." Clara could not help but smile as she looked down at her gown in disarray, her breasts still exposed and, she could not help but notice a sizeable bulge at the fall of his breeches.

"Then why are you waiting?" she raised a quizzical eyebrow.

Charlie took a deep breath before replying. The urge to take all she was offering was almost overwhelming. It would be easy to give in to what he knew they both wanted, but he was determined. Clara would be his wife; she would be treated with the respect she had so often been denied. Claiming her now would smack too much of the master having his way with his servant and that he did not want to do. Though when they were wed, he would very much enjoy making love with Clara in bed or out of it, clothed or unclothed, and in a variety of positions. He cleared his throat before his imagination got the better of him and his determination.

"Clara, sweeting, please believe me, I want to make love to you, to feel you come when I am inside you and to hear you scream my name as you do. But, God help me, I am not going to take you until you are well and truly my wife, which thank God, is to be soon."

"Then what are we doing?" she asked with a smile.

"Practising," he grinned. "There is more than one way to show physical love Clara, and this time it is all for you."

She raised her eyebrows, "I do not underst...oh."

Her eyes opened wide as his questing fingers found her most intimate place and stroked with increasing intensity. She gasped as his fingers dipped inside her and his thumb found the sensitive nub.

"Ah," he murmured, "the pearl of great price," and lowered his head.

Charlie could feel the race of her heart when his mouth replaced his fingers, heard her crying out as he slipped his tongue inside her. She gripped the sides of the sofa as sensation after sensation swept through her like an immense wave sweeping over her body, stifling her moans as best she could. Charlie raised his head to watch her, a satisfied smile on his face as he watched her body be overcome from what he could do to her. It was more than beautiful, it was enticing, and it was more arousing than he could have believed. "That's it my love, let yourself go with it."

"Oh, Charlie, I thought I was going to die," she gasped when she was able to string a sentence together. "I never knew."

Charlie smiled at her sparkling eyes and slightly flushed face. "There will be this and so much more," he promised.

She leaned up on one elbow. "And what about you?" she asked. "You have given me such pleasure, can I not do the same for you?"

There was a slight pause before Charlie's discipline and determination re-exerted themselves. "This was for you, Clara, but when you are truly mine and I yours, you will give me just as much if not more pleasure than I just gave you, I promise. For now, the taste of your body will fulfill me."

"But..."

"No buts, Clara, my control is hanging by the slightest thread as it is, but it is not indestructible. It is not often that I try to be a gentleman, but let this be one of those times," he replied firmly, knowing that most gentlemen of his acquaintance would have to conscience about taking what Clara was offering.

Within minutes, Clara's clothing was set to rights. "I imagine," she observed drily, "that should your businesses fail, you might gain employment as a lady's maid," she said as he finished lacing the back of her gown. "It would certainly appear that you have some experience in these matters," she added.

He swatted her lightly on the bottom. "I could not possibly comment," he growled, though she detected the humour in his tone.

"Oh no!" she exclaimed.

"What is it?" he asked, following her gaze.

"The box, it must have broken as it fell.

CHAPTER 38

Charlie picked up the box from where it had fallen. "Actually, I do not think it is broken," he said, examining it carefully. He drew in a sharp breath, his fingers stilled as he caught Clara's eyes.

"What is it?" she asked.

"There is some sort of secret compartment," he said quietly. "It must have activated the mechanism or something when it dropped to the floor."

Clara could barely breathe. "Is there something inside?" she whispered.

He held the box towards her. "If there is, it should be you who finds it."

Clara stared at the box. On the underside the corner of what looked like another drawer had slid partly out. She took the box with shaking hands.

"Come, sit and open it," Charlie guided her towards the sofa.

She looked up at him. "What if there is nothing?"

"Then you have lost nothing," he replied. "Whatever is in there may make some difference or no difference to your life, Clara, but either way you will not know if you do not look. I imagine," he added, "that there must be something of some importance for Mrs. Gowman to have gone to the trouble of both keeping it from you for all these years. In fact, keeping it until the time was right for you. It would appear that the time has arrived."

Carefully, Clara pulled the corner of the drawer, it slid out easily as though it had been used only recently. A parchment lay folded at the bottom of the drawer and on top was a small package wrapped in linen and tied with a silk ribbon. Delicately, Clara unfastened the ribbon and unfolded the linen to reveal four miniature portraits. An older and a younger couple stared back at her. The older couple were dressed in the fashion of an earlier age, both wearing powdered wigs and rich silks. The woman wore stunning diamonds and sapphires at her throat and ears along with a brilliantly matching tiara. The younger couple were also richly dressed but wore no wigs, the man's hair was longer than current fashion, dark and curly, held back with a black ribbon. The woman's hair was a rich shade of chestnut, swept back from her face and cascading over one shoulder. She wore the same diamonds and sapphires as the older woman.

Clara looked from one to the other. "Charlie do you think these could be my family?" she asked, her voice shaking with emotion.

"Clara, look in the glass," he replied. "You are exactly like this woman and, if you imagine the older lady without the wig, like her as well. I would say without a doubt that these are your parents," he pointed to the younger couple, "and these are your grandparents."

"But who are they?" she asked. "And why the need for so much secrecy?"

"That I cannot tell you, but we will find out. It is a puzzle to be sure, but now we have something physical to help us solve it."

"I think they are…" Clara began, and reached for her locket. Opening it, she gently eased out the inner frames.

"A perfect fit," Charlie finished. "Clearly the locket and the portraits are meant to be together."

"And they shall be," she replied, "but not until we have identified who they are," she explained. "It will be easier to do so if they are separate."

Charlie smiled at her practicality. "This does confirm one thing," he began, indicating the likenesses. "Clearly your family has, or at least at the time these portraits were painted, had wealth and I would surmise, probably a great deal of power as well. Their clothing and jewels would suggest so at least."

"But why give me up if they had wealth and power? Why was I so unwanted that they sent me to an orphanage?" Clara asked.

"Clara, perhaps there was another reason," he suggested.

"What do you mean?"

He took both her hands in his hands, which although were softer now, her hands had clearly known hard work. "It could be, Clara, that for some reason, your parents sent you to the orphanage in order to protect you."

"I do not understand."

"Think about it, you were left at an orphanage but there were lessons and gifts that suggest your family knew where you were. There was also the silver locket when you left, to be replaced by the gold one when you came of age. Then there is the warden's disappearance, even though she clearly wanted you to have this, and was sure that one day you would come for it, which leads me to believe that perhaps you were not sent there because you were unwanted, but because you were loved very much. So much that you were taken there for your protection."

"But who would want to harm a babe?" she asked, her eyes wide.

"Perhaps someone who did not want the babe to grow into an adult," he suggested. "Who for some reason, was a threat to them?"

"Me?" she squeaked. "How could I possibly be a threat to anyone?"

He looked at the box once more, "Perhaps the parchment will throw some light on the subject."

Clara nodded and carefully drew the parchment from its place. The only sound in the room was its quiet crackling as she slowly unfolded it.

"It is nothing," she sighed. "Just a jumble of dashes and lines."

Charlie took it from her and was silent for a moment while he examined it.

"Perhaps it was just placed there to protect the pictures," she suggested.

He shook his head. "I do not think so. I believe this is some sort of cipher and look," he pointed to the bottom corner. "This is a seal. Clara." His eyes met hers. "Once we break the code on this document, coupled with the portraits, we will find out who you truly are."

CHAPTER 39

There was a silence in the duke's book lined study, apart from the ticking of the ormolu clock on the high marble mantel. Pale winter sunshine filtered through the tall windows, highlighting one or two motes of dust as they floated to the floor. The duke's housekeeper would not be happy if she saw them, a housemaid or two would be given a stern word, though as Clara looked at them, neither he, nor Charlie seemed to notice. The duke's eyes were firmly focused on the parchment in his hand.

Clara could scarcely breathe as she waited for the old man's response. She started slightly as Charlie interlaced his fingers with hers, his reassuring look and smile calmed her shredded nerves. Finally, the duke looked up. "Most interesting," he said, turning his attention to the miniatures nestled in his other hand. "And these were all in some sort of secret compartment in the box?"

"Yes, Your Grace," Clara replied.

"Do you have any idea who they are?" Charlie asked.

Once more, the duke carefully examined the items before looking up. "One cannot but be struck by the uncanny resemblance of both the women in the portraits to Clara, so I believe without a doubt that they are your family." He turned to Clara. "In fact, I would say this is your mother and grandmother. I cannot imagine it could be otherwise."

"That is what we thought," Charlie put in. "But do you have any ideas as to their identities?"

For the third time, the duke paused before replying, "I believe I have an idea, though I am not completely certain and, until I have investigated further, I shall keep my own counsel. It would do no good to bandy names about until we are quite sure."

"What about the document?" Clara asked, nodding towards Charlie. "We thought it was some sort of code."

"Indeed," the duke replied, reaching for his magnifying glass. "But even more interesting, I believe, is that there is something else written in some kind of invisible ink. See," he held the glass and moved the candle. There were distinct but faint markings.

"But this makes no sense," Clara exclaimed.

"On the contrary, my dear," the duke replied. "I believe this is all beginning to make a great deal of sense."

"I should like to know, Grandfather, how it is that you came to know about invisible ink and codes and so forth?" Charlie asked.

The duke smiled. "I was not always an old man, and I have served my country in a number of ways," he replied.

Charlie raised his eyebrows. "You were an agent?"

"I was a diplomat," was all the old man said, with a smile.

Charlie returned his attention to the items on the desk. "What shall we do now?" he asked. "These are all clues to Clara's origins, but until we can piece them together, we have reached an impasse."

"If I may?" the duke turned to Clara. "I think I know a man who can help us decipher the document, and someone who is an expert on the art of the miniature. He will be able to tell us the artist, and, if I am not mistaken, probably the date and even, I believe will be able to confirm the sitters."

Clara's eyes shone. "Oh, could you, sir? That would be wonderful."

The duke smiled. "I only hope that as your story unfolds, you are not disappointed."

She smiled back at this man who had become so dear to her. "I will never be able to thank you enough for all that you have already done for me. Finding my family, whoever or whatever they are, would answer so many questions I have had all my life." She looked at the two men who meant so much to her. "You both know where you came from, you have your history and know where and how you fit in to it. With any luck, I shall soon begin to know mine."

There was a discreet tap on the heavy oak door before Betts, the duke's butler stepped into the room. "Excuse me, Your Grace, Mr. Hampton, Miss Burns," he bowed. "But a young person left this at the door and was most insistent that it be delivered immediately to Miss Burns." He held out a silver salver on which rested a small package wrapped in brown paper and tied with string. Attached was a label clearly marked 'For the attention of Miss Clara Burns.'

Clara hesitated. "Open it Clara," Charlie prompted, "I do not think it will bite," he added, smiling.

With trembling fingers, she pulled the string and unfolded the paper, inside was a small leather box decorated with gold. She slid the small hook out of its eyelet and opened the box. Inside, on a bed of black velvet was a gold ring. She looked from one man to the other. "I think it is the seal ring," she whispered, running her finger over its raised surface.

"May I?" Charlie asked, holding out his hand. He took a piece of paper and held the duke's sealing wax over the candle before dripping it onto the paper and pressing the ring firmly into it.

There, on the paper, there was no mistaking the circle containing the interlinked letters CB, surrounding the circle were other, tiny circles. There was silence, as they all looked from the print Charlie had just made to the parchment. "It is the same," he said.

"Betts. Fetch the person who delivered it," the duke commanded.

The butler looked at the floor as though wishing a hole would appear in the turkish carpet. "I am afraid that the young man left it with the footman, Your Grace, who brought it to me, but the young man ran off as soon as he handed the package over."

"Damnation."

"I apologise, Your Grace."

The duke shook his head. "There is no blame, Betts. Neither you, nor the footman, indeed none of us could know what was in the package, or whether it could be of importance. In any case, the messenger was probably employed just to deliver the package and did not know what was in it either."

"Did the man give a message?" Charlie asked.

"I believe he said, 'Give this to the woman calling herself Miss Burns,'" the butler replied.

Charlie and his grandfather exchanged looks.

"There is something else, Your Grace. Jones, the footman, said the man spoke with an accent. A foreign accent," he added ominously.

"Thank you. That will be all, Betts."

Clara did something she had never done before and thought she never would. She fainted.

CHAPTER 40

"Oooh miss, you gave us all such a fright," Lily said as she brushed Clara's hair. "I thought Mr. Hampton was beside himself, Carried you up here himself he did, and the duke, I thought he was going to have a fit of apoplexy."

"Well, Lily, I am quite all right as you can see. It was just a stupid faint, that is all," Clara replied. She could not think of the arrival of the ring yet, she would think of it later when she had time to consider what it could possibly mean.

"Pale as a ghost, you was. Mr. Hampton laid you on the bed like you was made of bone china."

"Mr. Hampton is very kind," she replied, a slight blush tingeing her cheek at the thought of him anywhere near her bed. Lily twisted the last strand of pearls in place. "I think Mr. Hampton feels more than kindly towards you Miss, if I'm not speaking out of turn. I've seen the way he looks at you when he thinks no-one is looking and," she added with a little smile, "the way you look at him, miss. It's very romantic."

"I think that had better be all, Lily," Clara said, drawing on her evening gloves. "On both accounts, the hair and your fertile imagination."

"That's my tongue running away with me again. As my mum says, 'Not everything in your head Lily, needs to come out of your mouth.' Apologies, Miss Clara."

Clara laughed. "Wise words we should all do well to heed. Now Lily, what do you think? Shall I pass muster?"

The maid looked Clara over from head to toe, taking in the chestnut curls interlaced with pearls with one tress over her shoulder to hide the birthmark Clara was conscious of. Matching pearls were at her throat and ears, their translucent sheen reflecting the smoothness of her skin. The gown was new, yet another gift from the duke. The pale green silk was overlaid with a fine, almost transparent net embroidered with seed pearls which shimmered in the candlelight. The skirt fell in soft folds and made a slight rustling noise like the wings of a small bird as she moved, and on her feet were matching slippers of the finest kid leather. Small, embroidered lilies of the valley in pale and darker greens decorated the waist, hem, and edges of the puffed sleeves. The neckline was lower than Clara was used to, revealing the creamy tops of her breasts, but it was, after all, an evening event and she had seen other ladies in necklines that were much lower.

"You look like a princess, miss," Lily replied, handing Clara the matching fine woollen cloak. "You be sure to wrap up in this, miss, or you'll catch your death. It's enough to freeze a brass monkey's tail off tonight."

"I certainly will." Clara smiled. as she took the cloak.

She was still smiling when she entered the salon. The room, she felt, perfectly reflected its owner: rich yet understated. The pale blue silk damask on the walls contrasted with the heavy indigo velvet drapes drawn closed to keep out the winter chill. The silver candelabras scattered around the room were reflected in the mirrors, giving light and warmth. A cheerful blaze burned in the hearth and in front of it stood Charlie, looking into the flames, one arm resting on the white marble mantelpiece. From his other hand dangled a brandy glass.

Clara's mouth went dry. He was always a handsome man, but in his formal evening clothes, he was completely devastating. The midnight blue jacket fitted him to perfection, emphasizing his broad shoulders and tapering down to his waist. She had been close enough to know that underneath the soft expertly tailored cloth, his body was hard. He was not a soft gentleman, he worked himself hard, both physically and mentally, and it showed. His matching evening trousers hugged his long, lean legs. There was nothing soft about this man at all. As he turned, that wayward lock of dark hair flopped delightfully over his eyes. At times, the high cheek bones and sharply angled planes of his face could make him look severe, but when he smiled, he was truly devastatingly handsome.

———

As he turned, Charlie could not quite believe the vision that stood before him. Clara was quite exquisite. Had she been a lady, launched into society in the normal way, she would have been one of the incomparables, a diamond of the first water. There was no doubt in his mind that suitors would be queueing up to propose and not a single one would be worthy of her. Come to think of it, he was seriously considering ensuring that Harper and Silcock never came within a mile of her, though they were his greatest friends.

He walked towards her and took her hand, raising it to his lips. "You are beautiful, Clara," he murmured, wanting to slide the silky fabric from her and feel the touch of her skin against his lips. In fact, he wanted nothing more than to remove every last stitch of her clothing and glorify her very body. Despite his varied affairs and liaisons, nothing could compare even remotely close to the depth of his feelings for Clara. Although he kept fighting the word, he knew it was love, this desire not just to possess her physically, but to engage her mind, to pass hours simply in her company. To hear her ideas and opinions, to stand beside her and be there to pick her up if she ever needed it, however rarely that may occur, and to protect her.

Charlie faltered slightly. Their recent discoveries of the portraits and the documents suggested perhaps that Clara may need more protection than she realised. Someone had gone to a great deal of trouble to keep her carefully hidden for most of her life. That suggested that she needed protection from something, but what or whom he did not know. The arrival of the ring worried him even more. Someone knew not only who Clara was, but where she was. Until he knew more, he would not let her out of his sight. The wedding would take place as soon as possible, he had the license, all he needed was to get hold of a vicar, but before that, they would endure tonight's musicale. He pasted a smile on his face. "Let us face the music."

CHAPTER 41

*T*he musicale was a bigger event than Clara had been expecting. "I thought there would only be a dozen or so people here," she whispered to Charlie as they were announced.

"The earl has only fairly recently inherited. I believe he is a distant cousin who had no expectations of any kind," Charlie explained. "He had to make his own money, which he did handsomely in shipping, mining, and timber. Now he has been somewhat unexpectedly elevated, he is trying to cement his position as a patron of the arts."

"Goodness, had the old earl run out of sons?"

"War wasted the lives of two of them, the third in a hunting accident and the youngest was stupid enough to challenge a better shot to a duel. Still," he nodded to their host as they approached the receiving line, "silver linings for the cousin."

Once they had greeted their hosts, they passed through into the Durham ballroom where, although sixty or so chairs had been set out, most of the guests were milling about. A pianoforte stood on a raised dais at the end of the room and musicians were already tuning their instruments.

"My lords, ladies and gentlemen, if you would be so good as to take your seats," a footman dressed in the yellow livery of the Durham house boomed, "the musicians are ready to perform."

"It is customary for the ladies and older gentlemen to sit," Charlie explained. "We younger chaps generally stand at the back."

Clara arched a quizzical eyebrow. "So that you can more readily escape and access the earl's wine cellar?"

Charlie chuckled. "You would be surprised were it not the case. Are they not the Grainger girls beckoning to you? It would seem their disagreeable father has, for once, allowed them some fun. Partly I imagine because he does not have to pay for it."

Clara made her way over and took the seat next to Verity. "We are so pleased to see you again, Clara," Verity began. "And we must apologise for Lady Elizabeth's behaviour at tea. Interrogating you as though you were some kind of master criminal," Ella added.

"I rather think Lady Elizabeth has taken something of a dislike to you," Verity went on. "Possibly because you seem to have attracted the attention of Mr. Hampton. He is quite the catch of the season."

"And no doubt Lady Elizabeth intended he should be caught by her." Ella laughed. "But truly, Clara," she added, her face grave, "beware of Elizabeth Morgan, I have known her since we were babes in arms and she can be a spiteful cat."

"I will," Clara replied, knowing even better than Ella just how spiteful Lady Elizabeth could be.

Further chat was curtailed as the rest of the audience were now settled in their seats and the music began. Three young ladies sang to the accompaniment of the chamber orchestra. One of the young ladies was joined in a duet by a young lord who was clearly besotted by her, the other two played the pianoforte. Then it was Lady Elizabeth's turn, she sang in a rich soprano before sitting at the pianoforte. She was an excellent pianist, there was no denying it. Where the other young ladies had played competently, Lady Elizabeth's fingers flew over the keys, her eyes often closed as she was completely absorbed in the music. She almost started when the audience applauded her at the end of her performance.

"Lady Elizabeth is very talented," Clara whispered to Verity, as the young woman made her way towards them.

"Indeed," Verity agreed. "I do not think I have ever seen her so contented."

"Brava, Lady Elizabeth," Ella exclaimed.

"It was a wonderful performance," Verity added.

"I had no idea you were such an accomplished player," Clara put in.

The young woman smiled. "Thank you, ladies, but I find after a performance I am quite in need of refreshment and perhaps a little air. Would you care to accompany me?"

The Grainger girls looked uncomfortably apologetic and Ella demurred, "I am sorry, Lady Elizabeth, but our father insists we must stay within his sight, and now that the dowager Countess of Alton has brought him refreshments, I doubt he will quit his seat."

Lady Elizabeth smiled gleefully. "Then I must rely on you, Miss Burns, to accompany me," she said to Clara.

"Of course, Lady Elizabeth, it would be a pleasure," Clara replied, hoping that she did not sound insincere, and wondering where Charlie was lurking and if he was witnessing the interaction.

Lady Elizabeth seemed to know the layout of Durham House, and before long Clara found herself in what she assumed must be the long gallery. Generations of Durhams gazed down dispassionately at the two young women, many of whom bore more than a passing resemblance to the current earl, distant cousin or not.

"Did you want to step outside, my lady?" Clara asked.

"Indeed not, the air is far too cold. Besides," Lady Elizabeth stepped further into the room, her heels tapping on the wooden floor and echoing around the large space, "these rooms were designed for ladies to take some exercise in inclement weather, back in the old days. We have one at Morgan Abbey." She turned from the portrait she had been studying. "But of course you know that do you not…Blackburn?"

CHAPTER 42

Clara swallowed, her heart was beating so loudly she thought Lady Elizabeth could probably hear it. She opened her mouth to say something, but Lady Elizabeth stopped her with an autocratic wave of her hand, "Do not bother to lie, Blackburn. I knew there was something familiar about you from the very beginning, but I could not put my finger on it, until the other day, but then…"

"Then I stood behind you as I have done a thousand times before, and you realised where you had seen me," Clara finished for her, there was no point in denying it.

"Indeed, in your proper place," Lady Elizabeth replied, tilting her head to one side as she studied Clara from head to toe. "And do you know what conclusion I draw from this little charade, Blackburn?" she asked.

"I have no doubt that you intend to tell me," Clara replied.

"It is and always will be 'my lady' to you, Blackburn," Lady Elizabeth snapped. "It is that no matter how expensive the gown or jewels in which you are attired, you were never a lady and you will never be a lady. You are a servant. You were born to serve your betters, though when I have finished with you, I doubt you will be able to work even as a tavern wench on the dockside."

"I suppose I should not be surprised," Clara shot back. "You always were a malicious piece of work, *my lady*," she said with scorn.

The other woman's eyes flashed, her grip on her fan turned her knuckles white. "How dare you speak to me like that."

"Or what?" Clara continued, anger flooding though her veins. "You have already told me you intend to ruin my life, so what else do I have to fear? So for once in your vain, spoiled life you are going to listen to a few home truths even though they come from someone so far below you.

"You started out with so many advantages a person like me could not even dream of: wealth, position, beauty, and yet it was not enough. You had to make yourself feel even better by making everyone else seem inferior. You once had friends and suitors by the handful, but one by one you drove them away with your vicious tongue and temper because you had to have all the attention, all the compliments. You could have had all you desired, Lady Elizabeth, but all you could be was cruel and unkind. I may only be a maid, born to be a servant, but I can tell you this, every single maidservant I have ever met has been more worthy of the title lady than you will ever be."

Lady Elizabeth stepped forward, her face white and contorted with rage. "You are a nobody, a nothing and you will come to regret every word you have just uttered." She raised her hand, but Clara caught it before she could strike.

"I think not, my lady," she said coolly. "Now, I believe you need to return to the company and begin to destroy me." There was no point in appealing to a better nature, Clara knew there was none.

The other woman gave a sly smile as she stepped back and straightened her skirts, quickly regaining her composure before looking at Clara. "No, I do not think I shall reveal you today. That would deprive me of a great deal of entertainment. One has to build up to the denouement, a little hint here, a small suggestion there, so that gradually, as you enter a theatre, assembly, ballroom, or some such society event, you will begin to hear whispers. Ladies will talk about you behind their fans, and slowly they will begin to turn their backs on you, until you are faced with the cut direct wherever you turn. No-one will receive you, not in London, Bath, or Brighton, in fact I doubt that you would be received anywhere."

"The duke and Mr. Hampton…" Clara began.

Lady Elizabeth snapped her fingers. "Oh, do you think they will protect you? Deluded girl, the ton always looks after its own. Besides, the duke's power is over, he is an old man and of little consequence to society these days, nor is his idiotic sister. As for Mr. Hampton, he may be as rich as Croesus, but his influence is not as great as he thinks, especially when it is known that he allowed himself to be duped by a maid."

"He will be duke one day," Clara put in.

"But for now he is not, and by the time I have finished he will no doubt be hoping that by the time he inherits, this unfortunate scandal of trying to pass off a servant as a woman of quality will have been forgotten."

Neither of them heard the opening of the door, Clara turned at the sound of footsteps, hoping to see Charlie, horrified to find Sir Taylor Rufford approaching.

"Elizabeth, a thousand pardons, I missed your performance my dear when the wheel came off my damned carriage and it took an age to get it repaired." He turned to Clara and bowed slightly. "Miss Burns," he said, coldly.

Lady Elizabeth's laugh was shrill as it echoed round the room. "You really do not need to bow to her," she said.

"I do not follow," he replied, looking perplexed.

"Do you remember a little while ago my maid, Blackburn disappeared?"

He nodded.

"Well, she stands before you, not as Blackburn, my maid, but as Miss Burns, ward of the Duke of Wensley and friend of Mr. Charles Hampton."

"But Miss Burns is the duke's ward," Sir Rufford repeated.

"Oh, Taylor, do not be so obtuse," Lady Elizabeth snapped. "Somehow, Blackburn managed to inveigle herself into the duke's life and he for some reason is passing her off as his ward. Either because it amuses him or he has gone senile."

Sir Taylor Rufford raised his quizzing glass. "Well, well and this is she? Comely little chit, but the little bitch damn near killed me when she kicked me in the balls at the theatre." He reached out a hand and ran his fingers boldly across the top of her bodice.

"And if you persist, Sir Rufford, I will do the same again," Clara said, "twice as hard."

Sir Rufford laughed. "My, my, what spirit. I have a good mind to show you here and now what happens to girls who do not know how to treat their betters."

"Get your filthy hands off my fiancée," Charlie's voice seemed to bounce off the walls as he strode into the room. "Or you will begin to long for the day the only pain you feel is bruised balls." He turned to Clara. "Are you all right?"

She nodded, "I am but…"

"Did you say your fiancée Mr. Hampton?" Lady Elizabeth's eyes glittered with malice.

"And does she know about the…?" Sir Rufford began, finding his voice and realising he could now claim his winnings.

"Taylor," Lady Elizabeth interrupted, "I feel a headache coming on. Would you escort me home? This evening has been too much." She turned to Clara and said with acid sweetness, "Good night, my dear. I cannot tell you how much I am looking forward to our next meeting."

CHAPTER 43

$\mathcal{T}$he ride to Wensley House was undertaken in almost total silence until they approached the gates when Charlie spoke, "We shall have the wedding tomorrow, everything is moving very quickly, Clara. The duke's investigators are getting close to finding out who you really are and I am worried that someone will do anything to ensure that your true identity remains a secret, one way or another."

"But what of Elizabeth Morgan?" Clara asked nervously. "She knows everything and is intent on telling the whole of society about the fraud I am."

Charlie took her small hands in his large ones. "Elizabeth Morgan is a distraction, an unpleasant one I grant you, but a distraction, nonetheless. Besides, she only thinks she knows who you really are, within a very short time, her so-called revelation will mean nothing and she will be viewed as a laughingstock."

"Then why the sudden rush to marry?"

He raised her fingers to his lips. "It is not a sudden rush," he said quietly. "I wanted to marry you the minute you said yes. I have been carrying around a special license for what seems like months."

"Charlie," Clara smiled, "are you really sure? Because we really do not know what might happen."

"Clara, sweeting, no-one knows what the future holds, that is part of life's adventure. But whatever it is, good or bad, we will both be stronger if we face it together." To the point, he was confident that he would always be able to protect her, the miracle that had been given to him to keep safe and cherish and for which he would be eternally grateful.

Clara's heart leapt. Could it really be that Charlie Hampton truly wanted to marry her? He did not love her, he had never said the words, perhaps in time he might, though she doubted that he would ever feel for her as she did for him, but it would be enough. It was more than she could have dreamed of a few short weeks ago.

"Well then," she replied, "we had best not let that special licence go to waste."

Charlie gathered her into his arms, "I promise my darling, neither you nor I will ever have cause to regret this."

Much to Charlie's frustration of both body and spirit, the wedding could not take place until the following week.

"Clearly your expectations were hopelessly optimistic," Lady Bea chided him as he complained that he could not see Clara for the third time in a week. "Clara is having a fitting for her gown," the dowager explained semi-patiently. "There is the gown, the wedding breakfast, the vicar, and a thousand other things to be organised. These things usually take several months at the least."

"Several months! I could have been to America, conducted business and be back again," he retorted.

"I daresay," the older woman replied. "However, you have never planned a society wedding."

"It is not a society wedding, it is to be a small affair here with you, grandfather, Harper, and Silcock as we both desire," he said and struggled to maintain an even tone.

"A small affair indeed, but still you want your bride to enjoy her day I take it?"

"Of course." He could not decide whether his great aunt was deliberately trying to annoy him or whether his frustration meant that he was just permanently irritated.

"Then go into the library and do something useful and stop getting in the way," she told him firmly.

"Would that I could," he replied, "but the whole place is in the same chaos as at my house." He looked round as servants scurried about with armfuls of greenery and ribbons. Swags of ivy already decorated the staircase and two footmen were on ladders, hanging garlands of holly.

"Well what do you expect?" Lady Bea asked. "What with preparations for the Christmas Ball, Christmas itself to prepare for, and you suddenly spring a wedding on us?"

"You may have a point," Charlie conceded. In his desperate need to marry Clara, he had forgotten about virtually everything else.

"Then go and find your grandfather, he has been asking for you. You can both moan together." Although her words were harsh, there was a twinkle in his great aunt's eye.

The duke was ensconced in his study, examining the document in his hands as Charlie walked in.

"Escaping the wrath of Bea?" he asked with a smile.

Charlie returned the smile. "Something like that. Why is it that when there is a wedding in the offing, women begin to act like Attilla the Hun?"

"Possibly because they are denied the power to make decisions in other spheres," his grandfather suggested.

"Wise words," Charlie acknowledged. "Words I would do well to remember as a married man."

"I very much doubt that Clara will allow you to do otherwise given her singular life experiences. She has not been brought up to be a mild mannered, obedient wife as girls of the ton are taught to be from the cradle. She has spirit and intellect; I doubt that she will sit for hours happily embroidering your shirts."

"Nor would I wish her to."

His grandfather regarded him solemnly for a moment. "Good. You are fortunate that your marriage is beginning with love." He raised his hand as Charlie was about to speak. "I have seen the way your eyes soften when you look at her. It is how I used to look at your grandmother and the way your father always looked at your mother. I have also seen the way Clara looks at you when she thinks no-one is looking. However, that is not what I wanted to speak to you about," he indicated the document on his desk. "I believe we now know at least part of the truth of Clara's identity."

CHAPTER 44

*I*t had been decided to hold the ceremony at Charlie's house, for which Clara was grateful. During her time there, she had found friends among the staff. Though from today forwards, she would have a different role in their lives and they in hers.

Clara paused at the top of the grand staircase. Shortly, she would become Mrs. Charles Hampton. Behind the doors to the library, she knew, waiting for her as well as Charlie were the dowager, Charlie's friends Harper and Silcock, and the staff, whom she insisted should be there in lieu of her family.

"It's time," Lily whispered, holding out the posy of flowers. "You look lovely, Miss Clara. A real lady you are and no mistake."

Clara looked at her maid, her eyes suddenly moist. It had taken an age before Lily had been satisfied with her appearance. From the curls pinned, not with diamonds and pearls as a bride of the ton might demand, but with small white stephanotis from the duke's hothouse. The dress was made of the finest white silk trimmed with Nottingham lace at the neck and sleeves and delicately embossed with flowers at the waist and hem. Around her neck she wore her gold locket.

At the door, Lily made the final adjustments as the duke appeared beside her. "You look exquisite, my dear," he said quietly as he tucked her hand through his arm. "My grandson is the most fortunate man in the world to have you as his wife."

"I hope so," she whispered.

"And I am fortunate to have you as my granddaughter-in-law. Now," he motioned for the footman to open the door. "Let us proceed with this wedding."

The library had been decked with holly, ivy and rosemary, with wreaths of greenery and fruits decorating the many candelabras around the room. It looked magical to Clara. A table had been covered with a snowy white cloth and candles to act as an altar and at it stood Charlie, a wide smile on his face as she walked towards him.

His eyes took in the dress which made her look ethereal. He was in truth, marrying an angel, to be his to love, cherish and protect until death. He smiled as she walked towards him, thanking God or the fates for the day she had fallen into his life. His reconciliation with his grandfather was, at least in part, thanks to her. He turned to the vicar as he began reciting, "Dearly beloved…"

The ceremony was over quickly and soon they were seated in the grand dining room. Clara knew that Charlie had arranged for the servants to have their own celebration later and was touched by his thoughtfulness. A few short weeks ago, she expected to have been there, celebrating his wedding to Lady Elizabeth. He leaned forward "I hope you are not disappointed that you did not have the grand society wedding."

"Not at all," she replied quietly. "I know nobody and no-one knows me, so I rather fancy my side of the church would have been somewhat empty."

"Believe me, now that you are married, the invitations and new friends will come thick and fast."

"Until they find I was once a maid," she said wryly.

"Anyone who is so small minded is not your friend," he replied firmly.

"Forgive me, I could not help but overhear," the duke put it. "Remember, that one day you will be a duchess, indeed, should Charlie wish it, there is already a title he may use as my heir, that will surely set the cat among the pigeons." He laughed.

Clara touched his hand, knowing that Charlie had no intention of taking any title before he had to. "Hopefully that will not be for many years to come."

"I certainly do not intend it to be," the old man smiled. "Not until there are a few great- grandchildren to gather at my feet and hear the tale of how their mother conquered society."

"Speaking of which," Charlie glanced at the company, "I believe it is time to bid our guests adieu."

Harper and Silcock were the last to leave, having partaken liberally of Charlie's port, among other things.

"Felicitations, Hampton. You managed to find yourself a beauty."

"A diamond of the first water. Even without our help," Silcock added.

"Rufford will be in the boughs." Harper laughed. "Make sure you make him pay." Silcock joined in the laughter as they stumbled towards their carriage. Harper turned, "A gentleman always settles his gambling debts before his creditors," he called out.

"Get him home, Silcock," Charlie responded tersely, "before he does any damage to himself, or anyone else."

"Certainly." Silcock bundled his friend into the carriage and it drew away.

"What on earth was all that about?" Clara asked as they walked back into the house.

Charlie hesitated a moment before replying, knowing now was the time to confess about the wager, while he could explain his stupidity himself, but he was afraid to ruin the moment. He did not want Clara's memories of her wedding clouded by his revelation. "Nothing, Harper's mouth flaps too much when he's taken a drink. He barely knows what he is saying when he is sober, let alone when he is in his cups. Now my love," he leered outrageously, "I believe the duke, Great Aunt Bea, and all the servants have made themselves scarce so that we may attend to the business at hand."

"Which is?" Clara could not keep from smiling.

"Why, the important work of consummating our marriage and producing an heir or at least practising until we succeed," he said, taking her hand and leading her towards the staircase she had nervously walked down only a few short hours before.

Charlie insisted on carrying her, giggling, over the threshold of his room before kicking the door closed.

"I gave your maid time off," he whispered into her ear, causing shivers to travel down her spine, "so that I could undress you myself." He gently nipped her ear lobe, sensually curling around the pearls, as he slowly released the buttons. She trembled as she remained still, allowing him to caress each inch of flesh as he revealed it, kissing his way down her body until her gown rippled to the floor. Her petticoat followed and soon she stood in her stays, silk chemise, and stockings.

He began to toy with the ribbons when she stepped back, enjoying the surprise in his eyes.

"One moment," she held up her hand. "Turnabout is fair play."

"I don't understand…"

"Well, I am almost naked and you are fully clothed, it hardly seems fair."

Charlie grinned broadly and held out his arms. "By all means, Mrs. Hampton."

With a glint in her eye, Clara slowly unwound his neckcloth and pulled off his jacket and waistcoat. As he had done, she tantalised him by kissing each spot as she unbuttoned his shirt and gently slid it from his shoulders. Her breath caught in her throat as she took in his broad shoulders and sculpted torso with a dusting of hair across his chest which narrowed as it drew her eyes down to the waistband where it disappeared from her gaze.

"My turn," he murmured as he turned her around so that she could see them in the cheval mirror. Within seconds, her stays and chemise joined her gown on the floor. he stood for a moment drinking in the sight, now that she was naked in front of him he could appreciate her entire body, the curve of her breasts, the narrow waist and her shapely legs as well as the intriguing tangle of curls between her thighs. "Exquisite," he whispered as he scooped her up and gently laid her on the bed.

He was determined to take his time with her, though he very much feared it might kill him. It was the least she deserved, although he already knew that she was a sensual woman. As his fingers trailed over the taut tips of her breasts, she drew in a sharp intake of breath. "You like that, I think," he smiled, lowering his head, "then you are going to love this." He lavished attention on her breasts, laving, stroking and gently nipping them with his tongue and teeth as his hands drifted lower finally finding the damp curls at the apex of her thighs.

Her breath came in gasps and moans, unable to form words, even his name. Every sound she made hardened him further, he had never experienced anything like this before, it was torture, but the most exquisite torture he would not mind experiencing until his last breath, which if he didn't have her very soon would be sooner than he anticipated.

He strained for control. "My God, Clara, what you do to me," he murmured, as his questing fingers found their goal, loving the small cries she made as he explored her, stroking and teasing further than he had ever dared to before, pushing a finger slowly into her damp entrance, delighted that she was ready for him, feeling her squeeze and melt around him. He could have spent the rest of his life doing this, knowing how much pleasure he was giving, hearing her whimper and strain with need and desire, her head moving from side to side as she writhed beneath him, knowing that she was searching for something only he could give her, finding, inexplicably, that giving pleasure to her was immensely pleasurable to him, a thought that had never occurred to him before with other women, but then other women were not Clara.

She whimpered when he removed his hand and trailed a string of kisses down from her breasts to her abdomen. Her eyes flew open when she felt his breath at her entrance. "Charlie…" but her voice stilled and her hips came off the bed as his tongue plunged inside again and again until she was almost crying with need. The memory of being able taste her from her source had driven him mad for more since he'd last pleasured her this way. Her flesh was delectable.

When he could stand it no more, he raised himself on his elbows, his cock gently probing her entrance. "I can wait no longer, dearest, sweetest Clara, I have to have you, to claim you and finally make you mine," he whispered.

"Yes, yes, yours, oh God yes, now!" Clara moaned, as he plunged into her. Despite both of their bodies urging him onward, he waited a moment, knowing that there would be a moment of pain, allowing her to adjust to the size and feel of him within her.

"Are you all right?" he asked, looking into her startled eyes. She nodded. "Don't stop now," she whispered back. "Please don't stop now. I need you."

It was all the encouragement he needed. He drove into her with a wild passion, deeper each time, pushing into her until their bodies merged again and again, driven on by her ecstatic cries he drove into her harder and harder as she moved instinctively with him, almost sending him over the edge of reason. When she tensed and held on tightly to him, gasping with amazement, he knew she had reached her climax and drove into her once last time as lights exploded behind his eyes. It had never, never happened like that before.

"Oh, Charlie," was all she could say as he drew her onto him so that her head rested on his chest, her glorious hair in a silken tangle across his bare skin. "I never imagined anything like that." She added, "It was exquisite."

"It is not always like that," he murmured thoughtfully. He never could have imagined that love and passion could have this kind of effect. It had been as Clara said, exquisite and he knew that before the morning came, he would have her again and again.

CHAPTER 45

*I*t took Clara a moment to remember where she was, but the sight of the naked man beside her quickly brought the memories of their wedding night flooding back. Charlie had proven himself to be a generous and thorough lover, ensuring her pleasure before taking his. Several times throughout the night he had reached for her and begun again, sometimes quickly and sometimes so agonisingly slowly that she almost cried out with frustration. It seemed he could not get enough of her body, nor she his.

Gently, trying to disengage from his grasp so as not to disturb him, Clara found herself again being gathered against his hard body.

"And where do you think you are going, Mrs. Hampton?" he leered.

"We must get up, Charlie," she replied. "What will people think?"

"We are a newly married couple, I imagine they know exactly what we were doing last night and what I fully intend to do again, right now," he said, pulling her closer and kissing her soundly.

It was at least an hour later by the time they had both bathed and dressed that they made an appearance for breakfast.

"I find I am quite famished," Clara declared, helping herself to a coddled egg and toast.

"Given your exertions last night, I am far from surprised," Charlie replied, piling his plate and coming to sit next to her. "Fulfilling the duties of a married woman is quite exhausting," he added, provocatively.

"And of course, as your husband, is it my honor to encourage you and teach you your wifely arts."

"There is just one thing I would like to say about that…" She leaned forward and breathed into his ear, "It was not a duty, Mr. Hampton, it was a pleasure. And it will be even more so, I believe, when I can teach you about your husbandly ways."

Charlie was instantly hard. "Witch," he whispered back "If you continue to provoke me, I shall be forced to take you upstairs, or even clear the table and take you here."

Clara's reply was lost in a commotion in the hallway.

"I tell you he will see me. Mr. Hampton owes me money and I have come to collect."

Charlie and Clara exchanged a glance, both of them recognised the voice immediately. The door was flung open and Pearson entered looking flustered, followed by Sir Taylor Rufford, who quickly elbowed him out of the way.

"I apologise, Mr. Hampton," Pearson began. "Sir Rufford barged in before anyone could stop him."

Charlie rose. "Do not apologise, Pearson. You are not responsible for this so-called gentleman's lack of manners," his voice dripped sarcasm.

"Come, come, Hampton," Rufford said, taking his seat without waiting for an invitation. "I believe congratulations are in order, Hampton. Harper and Silcock were carousing at White's on your behalf long into the night. Now that you are a married man, I must assume that you have conceded that I won our little wager. I have merely come to collect my winnings. A wager is a wager and as I pointed out to you before, a gentleman always settles his gambling debts."

"What gambling debts? Clara asked.

Rufford turned to her, raising his quizzing glass. "My dear, did you not know?" he asked with a sneering smile. "Let me explain," he sat back in the chair. "Some little time ago, Hampton here made a wager…"

"Rufford, this is neither the time nor the place," Charlie growled.

"The terms of the wager were that Hampton should persuade a lady to marry him."

"Which I did," Charlie put in. "Now get out."

"A lady of quality," Rufford continued, crossing one leg over the other. "As forfeit, should he not succeed he was to pay me £1,000," he paused and looked down his long nose at Clara, "and as we now know, you are not a lady at all."

Clara gasped. "Charlie, that is a huge amount of money. How could you be so idiotic?"

Taylor Rufford burst out laughing, but with little humour. "I agree, my dear," he said, "but there we are. Gentlemen are wont to make foolish bets and now I have come to collect." He turned to Charlie. "A banker's draft will suffice."

"You will have it this afternoon," Charlie spoke through gritted teeth. "Now get out."

"With pleasure." Rufford picked up his hat and strolled to the door. "Oh, by the by, Mrs. Hampton," he turned, his hand on the handle. "I nearly forgot, the other forfeit. Had I lost the wager I should be in debt to your husband by £1,000 and he would now own my racehorse, Rufford III."

"I do not understand what this has to do with me, Sir Rufford. This all happened before I even met Mr. Hampton."

"Of course you do not, but there were two forfeits, do you see? I stood to lose my racehorse if I lost," he paused.

"And?" Clara prompted.

He smiled, reminding Clara of a picture of a snake she had seen in a book. "I am so pleased you wish to know. Should Hampton have failed to persuade a young lady of the ton to marry him. He had to marry her maid." He placed his hat on his head. "Good day," he added and left.

There was a moment of silence before Charlie spoke. "Clara, let me explain…"

Clara held up her hand. "No, Mr. Hampton, I do not think you can."

"It is not as he said!"

"It sounded true enough to me. Is any of what he said untrue? You made a wager and you lost, and I am the price you paid for losing."

"Believe me, Clara, it is nothing like that." He started towards her.

She stepped back eyes wary. "Believe you? How can I believe you? How can I believe anything you say, ever again?"

"Surely, last night…"

"Last night was just pleasure, Charlie, was it not? With your… God I am not even a consolation prize. With your losings."

He strode towards her. "Do not say that. Clara, do not make what we shared sound tawdry and dirty. It was not just sex. I have never felt for any woman what I feel for you."

"Don't touch me, Charlie." She stepped further back. "I have to think about this."

"Clara, you are my wife," he said, desperately. Only yesterday they had made the vows, only last night they had consummated them.

"Only because you lost," she said quietly. "I wonder if that is all I will ever be, the woman you had to marry because you lost a bet."

"Of course not, please, listen to me."

She held up her hand. "No Charlie, not now. I will not be your plaything, your doll that you pick up and put down when you have tired of the game."

He reared back. "Is that what you think of me?"

She shook her head, sadly. "It wasn't. I thought you were different from the arrogant, self-centred lords I'd seen, because you have lived in the real world, like me. But money has given you that same arrogance to play with the lives of others. And through fault only my own, I allowed myself to be deceived and my future stolen from me."

"Please Clara…" he began. But she had gone, closing the door behind her, not with the slam he might have expected, but with a quiet click. The silence she left behind was deafening.

CHAPTER 46

"For a newlywed husband, you do not seem particularly happy," the duke said as he raised his coffee cup and took a sip, surprised that Charlie had joined him for breakfast a few days later.

His grandson regarded him from over the rim of his own cup. He had been married for less than twenty-four hours before the illusion had shattered like a fragile glass into a thousand pieces. He replaced his cup carefully on its saucer. "Clara found out about the wager," he replied.

"And not from you, I take it?"

"No," Charlie sighed. "Harper and Silcock went to White's after the wedding and when Taylor Rufford heard them, I had a visit from him come morning."

"But he knows nothing of Clara's background surely. As far as he and the rest of the world are concerned, she is my ward."

Charlie ran a hand through his hair. "Unfortunately not. Lady Elizabeth recognised Clara and Rufford now knows. Those two are as thick as thieves. When Rufford heard Clara and I were wed, he came to claim he had won the wager. In his eyes I had admitted to losing it by marrying the Morgan girl's maid."

"And Clara? Does she know of Rufford's claim?"

Charlie smiled ruefully. "Oh, he took great pleasure in telling her all about it."

"I take it Clara was not pleased."

At this Charlie let out a bark of laughter. "I think it is fair to say that Clara is furious. In fact," he added quietly, "I have barely seen her since the wedding."

"What do you mean?"

"It is like living with a ghost. Every time I enter a room I know she has been in I can sense her in the air, but she always manages to avoid my presence. If I am coming in, she is just going out, if I am going out, she is just coming in. She has barely spoken a dozen words to me since Rufford's visit."

The duke steepled his fingers. "And yet, this Rufford and the Morgan girl have not made their information public," he mused.

"Clara thinks they are waiting until we are at a large event, to cause as much embarrassment as possible, and if Rufford's malice is anything to go by, I would not be at all surprised."

The duke sat forward. "Surely not at the Christmas Ball? They would not dare."

Charlie sighed. "I rather think they would relish the opportunity to embarrass us at our own event. Lady Elizabeth despises both me for rejecting her and Clara for rising from her position as maid, Rufford cannot forgive the fact that I, a self- made man with no connections or assistance, have achieved greater wealth and position than he feels he is entitled to."

"Should we cancel it?" the duke asked.

Charlie considered the idea, then shook his head. "No. I would not give them the satisfaction and if they are going to spread the gossip and scandal anyway, we might as well get it over with. After the ball, people will retire to their estates for the festive season as usual, and when they return, perhaps the scandal will have died down, at least to a manageable level."

"For you and me, perhaps, if we are touched by it at all. Society is inclined to ignore the transgressions of a duke, and you have more than enough money to care what people think of you. It is Clara who will bear the brunt of this, particularly from the women. They will cut her to shreds. She has committed the ultimate sin of marrying not only out of her class, but by stealing away one of the most eligible bachelors of the Season."

Charlie paused for a moment, looking at his hands before he spoke. "She is strong. I just want my wife back."

The duke smiled for the first time since Charlie arrived. "You do I think, in fact, love Clara."

Charlie's head shot up. "Of course I do, she completes me. Without her I am only half the man I want to be."

"And you have told her this?"

Charlie shifted uncomfortably in his seat. "Not perhaps in so many words. But how could she not know how I feel?" It seemed inconceivable that she had not understood through the passion during their wedding night, the contentment afterward, their activities through the night had shown her how he felt more clearly than he could possibly express.

The duke chuckled. "Oh, to be young. Take it from me, my boy, a woman needs to hear the words, many times. You must go home and court Clara, but most important of all, you must say the words. She needs to hear them."

"I doubt Clara wants to hear anything I have to say," Charlie replied ruefully.

"Then you must make her listen," the old man replied firmly. "You are not a callow schoolboy, you are a man of the world, a successful man. If you cannot think of a way of doing it, you are not the man I thought you were. And if you love her as you say you do, you must fight for her."

For the first time since he arrived, Charlie looked calm. "You are right, of course. Of all the things in my life, Clara is the most important. If I do not fight for her, then I am not the man I thought I was either." He rose. "Thank you, Grandfather," he said softly, "I am glad that you are in my life."

Charlie left, unaware of the tears of joy in the old man's eyes.

Clara sat at the escritoire in the morning room, several crumpled pieces of paper lay on the desk as she attempted to find the right words to tell Charlie of her decision to release him from their marriage with as little scandal as possible, there would be no divorce, she knew that could not happen, but perhaps there could be an annulment. She blushed at the thought. Neither could claim that the marriage had not been well and truly consummated, but perhaps there were other grounds she could pursue. The duke had, after all, promised her a house and an income in the heady days when passing her off as a lady had seemed a jest. When she had nothing to lose, before she married Charlie, before she had fallen in love with him.

Perhaps she would even have to go abroad to make a completely fresh start. She could not help the tears that slowly traced their way down her cheek. To be separated from the duke and Lady Bea, the Grainger girls and Lily, the people who had almost become the family she had never had, was devastating. Leaving Charlie was almost too much to bear but bear it she would. If loving him meant walking away so that one day he could take up his rightful position as duke, without a scandal lingering over him, then that is what she would do.

So lost in her own thoughts was she that she did not hear the quiet click as the door opened as Charlie walked into the room.

CHAPTER 47

"Please," Charlie held up his hand. "I know I do not deserve your forgiveness, but please let me at least try to explain."

Clara nodded. After days of avoiding him, she wanted to feast her eyes on him one last time before she bowed out of his life. She moved to sit on the pale green sofa in front of the fire. Charlie stood looking into the flames before turning to face her. "There is no excuse," he said quietly. "I had been with Silcock and Harper, our talk somehow got onto the topic of marriage and they offered to help me find a wife. God help me." He glanced at Clara, but her expression remained neutral. "Anyway, at some point Rufford overheard enough to butt in. It was he who added the forfeit. The three of us thought he was jesting, but, as we now know, Rufford never jests."

"So that is why he and Lady Elizabeth were trying to trap you into marriage?" Clara mused.

"Indeed, and when it became obvious that was not going to happen, ever, I had a visit from both of them. At that point I thought I had scuppered the ridiculous notion of the so-called forfeit. In fact, I told him so, but Taylor Rufford is like the plague. He will twist and turn my words until he has done enough damage to your reputation. I underestimated how determined he was to try to wreak revenge on me. I am sorry that you were caught up in this."

"But, because he knows I was Lady Elizabeth's maid, he claims to have won the wager."

"Exactly. I did not marry the lady, but I did marry her maid. What he really needs is the money one way or another. Thinking he can humiliate me in front of the ton is just the icing on the cake." Charlie cleared his throat before adding, "For what it is worth, I never actually agreed to this wager and was pushed into continuing the farce by my peers. Nevertheless, I consider that I actually won the greatest prize a man could hope for: A wife who is not only beautiful, but intelligent, wise, and kind, and if she will but give me a chance to redeem myself, I will spend the rest of my life trying to prove myself worthy of her." He cleared his throat anxiously. "What I am trying to say is that I love you Clara, only you. Body and soul. Without you, my life would only be half a life. If you cannot bring yourself to love me, then so be it. I just ask you to give me time enough to show that I am worth a second chance."

Clara raised her head, her eyes bright with unshed tears. "Oh, Charlie," she said, "I was angry, furious in fact that you thought of me as a thing to be won or lost. But once I had calmed down and thought about it, I realised there is just one thing to do."

The hairs on the back of his neck rose. "And that is what?"

She gestured to the escritoire. "I have been trying to write a letter but it is better to tell you face to face."

"Tell me what?" he could barely squeeze the words from his throat.

Clara took a breath and twisted her hands in her lap. "This is never going to work, is it, Charlie? I was a naive fool to ever think so. You will be a duke one day, a man to whom people will look up to and respect. But with me as your wife, the scandal will never go away. There will always be gossip and it will detract from the important work you want to do in improving the lives of others. So I have decided to go away, to disappear. The duke offered me a house and an income when we started this charade. I plan to go and live quietly in the country somewhere where people have never heard of us, and if that is not sufficient I will go and live abroad, in Europe or even America. As a peer of the realm, you will be able to claim my death or abandonment of our vows and obtain a divorce and continue with your rightful life," her voice cracked.

Charlie knelt at her feet. "No, Clara, you cannot make this sacrifice. I refuse to allow you to destroy us, to destroy me. What would I do without you? I love you, Clara, with every ounce of my being and I refuse to live without you. Society be damned, we shall prove to them that their rules are ridiculous. This notion of superior breeding is nonsense, we know it and they know it. It is nothing but a way to gain and keep wealth and power to themselves, and if breeding has anything to answer for, it produced the likes of Rufford and the Morgan girl. Hardly the greatest recommendation."

Clara's eyes met his. "You do truly love me?"

"I love you," he replied. "I will say it and keep on saying it until you believe me. I love you so much." He raised her hand to his lips, his eyes never leaving hers. "If you believe nothing else of me, please believe that."

Clara flung her arms around him. "Oh Charlie, I do so love you, I have loved you almost since the moment I met you, but I never dared hope that you could or would ever love me. When you suggested marriage as a convenience, I hoped that one day you would come to care for me. Even though you were clear on your opinion of love from the start."

He gathered her gently into his arms. "Oh, my darling, I said some truly foolish things. The only example I had of love was my parents and step-mother and the trail of destruction it wrought. I tried to close my heart, but I could not close it against you."

"But are we strong enough for the scandal that is about to break on our heads?" she asked, her green eyes dark and troubled.

"It will be difficult, I shall not deny it, but we will face whatever comes together, for the rest of our lives." He stood and held out his hand to her. "Come," he said, "I have for too long neglected my husbandly duties of showing my wife how much I desire her, body and soul."

Clara gave a seductive smile as she took his hand. "Your wife is looking forward to it," she said boldly. "Though it is possible that your wife shares your desires, you may need to convince her."

In the bedroom, Charlie locked the door, before taking her in his arms and taking her lips in a searing kiss. Her gown, stays, and chemise were swiftly dealt with, buttons flew as he quickly divested himself of boots, shirt, and trousers, doing his best to attend to her with light kisses as he did so. When they were both naked, breathing raggedly, chests heaving, eyes wild with desire, he stood behind her in front of the cheval mirror, cupping her thigh with one hand and stroking the undersides of her breasts with the other, ensuring that she could feel press of his thick desire against her body.

"This is us," he whispered into the silence broken only by the ticking of the clock, "nothing between us, skin to skin, no secrets, nothing to hide, ever again." He brushed the hair from her neck and kissed her while his hands reached round and cupped her breasts, his thumbs grazing their sensitive buds. Clara's breath caught and she could not help but gaze in the mirror watching as one hand drifted lower and stroked her most intimate place.

"You can feel how much I want you," he murmured as he began to rub his body against hers, "and I can feel how much you want me." His voice dropped to a whisper as he slipped a finger inside her.

Clara was mesmerised by the sight of him pleasuring her from behind, looking into his eyes as he watched her, but it was not enough. "I want you Charlie, inside me. Now," she commanded breathily.

"Grasp onto the sides of the mirror," he said, positioning himself before entering her. "Look as us, Clara," he murmured as he drove into her again and again, filling her completely. Neither of them could look away, nor did they want to. Watching their movements, seeing how they affected each other, drove them both to higher joys. His questing fingers continuing to stroke and pleasure until her limbs began to shake and she screamed his name.

Whether he carried her to the bed, she could not say, but once again the room soon filled with cries of passion, whispers of desire, and sighs of pleasure.

CHAPTER 48

*C*harlie awoke as the weak rays of the winter sun filtered through the drapes. He did not move, not wanting to awaken Clara who slept on, nestled in the crook of his arm, her chestnut hair spread across his chest, her breasts, still pinked from his attentions, smoothed against his arm. In repose, she looked like a sleeping angel, her eyelashes fanned her cheeks, hiding those magnificent emerald eyes. Emeralds would be perfect for the Christmas Ball, Charlie thought. His thoughts drifted to how she would look in emeralds and naught else, but he pulled his mind away before he was driven to wake her. The ball, though, would be less than purely pleasant. God alone knew when those two vicious vipers, the Morgan girl and her odious cousin, would strike. But he would protect Clara from it if it was the last thing he did.

"My goodness," a sleepy voice interrupted his thoughts. "What dark thoughts are going through your head to elicit such a fierce expression?"

"I was thinking of Rufford and Elizabeth Morgan," he replied.

Clara propped herself up on an elbow. "Why would you want to spoil a lovely day thinking of them? Have you nothing more...enjoyable to entertain your mind?" she asked coquettishly.

"Oh, vixen," he groaned. "That I could. But despite how much I would prefer to engage in making love to you, the Christmas Ball is fast approaching and, much as I hate to admit it, they are from old families, and regardless of the fact that their coffers are much depleted, they do have some influence among the ton."

Clara raised an eyebrow. "But surely the duke has more."

Charlie shook his head slightly. "A generation ago yes, but he withdrew from society when my mother disappeared in scandalous circumstances. In reality, I believe, even though he is a duke, his influence is not what it was." He traced a finger down her cheek, unable to stop it from continuing its path down her neck until she gripped his hand within her own. "Do you want to cancel the ball?"

Clara thought for a moment. "No," she said, resolutely, "I will not run away. It is the same reason I would not want to rescind their invitations. We must face Lady Elizabeth and Sir Rufford at some time. Let us do it now and lance the boil of their venom."

"Are you sure?"

"Of course. If they want a fight, then a fight they shall have."

He could not help but chuckle. "I am beginning to wonder what sort of woman it is exactly that I married."

"One that grew up in an orphanage. Lady Elizabeth might have had the advantage of a ladies' boarding school, but I believe the orphanage prepared me better for the metaphorical bare-knuckle fighting she has unleashed."

At this, Charlie threw back his head and laughed. "Remind me never to cross you again."

Her eyes danced. "Very wise," she replied. "But I am at a loss to understand why they want to bring you down. What could you have possibly done that makes them so determined to punish you?"

"Lady Elizabeth was prepared, for the sake of my wealth, to hold her nose and marry me, as you know. I became more attractive when she learned about my grandfather. However, she is the last woman on this earth I could ever consider marrying, and when I more or less said so, her pride was wounded."

"An understatement I imagine," Clara replied. "She once sacked a maid because she brought her morning chocolate in the wrong cup. She is used to getting her own way and does not care to be thwarted as I know from first hand."

Charlie nodded. "They are both on the brink of financial ruin, the only difference being that Rufford knows it. They both need to marry money, and desperately. Lord Morgan's situation is not yet widely known, and I am still willing to apply some pressure to Elizabeth's father so that he might control his daughter."

Clara shook her head. "I think Lord Morgan relinquished control over Lady Elizabeth years ago."

"In any case, Rufford's creditors are starting to become impatient."

"So that is why the wager was so important to him."

"And why he tried to rig it."

"But his dislike of you seems to go much deeper than the wager," Clara mused.

Charlie shrugged. "Rufford has been brought up to believe that there is a natural order of society. That those born at the top are vastly superior to those at the bottom. In short, he believes he is naturally superior to those below him."

"Including you?"

"Including me, and furthermore, the fact that I have worked and made myself wealthier than him fills him with fury. In his view, I am and always will be an upstart who should be put in his place and kept there, under his boot. I believe he fears that self-made men like me are in the vanguard of the sort of revolution that saw heads roll in France not too many years ago."

"Did you send him the banker's draft to pay the wager?" Clara asked, suddenly.

Charlie shook his head. "When I thought I had lost you, all else lost importance. I did not think of it until this moment."

"Then do not send it."

Charlie's head shot up "What do you mean?"

"I understand that a gentleman always pays his gambling debts, but if that horrible man thinks he is going to take your money and then enjoy himself by trying to turn society against you, because you married beneath you. Then he can whistle for it," she finished, her cheeks pink with indignation.

Charlie looked at her with admiration. "That is the spirit. I had only thought to pay the bounder in order to spare you embarrassment. It seems that I was wrong to think you needed that kind of protection. In fact, my little spitfire," he said, pulling his hand from hers to pull her against him, "I rather think Taylor Rufford is going to need protection from you."

"The two of them are bullies and it is high time someone took them on," Clara replied firmly.

The conversation was terminated by a discreet knock on the door.

"I am sorry to bother you, sir, but His Grace has arrived and needs to speak you," Pearson's voice hesitated, "both of you on a matter of some urgency,"

Within minutes they entered the green salon to see the duke pacing up and down the Aubusson carpet.

"What is it that has you wearing a hole in my floor?" Charlie asked with a smile.

"This," the duke held out a piece of paper. "It arrived not half an hour ago," he paused. "It is a letter from Mrs. Gowman."

CHAPTER 49

Clara sat down, her legs unable to support her. "What does it say?" she croaked. The duke passed the letter into her shaking fingers. She instantly recognised Mrs. Gowman's flowing hand.

To the Duke of Wensley,

Sir,

It is with some relief that very shortly I shall be able to reveal the true identity of Miss Clara Blackburn who has been recently masquerading as your ward, Miss Burns. Her story is, as I am sure you have surmised, complex, and not without a degree of tragedy.

It goes without saying that Miss Blackburn's true identity would, until now have placed her in some degree of danger. To that end, I must ask that no word of this letter be made public until I return. I shall arrive in London on the twelfth of December and proceed to your home, where all will be revealed.

May I thank you and Mr. Charles Hampton for protecting Miss Blackburn in the interim.

Yours sincerely,
    Mrs. H. Gowman

"Well, what do you make of it?" the duke asked.

"It is Mrs. Gowman's hand," Clara replied. "I would recognise it anywhere. And danger?" she added. "Why would I have been in danger? I was a lady's maid, what threat could I possibly be to anyone?"

"I think," Charlie took her hands in his, "it is now more than likely that until recently at least, your existence proved to be a threat to a person or persons with some degree of power. But who that is and why, we must wait for this Mrs. Gowman to enlighten us."

"The twelfth?" the duke cut in. "That is the day of the ball. I shall cancel it immediately."

"No," Clara replied. "The ball should go ahead. We must try to keep a semblance of normalcy. The servants have already worked hard with the preparations, it would be a shame if all that hard work was for naught. In any case," she added. "I believe it will be quite a night for surprises all round."

"How so?" the duke asked.

"Rufford and the Morgan chit are threatening to expose Clara as a fraud," Charlie explained.

The duke looked at Charlie. "Can you not stop them? What of your leverage with Morgan, or Rufford's creditors?"

Clara glanced at Charlie before replying. "They are going to have their moment and I would rather it was when we are there to hear them, than hear it third-hand from behind someone's fan. Let them spit their venom and be damned," she paused before adding, "my apologies for my bad language, duke."

"Not at all, my dear." He smiled. "It is nothing I had not heard on the playing fields of Eton. I quite agree, let them speak and be damned."

Clara kept herself busy in the remaining days before the ball by throwing herself into the preparations. Every day she arrived at Wensley House and along with Lady Bea and Lily, made garlands of greenery for the grand staircase and a multitude of wreaths of apples, oranges, candles and spices for all the public rooms, as well as for the private apartments.

"This is the smell of Christmas most definitely," Lady Bea announced, breathing in deeply as she deftly twisted an ivory ribbon into position. "I was always thrilled to help with the decorations and when we were children, we were allowed to sit at the top of the staircase with nanny and watch the guests arrive in their finery for the ball. Later, Mama would arrange for a plate of sweetmeats to be brought up to the nursery. It was always so exciting."

"This one promises to be more exciting than most," Clara commented drily.

Lady Bea put down her scissors and faced Clara. "Now we shall have none of that, Clara, if you are, as I imagine, thinking of that dreadful Morgan girl and her cousin. You are part of the Wensley clan now. We stick together and protect each other. Furthermore," she added. "I believe you will find I am more than a match for the Morgan girl, her parents, and that odious cousin of hers. Believe you me, by the time I have finished with him, he will be Taylor Well and Truly Ruffled." She picked up her scissors and snipped off a straying twig.

There was a bark of laughter from the doorway, where Charlie leaned against the frame. "I believe, Aunt Bea, that Rufford will be begging for mercy from your whiplash tongue before the end of the first dance. However, I think we had best ensure that you are nowhere near sharp objects at the time," he laughed again.

"Have you come to help?" Clara asked, waving a piece of holly at him, "or have you come to distract?"

"I have come to distract you," he admitted. "Young Lily here happened to mention the lack of mistletoe earlier. I thought we might take a walk to the orchard and see if we can find some."

Clara jumped up. "Oh yes, that would be wonderful," she turned to the other two women, "If you do not mind."

"Of course not," Lady Bea replied. "The fresh air will do you good and Lily here can tell me the latest gossip in the servants' hall."

Charlie ensured that Clara was suitably clad in a warm cloak, bonnet, gloves and winter boots. He carried a large basket for the mistletoe as they stepped out. There had been a hard frost during the night which the weak winter sun had not been able to penetrate.

"Do you think we shall have snow for Christmas?" Clara asked.

"Possibly, but I should say at the moment it is too cold and dry. However, that is not the reason we are here," he replied.

"I know, we are collecting mistletoe."

He looked down at her and could not resist dropping a kiss on her nose. "That too, but we are here because there has been another message from Mrs. Gowman. She will arrive in the evening of the twelfth as she said," he paused "and she will be accompanied by another."

"Who?" Clara asked, breathlessly.

"She did not say," he replied. "But clearly it is someone who is a part of your unknown story."

"Could it be?" she paused, taking a deep breath, "do you think it could possibly be my mother?"

Charlie gently grasped her shoulders and pulled her towards him until his forehead rested against hers. "In all honesty, my love, I do not know and I do not think it wise to raise your hopes. It is someone relevant but I think we must wait and see."

CHAPTER 50

*C*lara stood transfixed at the entrance to the ballroom. The duke's servants had transformed it into a magical place. Candles burned from shining candelabras and the three huge chandeliers hanging from the ceiling, glittered, the crystals reflecting a myriad of tiny flames. Every surface was adorned with greenery, intertwined with the ivory ribbons and dried flowers that Clara, Lady Bea, and Lily had worked to produce. Garlands of greenery had been strung overhead giving the impression that the ball would take place in a fairy glade.

At one end of the room, a small dais had been erected for the musicians who would be arriving shortly. Clara turned at the sound of the footsteps, knowing, even before she turned it would be Charlie. He came to stand beside her. "It looks lovely," she said, leaning back against him.

"Indeed it does," he agreed. "Back in the day, Grandfather's ball was quite the highlight of the season, before people went to their country estates for Christmas. I think it is a tradition we must continue."

"Oh yes," Clara replied.

"And as this is your first ball as hostess, I have something for you." He reached into his pocket and handed her a velvet covered box. Clara opened it slowly, her eyes widened as she took in the diamond and emerald bracelet and earbobs. "Oh, Charlie," she said softly, "they are beautiful."

"There is a tiara which your maid is itching to put in your hair," Charlie said and smiled down at her, "and as for the necklace which completes the set, I rather thought you would want to wear your own," he gestured to her gold locket. "Especially tonight."

Clara reached up and kissed him. "I shall treasure them. But you do not need to buy me expensive gifts, Charlie. I have all the treasure I could want. I have the duke, Great Aunt Bea, and you, the family I have always wanted, and who knows? After tonight, I might find out even more about my own family."

Her modesty did not surprise him, but it did humble him. She brought to mind faint memories of his mother, the two of them the only women who had never counted their gifts in terms of gold and silver. He bent his head and took her lips in a searing kiss. "I know you do not need baubles, but it pleases me to give them to you. So I am afraid you must indulge me." He smiled. "Now go and get ready, this is to be your night."

Her smile wobbled. "Even with Lady Elizabeth? I must be honest, now that it is upon us. I am not sure I am as strong as I imagined."

He rested his hands on her narrow shoulders. "You are the strongest woman I know. You survived your upbringing and worked to support yourself, for a woman who would have destroyed someone with less spirit than you. I believe you will triumph tonight. You will charm and sparkle and society will be in awe of you."

"Do you truly believe even half of that?" she asked, biting her lip.

"I not only believe it, I know it," he replied, lightly swatting her bottom. "Now go. Lily told me to send you straight up, and I don't know about you, but when a valet or maid says jump, one does."

Clara found that Lily had worked her magic, as had Madame Flaubert. Her gown was of the palest green watered silk with the finest Nottingham lace overskirt shot through with gold thread. The square cut neckline was embroidered with lilies of the valley as was the hem and sleeve edges. Lily had, as ever teased Clara's hair into the latest style, piling some curls on the top of her head, which set off the magnificent diamond and emerald tiara to perfection. As ever, one tress curled over Clara's shoulder. As she drew on her white satin evening gloves, Clara took one last look in the mirror. "Thank you. Lily," she said simply.

"Miss, you look like a proper princess, and no mistake," the maid replied.

Clara smiled back. "Well, I think it is time for this Cinderella to go to the ball."

Charlie's heart almost stopped beating as he watched Clara walk down the grand staircase. "Remember to breathe, dear boy," the duke said, quietly.

"She is magnificent, is she not? Every time I see her, I fall in love with her even more." Charlie looked at his grandfather, expecting him to laugh.

"You are a lucky man, for your marriage is based on love and affection. I know you had your troubles at the outset when you told Clara about your ridiculous wager. But if you cannot make Clara as happy as she makes you, then there is no hope for any couple. Though," he added with a twinkle in his eye, "to be honest, I have no doubts on that score, for some reason she seems as smitten with you as you are with her."

Before long, they were standing in the receiving line as guests began to arrive. When Clara was introduced as Charlie's wife, there were one or two raised eyebrows, but most people immediately welcomed her. There was no doubt that the ton were as curious about the duke's recently discovered grandson as they were about his new wife. As the guests gathered in groups and the chatter grew louder, they could not help but hear their names mentioned. However, the tone was positive and when people turned and caught Clara's eye, they smiled and nodded which she returned with equal warmth. They saw a lovely young woman on the arm of her handsome and adoring husband, both of them looking happy and carefree. If only they knew Charlie could feel Clara's tension as she anxiously glanced at the elaborate doors. Whether it was in anticipation of Mrs. Gowman or the Morgans and Rufford, he couldn't say.

The room was almost full when Betts announced, "Lord and Lady Morgan, Lady Elizabeth Morgan and Sir Taylor Rufford."

"I see they have come en masse," the duke whispered to Clara as they approached. "Have courage, my dear."

Lord Morgan nodded briefly to the duke. "Wensley," he acknowledged, before moving on to Charlie whom he viewed with distaste. "Hampton." Then his eyes lit on Clara. "So, this is the duke's ward is it? Caught yourself a pretty one at least, Hampton." He bowed over Clara's hand, clearly having no idea that she had lived under his roof for a year at least. Lady Morgan followed, barely looking at any of them, then it was the turn of Lady Elizabeth and Rufford to be received.

CHAPTER 51

s Rufford approached the receiving line, Lady Bea tapped Clara's arm with her fan. "Chin up," she said. "I always find it helps to imagine one's foe naked."

"I'm not sure I want to do that," Clara whispered back.

The older woman's eyes narrowed as she looked at Rufford, "I don't blame you, looking at this specimen is quite enough to put me off my sausages." Clara could not help but giggle, which came out as an unladylike snort and drew a frown from Sir Rufford.

He bowed over her hand. "I am so looking forward to this evening," he said with heavy irony.

"As am I," Lady Elizabeth followed, giving the briefest nod to Clara. "It should prove to be the highlight of the season."

As they moved away, their heads together, Lady Bea leaned over to murmur, "Quite the two most unpleasant characters in society. I cannot for the life of me fathom why Andrew even invited them. Were it up to me, I should happily set the dogs on them." Clara smiled at the thought of Lady Bea's rather overweight lap dog biting Sir Rufford's ankles.

"The invitation list was an old one, we decided that we would rather have them here, knowing what they were saying, than let them spread the story unchallenged," Clara murmured back while smiling graciously at a lady who had just arrived.

"Well, I hope you are right, my dear. Now, I spy the Duchess of

Darton, I have not seen her since she buried the late duke. I must say she looks happier now that she did all the time they were married." She moved off, like a stately galleon, the feathers on her headdress bobbing as she made her way through the throng.

As Lady Bea disappeared, Charlie appeared by Clara's side. "It is going rather well so far," he commented, surveying the room.

"I imagine because the terrible twins there have not begun their mischief."

Charlie pursed his lips and nodded. "Possibly so, but the buzz of conversation sounds happy and everyone I have spoken to has congratulated me on my beautiful and charming wife." He smiled. Catching the line of Clara's gaze, he added, "It does not matter how often you look at the doors my love, it will not hasten Mrs. Gowman's reappearance."

"I know," Clara sighed. "But what if she does not come? What if there is a problem and she cannot get here?"

"For the first point, we have no reason to doubt that Mrs. Gowman will come. She has clearly gone to considerable trouble to ensure that she does. As to the second point, I imagine that, should there be a problem, the lady will get a message to us and come as soon as she can."

"You are right of course," Clara replied. "I just feel agitated."

"It would be unnatural to feel anything else. However," he held out his hand, "the perfect distraction is here. Dance with me, dear wife, and I know you can do this particular dance because I taught you myself." He grinned.

"I have not done it before the massed ranks of society," Clara replied.

"There is a first time for everything and I refuse to take no for an answer. If I must, I will invoke your promise to obey me, given a very short time ago." He waggled his eyebrows in an outrageous leer.

"You are incorrigible," she replied. But just talking with this handsome man who had chosen her to be his wife was making her feel somehow lighter. As though her worries were out of proportion.

"I certainly hope so."

Once on the dance floor Charlie held her close, pressing forcefully against her back and drawing her against him scandalously close even for a married couple. "Just try to relax and follow my lead," he breathed into her hair, savouring the delicate scent of violets and vanilla. Little by little he felt the tension begin to leave her. He had been aching to hold her in his arms all evening, since he had seen her make her appearance. Soon, the hubbub of the guests fell away as he and Clara moved together as one. From his vantage point of height, he had a spectacular view of her decollete and almost groaned aloud as he brushed against her breasts. His body instantly hardened and all he wanted to do was carry his wife off to bed and make love to her all night until she cried out his name over and over. He would remove the gown, stays and chemise until she stood before him, naked, except for her stockings and the emeralds. Then, he would lay her on the bed and kiss and caress every inch of her.

"Charlie," his delightful reverie was interrupted for which he was a little grateful, much more fantasizing and there could have been a real scandal on the dance floor.

"Charlie," Clara repeated as she dropped a curtsey at the end of the dance. "Listen."

He held out his arm to escort her from the floor. "I don't hear anything other than a lot of people, some of whom have already had too much to drink, talking inconsequential nonsense, like they do at every ball."

As they walked towards the duke, the guests parted to let them through. "No, it is different," Clara said. "Before, there was joyful laughter, now the tone is, I don't know, hostile. The hum of conversation is now a hiss." Any laughter they heard, had a sneering edge.

"Clara," Charlie said gently, "you are reading things into it that are not there."

"Am I?" she replied. "Let us see."

She smiled at Lord and Lady Whittington who gave the briefest nods before turning quickly away. Sir Bertram Stephenson quickly followed suit, almost down the length of the ballroom guests did not or would not look them in the eye. Or, if they did look, they glared at Clara as though willing her to turn to stone.

"This is outrageous." Charlie was furious. "How dare these people, guests, behave like this."

Clara shook her head; the only unforgivable sin was for someone of lower class to try to get into society. A titled woman's husband would overlook her affairs if they were with men he had been to Eton and Oxford with, but she would be shunned were she to take up with anyone of lower status.

"I would say," she said, feeling strangely calm, "that Lady Elizabeth has done her worst."

"I should like to wring her blasted neck," Charlie replied, his eyes searching the crowd.

It did not take long to find both Lady Elizabeth and her cousin at the centre of a large clique.

"Is it not too amusing?" Rufford was saying, "having failed to win the hand of a lady, Hampton was forced to marry a common maid to fulfil the terms of the wager."

"And I can verify that she is indeed a maid," Lady Elizabeth added. "However, much they try to pass her off as a lady, the duke's ward or whatever, for she was, in fact, my maid."

CHAPTER 52

here was a burst of sneering laughter from the group. "Perhaps your wife might fetch my hat," one of the young blades ventured.

"Or fix my wife's hair," another laughed.

"Perhaps she might attend mine in the retiring room," said a third.

"Where she belongs," Lady Elizabeth added with a sneer.

"That is enough," Charlie growled, his fists clenched at his side.

Clara said quietly, "Do not reward them by responding." Turning to the group she stood tall. "It is true. I was Lady Elizabeth's maid, and the only difference between people like you and people like me, is that you, by accident of birth were born with a roof over your heads, food on the table and money to indulge yourselves. Well, let me tell you I am proud to have more independence that you will ever have, because you live in a cage, richly gilded though it might be. Some of you women are sold into marriage to the highest bidder to keep your fathers' estates from failing, and some of you men must marry a woman with a large dowry to service your debts. So, a servant I may have been, but let me tell you I am more free than any of you."

There was a stunned silence, not only among the group in front of her, but in all the other knots of people nearby.

Rufford recovered first. "You forget yourself madam. Hampton only married you because he lost the wager."

Clara turned the full emerald fire of her eyes on him. "A wager which he never actually agreed to, but which you insisted he had made, which shows only how bereft you are of honesty and honour. Charlie believed you to be jesting, but as everyone here is aware, you are as bereft of a sense of humour as your coffers are of money."

There was a collective gasp at her words, and Charlie's arm slid around her waist. "Bravo, my sweet, but I now think we should step away and leave Rufford to choke on your words," he said quietly.

Rufford's face went from red to puce. "How dare you speak to me like that you jumped up little…"

"She dares," a new voice rang out, "because she is Her Royal Highness, Clara Alexia Therese, Grand Duchess of Cordavia."

A pin could have dropped and no-one would have heard it or moved one inch, no-one in the entire room spoke, even the air was still.

Clara stepped forward, her gaze settled on an older woman. "Mrs. Gowman?" she said, uncertainly.

The woman curtseyed. "No, Highness. I am Baroness Growinski. I came here with you when you were a baby to ensure your safety."

"I am not sure I understand."

"I am not sure any of us understands," Charlie put in.

"Why should you, Highness? Everything you thought you knew about yourself is false, but it had to be so in order to protect you."

Charlie tightened his arm around Clara's waist to support her both physically and mentally. "This conversation would, I think, be better taking place in private. Please," he raised his voice and addressed the crowd, "continue with the ball, dance, eat, drink and enjoy yourselves. My wife and I will join you as soon as we can." He nodded to the musicians who struck up immediately with a lively dance. As they left the room, the buzz of conversation that had begun with the words 'maid' and 'wager' were now replaced with 'duchess' and 'royalty' amid gasps.

At the door to the blue salon, the baroness turned, with her hand on the door handle. "Before you enter, Highness," she said. "Apart from the duke, there is someone else in this room who has been waiting to meet you. She is the one to tell you of your story."

Clara's eyes were wide with shock and surprise as she walked slowly into the room. Seated on one of the sofas was the duke, next to an old lady. Her hair was fashionably styled, but completely white. Her face, though now lined, still showed that she had been a great beauty in her youth with high cheekbones and bright blue eyes which sparkled with intelligence as she smiled at Clara.

The duke cleared his throat. "Clara, my dear, allow me to present Her Royal Highness, the Dowager Grand Duchess Therese Maria of Cordavia, your grandmother."

"Come, my dear. Come and sit beside me," the duchess spoke, her voice low and rich.

When she was seated between them, Charlie took a seat on the opposite sofa, next to the baroness.

"I have so longed to meet you, Clara. You are the image of my daughter."

"And of you, Therese," the duke added. "I saw the resemblance at our first meeting. Little did I know what it would lead to."

"But how do you know I am who you all think I am?" Clara asked.

"Because my darling, the baroness brought you here smuggled out of Cordavia in a hat box and has been with you ever since. I also know that beneath that tress of hair over your shoulder is a little heart shaped birthmark, as have I and so had your dear mama."

"Had? Is my mother…?"

"Dead? I am afraid so my darling, but I must begin from the beginning."

"Are you sure you want to do this now, Highness?" the baroness leaned forward. "We have travelled many miles. Would it not be better to wait until morning when you are rested?"

The older woman smiled. "No, baroness. I have waited many years to see my granddaughter, my only grandchild, with my own eyes. And I think she is as eager to hear her story as I am to tell it.

"Cordavia is a small duchy in the middle of the continent, so small that here in England I doubt many have heard of it," the duchess began. "It is surrounded by Oldova, Morabia and Erinzka on three sides, with the Koravan Sea on the other. We have always managed to remain independent, rarely through war, mostly through making alliances of marriage. Your parent's marriage was one such, but fortunately it was also one of love. My daughter, your mother, the Grand Duchess Sophia married Leopold, the younger son of Prince Uzertz of Erinzka."

The old lady smiled and gently stroked Clara's cheek. "When you were born there was great rejoicing in Cordavia. In our country, it is always the firstborn who is named heir. Our people have always felt they prospered when a woman wore the crown. However, I digress, our joy was short-lived. Within a week of your, birth Prince Uzertz died and his older son, your uncle Artur had taken the throne. A throne which was not big enough for his towering ambition, he wanted to rule an empire such as Napoleon's. He declared war on his neighbours and expected his brother, your father to be the first to bend the knee and make Cordavia a vassal state. Naturally, your mother and father refused, and that is when our troubles began."

CHAPTER 53

The duchess took a grateful sip of the sherry handed to her by Charlie before continuing. "Your father and his brother had never agreed about the duties and responsibilities of a ruler. As your mother's consort, your father had quickly become loved by the people. Together, they were reforming some of the archaic and ancient traditions and practices, and small though it is, I believe they would have brought Cordavia to its rightful standing in the world." The old lady paused for a moment, lost in memories which etched pain on her face.

"What happened, Your Highness?" Clara asked.

A smile instantly transformed the duchess' face. "Please, Clara, I am your grandmama. You do not need to address me formally." She patted Clara's hand.

Clara smiled back. "I am sorry, it is just that this is all so much. It will take a little getting used to," she paused, "Grandmama."

Tears welled in the old lady's eyes, but she straightened her spine. "You were a babe of but seven days when Prince Artur sent in his army. Our own soldiers bravely held them off for a week, during which time the baroness was able to smuggle you out of the country before the borders were closed. I went to my dear sister in Austria with many of our family jewels sewn into my clothing and the crown jewels disguised as a warming brick at my feet."

"And my parents?" Clara could barely bear to ask, but she had to know.

The duchess suddenly looked older and a single tear traced its way down her cheek.

"Sophia and Leopold intended to escape over the Pazzian Mountains to Morania. However, they were betrayed, there was an ambush, and they were pursued. The mountain roads are narrow and steep, the horses bolted and their carriage went down the mountainside. I am so sorry my dear, no-one survived. You and I are all that is left of our family."

The duchess stiffened her spine once again. "Prince Artur, your uncle, was furious that you and I had escaped. Even distant relatives were rounded up and stripped of their titles and lands, some of them were shipped off to exile and others simply disappeared. But you and I threatened his position. I, because I am a cantankerous old lady who refuses to be browbeaten by that young upstart."

"And I?" Clara interjected.

"You, because you represent the greatest threat to his ambitions. As rightful heir, you were a symbol, someone for Cordavians to unite behind. As long as you were alive, Artur would always be looking behind him to see if you were about to lay claim to his throne. He was rightly despised and hated by loyal Cordavians, which of course added to his fear."

"We put it about that you were dead of course and, in fact, so did Artur, claiming that you had been killed along with your parents. But the people remained suspicious and he knew you were alive and sent spies all over the continent to try and find you. Fortunately, the baroness is a resourceful and intelligent woman. She had contacts and friends in London. When news reached England about the trouble in Cordavia, she went to her friends on the committee of the Foundling Hospital. As a poor emigree, she said she had lost everything and needed to work, so she became the warden of the orphanage where you grew up and was able to hide you in plain sight as it were, along with the other orphan girls."

"But the extra lessons and gifts? Did they not risk giving me away?" Clara asked.

The duchess shrugged. "The story that your mother was a lady who had birthed a child out of wedlock was neither unbelievable nor unusual and satisfied any curiosity. Besides, we always hoped that one day you would be restored to your rightful place and would need the skills and education befitting your position. In fact, I believe your education by Rev. Dacre was much better than that received by many young gentlemen who attend universities."

Clara smiled fondly at the memory. "Rev. Dacre was indeed a wonderful teacher."

"As you grew up, the baroness became worried that you might be recognised. You are the image of dear Sophie."

"Who was the image of you Therese," the duke spoke for the first time, "which could have aroused suspicion among the older peers who might have recalled you." The two older people exchanged a look before the duchess continued, "Not only that, you have the birthmark which runs through the family. The baroness decided that as we could no longer keep you at the orphanage, which might have raised some questions, that you must go out into the world. Making you into a lady's maid was an inspiration. No-one in society would notice you as servants, rather like children should be seen and not heard and seen rarely, if at all. I understand there are some homes where there are corridors between the rooms where the servants appear and disappear through hidden doors when their tasks are done, and one lord's servants have to face the wall when he appears."

"It was not quite that bad at Lord Morgan's," Clara put in.

"Ah, yes. Your position in the Morgan household was carefully thought out. The Baroness knew the girl by reputation and it seemed a good position. She would be quite determined that her maid be kept out of sight as far as possible, though I must confess, we had no idea quite what an unpleasant piece of work she is. We must apologise for that. I am so sorry my dear, that you had to put up with her."

Clara shook her head. "It does not matter, Grandmama, in fact it seems a long time ago now and," she smiled at Charlie, "it was because of the dreadful Lady Elizabeth that I met Charlie. And I suppose for all her faults, inadvertently, Lady Elizabeth kept me safe."

"There is that," Charlie agreed. "And I will never forget the look on her face when the baroness announced who you really are." He paused before adding, "But why now? Is Clara safe, because we know there were others looking for her."

"We would never have revealed her highness' whereabouts were it not completely safe," the baroness replied.

"Your uncle, Prince Artur is dead," her grandmother stated. "Killed by his own bodyguard, his ambition and madness for power had caused so much bloodshed. So should you wish to return to Cordavia, it is now safe for you to return and claim your throne."

CHAPTER 54

*V*ery gently, so as not to disturb her sleeping husband, Clara eased herself off the bed and donned her discarded nightrail and robe. She could not sleep. The events of the last few hours were whirling around in her brain. Lighting a candle, she found her slippers and quietly crept from the room.

Apart from the odd creaks and groans of the house settling, the rooms were deserted, even the servants were in bed. There were the remains of a fire in the library which, with a little encouragement, Clara soon had blazing cheerily as she curled up in one of the armchairs to think. Only this morning she thought she had known who she was, Mrs. Charlie Hampton, the wife who was once a lady's maid. Even that elevation which had seemed enormous, paled into insignificance compared to her newly found grandmother's revelations.

She smiled at the memory of returning to the ball and bidding their guests goodnight. This Christmas Ball would certainly be gossiped about for years, but not for the scandal of a maid being passed off as a lady. The revelation of a secret grand duchess eclipsed everything. No doubt the scandal sheets would be full of it, and from being someone who was never noticed, Clara knew her life would never be the same again.

She walked over to a shelf and took down an atlas, turning the pages carefully, until she found Cordaviat. As her grandmother had described, it was bordered by other countries and an inland sea. It was also the smallest country in the whole of Europe though its position in the centre of the continent gave it some strategic importance, hence the ambitions of Prince Artur. She traced the outline of the border with her finger, it was almost beyond belief that she, who up to a few weeks ago owned two dresses, a piece of cracked mirror, and a silver necklace, could now, in theory at least be the ruler of a country.

Even before the door was fully opened, her heightened senses told her it was Charlie. He too held a candle and his feet were bare underneath his robe, and, as she now knew, the rest of him would be equally naked.

"Difficulty sleeping?" he asked, setting the candle on the small table. She nodded.

"It is hardly surprising, given tonight's revelations."

"I suppose not."

"Come, sit beside me." He sat on the chesterfield. "You should have awakened me and we could have had this conversation in the warmth and comfort of our own bed," he chided gently. When he had settled her against him, her head resting against his chest, his arm around her where it should be and a soft blanket over them, he breathed in the scent of her hair. If she could preserve this moment he would, the hustle and bustle of life receded, and they could just be together. Just being of course would never happen, not in the real world and even less so in the surreal world they now found themselves in.

"So what are you going to do?" he asked.

"About going to Cordavia and claiming the crown?

He nodded.

"In all honesty I do not know. I should like to visit one day, of course. But to claim the crown?"

"According to your grandmother, the crown is rightfully yours," he pointed out.

"And yet it seems to have brought my family nothing but death and disaster," she replied. "Besides, the country, according to grandmama, is for the moment at least stable now with an elected governing committee. Surely they would not wish further disruption."

"Then how about this? We plan a visit to Cordavia o visit your family home. If you wish, we might even have a home there for some part of the year."

Her eyes shone as she looked up at him. "You would do this for me?"

He dropped a kiss on her forehead. "Of course, I love you, Clara, I only want to make you happy."

"But what about your work? Your business?"

He smiled, "Business is business no matter where it is enacted. In fact, there will no doubt be opportunities in Cordavia and surrounding countries now that Prince Artur is no longer threatening endless and wasteful war."

Clara frowned. "But I do not speak a word of Cordavian, nor do you."

"Nor does anyone. I believe they speak a mixture French, German, and for some bizarre reason, there is English spoken as well. As for the crown," he continued, "it may be that although there is an elected government, they would like a Head of State who is neutral. I imagine a young woman would be a powerful symbol of a fresh new chapter in the country's history."

Clara looked at him askance. "You do remember that a few weeks ago I was the orphan lady's maid to Lady Elizabeth, do you not?"

He laughed. "Of course, and one of my fondest memories of this evening will be the regal way you walked down the ballroom, like a queen, graciously acknowledging the bows and curtseys of the cream of London society as though you had been born to it. Which of course we now know you have."

Clara joined in with his laughter. "Lady Elizabeth curtseyed so low I thought she was going to fall over," she paused, "or out of her gown."

"And Rufford could only look at his feet, as though they were about to reveal the meaning of life. I imagine, given their earlier mischief before the baroness' appearance they will never dare show their unpleasant faces in society again. In fact," he added thoughtfully, "it would not surprise me were they to be already on a boat bound for South America."

Clara laughed ruefully.

"Now, my dear wife," he whispered, with a gleam in his eye, "I think it is time we returned to our bed. I have a notion to make love with a particular Grand Duchess of Cordavia."

"Do not forget," Clara said with a brilliant smile, "that you will be a duke one day."

"But not for many years, I hope, and I believe your grand title out dukes me in any case."

Clara's eyes danced. "Then you may proceed, by royal command."

He chuckled. "As ever, my lady, your wish is my command."

EPILOGUE

Two years later

Charlie's heart swelled with pride as he watched the Archbishop lower the crown onto Clara's head. Cordavia would never have a more worthy ruler. He glanced down the row to where his grandfather and newly acquired grandmother stood, noting that their hands were intertwined, not quite covered by the folds of the duchess' gown, knowing that the two old people did not care who saw them. After almost half a century of separation by protocol and royal decree, they had found each other again and were not going to waste what time they had left together. He smiled as they exchanged a loving look and the duke raised his duchess' hand for a kiss.

The organ swelled and Charlie's attention turned back to Clara. She looked magnificent as she began the long procession down the cathedral. The cream silk gown was embroidered with thousands of stars and violets, the national flower of Cordavia, each with a small diamond at its centre. The Cordavian state crown consisted of many stars, each set with diamonds on a narrow stem attached to the frame. It looked as though Clara was wearing a halo of stars, which glittered and shimmered with every step. As she approached his seat, she paused and beckoned him. It was not what they had done at the rehearsal and a break with protocol, but from the outset, Clara had been determined to do things her own way.

His mind flashed back to their first visit, two years ago when they had received an invitation from the Prime Minister. Although in theory she wanted to visit one day, Clara had been reluctant to come, but he had persuaded her that she ought to see the land of her birth and heritage. At that visit, the Prime Minister had asked on behalf of the Cordavian government if she would take the crown.

The country had been through much turbulence in the years since her parents' deaths and the government felt that a new, young duchess on the throne would serve to unite the country. Indeed, he felt she was the only one who could unite the people.

Clara's first instinct was to refuse and pointed out that although royal by birth she had not been raised or trained in the role of a monarch. Besides, her life was with her husband in England. The government would be willing to accept her on any terms, even if she only spent half of her year in Cordavia. It was Charlie who had quietly persuaded her that she should take on the mantle of leadership. "Look at how you can change lives," he had suggested, "especially of women and the poor. This is what you were born for Clara, this is your destiny. Your life was saved for a reason, people risked their lives to keep you safe. You have so much to give, now you will be in a position to make real change. Not only that, you have lived the life of the poor, how many kings and queens can say that? You know what needs to change and you can make it happen."

"But what of our family? The duke, Lady Bea, Grandmama? And what of your business?"

Charlie had kissed her soundly, her care for others was exactly what would make her a wonderful ruler. "Grandfather and your grandmama will not be separated now that they have found each other again. I believe they intend to spend time in both countries. As for Great Aunt Bea, she will do as she has always done, which is to do exactly as she pleases. In terms of business, now that there is peace in Cordavia, there are in fact plenty of opportunities for business and my knowledge may even be of some use to your government."

Having made the decision, Clara threw herself into learning as much as she could about Cordavia, this country she had not even heard of until she became its heir. Baroness Growinski and her grandmama were able to teach her its history and constitution and it was in one of their lessons that her grandmother said, "Clara my dear, I do not wish to be indelicate, but you have been looking a little peaky recently. Are you quite well?"

"Of course, Grandmama, I am rarely ill. I just seem to have eaten things that disagree with me recently."

The duchess shook her head. "Do you not think, my dear, that you could be with child?"

Clara's hand shot to her mouth. "Oh, how could I have been so stupid, now I think about it…"

And so, despite the fervor of educating a new ruler, settling in a new country, and moving businesses, it was decided that the coronation would be delayed until Clara had given birth to their twins, Eleanor and Jack, just two months prior. They were unable to witness the auspicious rise of their mother, instead remaining at the palace in the care of their nanny and supervised by Lily who guarded them fiercely. Charlie smiled at the thought of his children, for not only had Clara's life changed beyond anything they could have imagined, so had his own. He had a dear grandfather he had never expected to know, a new grandmother as well, a wife he loved beyond the reason and logic that he'd once held in such high esteem, and now children of his own. His life was complete.

Suddenly back in the present, he saw Clara hold out her hand. He took it, bowed to the queen of his heart, and raised it to his lips, then tucked it in the crook of his arm. As they walked to the great west door of the cathedral, the crowds outside could already be heard cheering. Charlie turned to Clara and whispered, "The people already love you almost as much as I." She smiled back "And to think I was once told I never was and never would be a lady."

"Lady Elizabeth perchance?" he raised an eyebrow. "I believe she fled to Canada where she and her odious cousin are eking out a living running some kind of hostelry for fur trappers. The work is hard, as is the life she now leads, which some might feel is a just punishment. Never a lady? You were always a lady, and now you are a queen."

They smiled at each other and turned to wave at the crowds as the cheers swelled.

Don't miss out on your next favorite book!

Join the Satin Romance mailing list
www.satinromance.com/mail.html

ACKNOWLEDGMENTS

To all at Melange for their patience, professionalism and dedication in making me a better writer.

To my family for their encouragement and occasional nagging to stop procrastinating.

THANK YOU FOR READING

Did you enjoy this book?

We invite you to leave a review at your favorite book site, such as Goodreads, Amazon, Barnes & Noble, etc.

DID YOU KNOW THAT LEAVING A REVIEW...

- Helps other readers find books they may enjoy.
- Gives you a chance to let your voice be heard.
- Gives authors recognition for their hard work.
- Doesn't have to be long. A sentence or two about why you liked the book will do.

ABOUT THE AUTHOR

Anna lives in a lovely village in Hampshire England with her own romantic hero, otherwise known as her long-suffering husband and has two grown up children. An ex-teacher, she has taught many subjects from religion to drama but has always had a passion for history and would love a time machine to experience life in Georgian England, though suspects she would have been one of the maids washing the cups rather than delicately sipping tea from them.

When she's not thinking about life in the nineteenth century, she enjoys travelling and learning about different customs and cultures, especially the food. Anna also loves to walk in the beautiful Yorkshire Dales which provides much inspiration for her writing. She also plays the piano and it's her ambition to be able to play well enough so that the cat doesn't leave the room.

ALSO BY ANNA AYSGARTH

Unsuitable Brides

A Bride for Christmas

The Marquess Meets Miss Nobody

Never a Lady